Also by Ellen Crosby
Moscow Nights
The Merlot Murders

THE CHARDONNAY CHARADE

A Wine Country Mystery

ELLEN CROSBY

SCRIBNER

New York London Toronto Sydney

SCRIBNER
1230 Avenue of the Americas
New York, NY 10020

DESIGNED BY LAUREN SIMONETTI
Text set in Bembo

Manufactured in the United States of America

1   3   5   7   9   10   8   6   4   2

Library of Congress Control Number: 2006100907

ISBN-13: 978-0-7432-8992-4
ISBN-10: 0-7432-8992-7

For Juanita Swedenburg,
and in memory of Wayne Swedenburg, with thanks;
and in memory of Skipp Hayes, with gratitude.

I could not stay another day,
To love, to laugh, to work or play;
Tasks left undone must stay that way.
And if my parting has left a void,
Then fill it with remembered joy.

—From "Remembered Joy,"
an Irish prayer

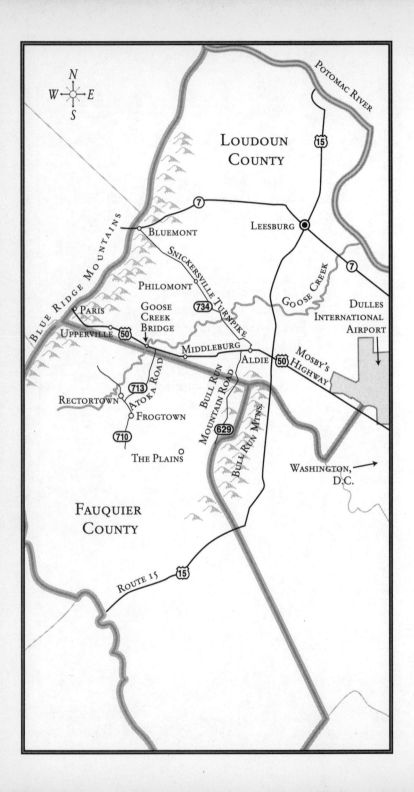

Montgomery Estate Vineyard

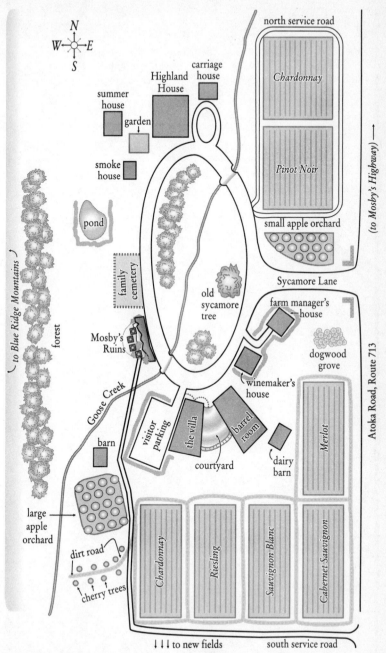

THE
CHARDONNAY
CHARADE

If God forbade drinking, would he have made wine so good?
—Armand Jean du Plessis,
Cardinal Richelieu

CHAPTER 1

⸺⚬⚬⚬⸺

Some days I wish my life ran backward, because then I'd be ready for the catastrophes. Or at least I'd know whether there was a happy ending. I own a small vineyard at the foothills of the Blue Ridge Mountains in Atoka, Virginia, where our winters are cold, our summers hot, and spring is the blissful season of growth and renewal. But not this year.

On what should have been a balmy May night, a warm air mass moving up from the Gulf of Mexico looked like it was going to smack into arctic winds sweeping down from Canada, causing temperatures to plummet below freezing. A week before Memorial Day, and Jack Frost nipping at our nose like early March. The weather forecaster on the Channel 2 news at noon recommended bringing tender young plants indoors for the night, "just to be sure." A fine idea, unless you had twenty-five acres of tender young grapes.

A lot of science and math go into making wine, but most people don't realize it's also a hell of a crapshoot, meaning a hearty dose of guessing and finger-crossing figure into the equation, too. Mother Nature can always pull a fast one when you least expect it, and suddenly you're scrambling—like we were this afternoon.

Normally I play it safe with my money and my business. Last fall, though, an unexpected financial windfall landed at my feet and I did something I swore I'd never do. I spent it. The money would go into clearing more acreage and planting new vines come spring.

Literally a bet-the-farm gamble, since we were trying grapes we'd never grown before.

I'd expected Quinn Santori, my winemaker, to be as gung-ho about the decision as I was. Of the two of us, he was the risk-taker. Imagine my surprise when he made a case for planting less and using some of the cash to install wind turbines. Quinn had moved here from Napa eighteen months ago and he was still hard-wired for California, where turbines, which protect the grapes from late-season frosts, were common. I'd lived in Virginia for most of my twenty-eight years and we got that kind of killing frost once in a blue moon.

And since my family's name was on every bottle of wine that left this vineyard, we did it my way. For the past few months we'd cleared land and plowed new fields. Thank God we hadn't started planting yet.

Quinn never said "I told you so" once we heard that weather forecast, but he came close. My father had hired him shortly before he died last year and it had been a marriage of convenience. Leland needed someone to work on the cheap, freeing up money for his gambling habits and low-life business deals. Quinn wanted to make a new start in Virginia after his former employer's decision to add tap water to his wines—boosting production for a black market business in Eastern Europe—had earned the ex-boss free room and board at a California penitentiary. When I took over running Montgomery Estate Vineyard nine months ago, I quickly found out that Quinn had a macho streak as wide as the Shenandoah River, a problem with authority, and a habit of speaking his mind with a candor polite folks would call unvarnished. If you happened to be a woman and also his boss, you would call it mouthy.

"Now that we've got our back to the wall thanks to you," he said, "the only way we're going to save our old vines is if we move that freezing air away from the grapes. Since we didn't install turbines, we'd better get a helicopter in here. Expensive as hell, but beats waking up and finding we've got a few acres of frozen grapes we could use for buckshot."

I closed my eyes and wondered how much "expensive as hell" cost—not that it made any difference. If I couldn't hire a helicopter, we'd kiss about forty thousand dollars' worth of wine goodbye in one night. At least we were only talking about the whites, since they were farthest along.

"I'll get someone," I said. "Don't worry."

"You'd better," he said, "because I look pretty stupid strapping wings to my arms and flapping 'em around the vines like the *paisanos* do back in the old country. Besides, I got my hands full with the pesticide guys over in the new fields. They gotta get those protective tarps down right away."

"They don't really use wings and flap their arms in Italy, do they?" I asked.

He tucked his fists into his armpits and moved his elbows up and down. "Are you going to make those calls or aren't you?"

I made the calls. Finally Chris Coronado from Coronado Aviation in Sterling said he'd take the job. "I'm not cheap, Lucie," he said, "but I'm good. I've done this before."

He flew to the vineyard later that afternoon to see the fields in daylight and mark the coordinates in the helicopter's GPS navigation system so he could find them in the dark. His partner arrived in a Dodge pickup, towing a bright yellow fuel truck, which he parked near the Chardonnay block in the south vineyard. The pleasure of their company came to seven hundred and fifty dollars an hour for the helicopter, with an extra two-fifty for the fuel trailer.

Chris reckoned the temperature wouldn't dip below thirty-two until three or four in the morning, meaning they would only be in the air for a few hours until dawn. So about thirty-two fifty for the night. Anything a smidge above the freezing mark and we were home, but not free—they still collected a thousand-dollar retainer and got to spend the night in the warm comfort of Quinn's spare bedroom instead of fighting vertigo flying in near-total darkness above our vines.

So that Chris could see where he was going, we needed to put flashlights around the perimeter of the fields he would strafe, our own version of airport runway lights. I figured about forty would do the job. We owned eight.

Randy Hunter, one of our part-time field hands, walked into the tool room in the equipment barn while I was checking the batteries. Good-looking in a rough, tough cowboy way, mid-twenties, with bright blue eyes, curly blond hair, and a few days' worth of grizzle that said sexy, not scruffy. When he wasn't working for us, Randy delivered furniture for an antique shop and groceries for an upscale supermarket. In his spare time he worked out and played local gigs with his band, Southern Comfort. Maybe it was the slow, languid Louisiana drawl or maybe the way those ocean-blue eyes could caress, but Randy had a way of looking at a woman—any woman—like she'd been created just for him on God's best day.

"What're you doing, Lucie?" He set his heavy-duty gloves on the workbench and took off his leather jacket. I couldn't help staring. Looked like he'd added another tattoo, this one around his muscular left bicep. Lightning bolts.

"I'm trying to figure out where I can get about thirty more flashlights in the next few hours," I said.

"You could buy 'em in a store," he said with an easy smile, "like most folks do."

"They sell them in stores?"

His eyes flashed appreciatively as he laughed. "What's the rush, needing so many?"

"We need to put them around the boundaries of the Chardonnay and Riesling blocks so they can be seen in the dark. I'll be driving to every hardware store in two counties before I'm through."

"I'm supposed to be moving that shipment you got from Seely's, but if you need to, I can help here instead," he offered. "Long's I have enough time to set up for your party tonight."

I liked the lilt in his voice.

"That'd be great. I could really use a hand," I said. "We'll worry about the plants later."

The sound of furious fiddling came from somewhere near his belt. He pulled a mobile phone out of the pocket of tight-fitting jeans and squinted at the display.

"'Scuse me. I gotta take this. Be right back." He flipped the phone open, cutting off the tune. "Hey, darling. Been thinking about you."

I could see him outside through the window, pacing back and forth as he talked to his lady friend. When he returned, I was struggling with a balky flashlight, trying to unscrew it so I could remove the dead batteries.

"I got that." His fingertips brushed mine and he opened it like the threads had been greased. "There you go."

His frank, wolfish eyes held mine, flustering me so the flashlight slipped through my fingers. It hit the floor and the batteries ejected like torpedoes. He winked and reached down for them, clearly enjoying the sight of my face turning the color of a hot chili pepper.

"So what's that song on your phone?" I needed to divert his attention.

"'The Devil Went Down to Georgia.' Charlie Daniels." He grinned and set the batteries on the workbench.

"You playing it tonight?" I gave up and smiled back at him. That much flirtatious charm ought to be illegal.

"We don't got a fiddler," he said. "And we're nowhere near as good as old Charlie. Besides, we're country rock 'n' roll, not redneck. But we are gonna play 'Georgia on My Mind.'" Another sly wink. "By way of saying thanks."

I laughed. "Good career move."

Georgia Greenwood had wanted Southern Comfort to play at the vineyard tonight at the black-tie fund-raiser, which we were hosting for the local free clinic. The band didn't have the polished sound I would have chosen for this well-heeled philanthropic crowd, but Georgia's husband, Ross, the doctor who once saved my life and now ran the clinic, was paying the bill. He adored his wife. What Georgia wanted, Georgia usually got.

Randy and I divided up the hardware stores and headed in opposite directions.

The errand didn't take as long as I'd reckoned, even though we bought out two stores. When we got back, he came out to the fields to help me. While I attached temperature sensors to the wooden trellis posts, he dug shallow holes and stuck the flashlights in them so the light pointed skyward.

"You sure this is gonna work? A helicopter?" He was on one knee, tamping the earth around the last flashlight. "Kind of seems like burning green wood for kindling, if you ask me."

"The alternative is a pair of wings," I said. "It has to work."

Randy smiled his slow, lazy smile again. "I hope so for your sake. You been working like a dog to get this place running good again ever since your pa died."

"Thanks. I'm trying to."

He stood up and stripped off his work gloves, banging them against a post to loosen the dirt. "If you're all set here, I'm gonna head over to the barn and get my things for tonight."

I knew he meant the old hay barn, which we let him use for band practice. The nearby cows and horses didn't seem to mind the loud music the way his neighbors used to. In return he worked a few extra hours for us off the clock.

"You and Quinn finish down at the new fields today?" I asked.

"Yes, ma'am. I nailed up a bunch of 'Keep Out' signs when Quinn took off to talk to your pilot. I'm glad that spraying chore is over with. Nothing's gonna live in that dirt with what that dude put in it."

"No bugs, at least," I said. "The vines won't mind."

"People mind. That stuff can kill you dead."

"It'll dissipate in three days under those plastic tarps," I said, "but I agree with you. It's nasty."

He shook his head. "Can't figure out why it doesn't kill the vines, if it kills everything else. Anyway, have yourself a good one, Lucie. See you later."

The fund-raiser for the Patowmack Free Clinic had originally been planned as an outdoor garden party. We were holding it over at the Ruins, the burned-out red brick tenant house we'd converted into a stage for plays, concerts, and wine events. More than a century ago the house had been a hideout for Colonel John Singleton Mosby, the Confederacy's legendary guerrilla commander, known as the Gray Ghost. Along with his group of Partisan Rangers, Mosby terrorized Union soldiers in our neck of the woods with surprise raids on their supplies and horses. The tenant house had been one of his many bolt holes until soldiers in blue coats burned it one winter night, trying to flush him out.

Evening gown notwithstanding, the fund-raiser was all work for me, with the ominous distraction of Quinn's regular phone calls reporting on the tumbling temperatures in the fields. As soon as possible I left the catering staff to clean up and joined him at the winery.

"How 'bout we take that candy-cane car of yours out for a spin to see what's happening up close?" he said. "At least we'll be warm when we're sitting in it."

"No making fun of my car or you can check those vines in the Gator," I told him.

I'd bought the red-and-white-striped Mini Cooper convertible from a friend after taking it for a test drive through the vineyard, where it easily navigated the narrow space between the rows of vines. It was the perfect car for zipping through the fields, though I'd learned to slow down on the corners after wrecking the side mirrors one too many times. Tonight the heater alone made it worth the price. The only way to keep warm if you were out in the Gator—which looked like a tractor bred with a golf cart—was by laying your hands on the engine hood.

"Damn, it's cold," Quinn said as he got in to the Mini.

"I hope we can pull this off." I started the car. "We've had it if the fruit freezes."

"Talking about freezing, Jennifer Seely called from the nursery while you were at the fund-raiser, all bent out of shape. She dropped off a shipment of bedding plants at the winery this afternoon. Said Randy was supposed to take care of them. She wanted to make sure he'd moved them inside tonight or they'll die. I couldn't find 'em. Did you do something with them?"

"No, and Randy didn't, either. He helped me buy the flashlights and then stuck around to set them up. Maybe Sera did. It was her plant order. Everything she wanted for the border gardens next to the villa and the baskets and wine casks in the courtyard."

"Well, somebody took care of them. There was nothing on the crush pad." He shrugged and changed the subject. "How did the party go?"

"Fine, until the end." I shifted into third as we motored down the dirt service road. "Harry Dye got loaded and decided to give Georgia Greenwood a piece of his mind."

Quinn picked up the thermos I'd filled with coffee and chuckled in the darkness. "Good for Harry. She had it coming. Every vineyard owner around here hates her guts. She'll shut us all down if she gets elected in November and takes that dumbass plan of hers to Richmond."

"First she has to win the primary," I said. "It's not a sure thing."

"She's picking up votes," he said darkly, pouring coffee into the plastic thermos cap. "She could win."

Georgia's dumbass plan—supported by civic groups, churches, and school PTAs—would stop vineyards from selling wine directly to restaurants and stores, forcing us to go through wholesalers as middlemen. It would be the death knell of the little vineyards—family farms, when all was said and done—whose profit would be wiped out if they had to add one more link to the distribution chain.

But Georgia had invoked Prohibition, claiming it meant less "demon alcohol" out there for our children to get their hands on. In my humble opinion, most kids' choice of beverage was ruled by their wallet, not their palate. I wasn't too worried about a fifteen-year-old with Mom or Dad's credit card trying to con me into selling him a case of twenty-dollar-a-bottle Pinot Noir over the phone. Shutting down vineyards that made pricey boutique wines wasn't going to change teenage drinking habits. They'd still drink whatever cheap rotgut they could get their hands on.

"I don't think she's going to win," I said. "Not after what she did to Noah Seely."

"It was a pretty stupid move," Quinn agreed, "going after Santa Claus."

"Generations of voters sat in his lap and told him what they wanted for Christmas. He fixes up that nursery like you always imagined the North Pole would be when you were a kid. The only thing worse would have been attacking motherhood or the flag."

"Didn't seem to bother Hugo Lang. He just endorsed her." Quinn poured more coffee into his cup. "Wonder how she pulled off getting a U.S. senator to do that. Wait until Hugo gets the VP nod at the convention in August. He'll have coattails from here to the moon."

"He stopped by tonight." I turned on my high beams so I could see in the inky darkness as we went off-road toward the fields. "Right before Harry went nuts. God, that was embarrassing."

"Who cares? Good old Harry. The only vineyard owner around here smart enough to put in turbines." Quinn finished juggling the thermos and cup and leaned his back against the door of the small car so he was facing me. "Where was Ross? Wasn't he around to defend his wife's honor?"

"He left early. Medical emergency. One of his patients went into premature labor with twins. Was that another dig about the turbines?"

"Would I do that?" he asked unconvincingly as I pulled over by the Riesling block and parked. "Here. Have some coffee. It's going to be a long night." He handed me his cup and unscrewed the bottom cap from the thermos for himself.

"Thanks." I warmed my hands on the cup and blew on the steaming liquid. "Hugo spent a long time talking to Georgia. He didn't look too happy about it, if you ask me. They left together, too. It was odd. The whole endorsement thing is odd."

"Odd, how? You think they're screwing?" Quinn perked up. Sex interested him. "Georgia's a knockout even if she is a bitch, but I don't think Hugo'd bang a married woman. The guy's a Boy Scout."

"You can be so vulgar sometimes, you know?" I said. "You never knew Hugo's wife. No one could take her place. He's definitely not . . . banging . . . Georgia. Or anyone else."

He laughed, unrepentant, and set the thermos on the floor. "She's doing it. You can tell. She puts out vibes. If you ask me, she's got something going with Randy."

"No way." Our body heat and the steam from the coffee had fogged the windows so it was like being in a cocoon. I turned the defroster on high and raised my voice to be heard over the gusty roar. "Randy could be her son. He'd be more likely to go out with Mia than Georgia."

"Sweetheart, this may come as a news flash to you, but there are some men who sleep with more than one woman at a time. He could still date your sister and have a little on the side with Georgia."

"Georgia shops at Saks and Tiffany's. She and Ross have a Picasso in their living room. Randy's an Elvis-on-velvet NASCAR kind of guy. Sorry. I don't see it. He could be sleeping with ten women, but she wouldn't be one of them."

Quinn made a bad job of whistling "The Devil Went Down to Georgia," then said, "That phone of his goes off all the time. And the song is no coincidence. It's hard not to overhear sometimes. I think he's been talking to her a lot."

"She got him the job playing tonight. Why wouldn't they be talking?" I turned the defroster down, since it had worked its magic.

"Where there's smoke there's fire. You heard it here first." In the newly quiet darkness, one of the sensors went off and we both jumped. "Damn! First one to go. I'll check it out. You stay put. I'll be right back."

I watched his dark, solid figure disappear in the star-filled night. The waxing quarter moon's silvery light caught the tops of the nearby vines so they already looked frost-covered. Hopefully only an optical illusion. Otherwise it would be the beginning of the end. Quinn opened the passenger door a few minutes later, bringing frigid air into the car.

"Show time," he said. "Thirty-two degrees and it's not even three a.m. I called Chris and woke him up. He's on his way. We'd better turn on those flashlights." He reached in the backseat and picked up what looked like two sets of earmuffs, handing one to me. "Here. These are from Chris. Make sure you wear them or you'll go deaf." He paused, then said, "You know, it's going to be really hard to see in the dark. Maybe I should call Hector."

"No. He hasn't been looking too well lately. I'm worried about him. Let him sleep and he can take over in the morning." Hector Cruz, our farm manager, had been with us ever since the first vines were planted twenty years ago. Now he and his wife, Sera, were the only ones left among our employees who remembered every one of our harvests.

"You sure?" Quinn asked quietly.

I appreciated the fact that he didn't glance down at my feet, even if we both knew what he was talking about. It had been nearly three years since a car driven at high speed by an ex-boyfriend plowed into the stone gate at the entrance to the vineyard. Only one of us walked away from that accident and it wasn't me. In fact, I did not walk again for a long time—and the reason I did was due, in no small measure, to Ross Greenwood. Even so, after I got out of the hospital there were

months of therapy, then a wheelchair, walker, and finally graduation
to the cane I will need forever because of a now-deformed left foot.
Quinn and I rarely discussed my disability, and though I knew he
thought my knowledge of wine making could fit on the head of a
pin—with plenty of room left for the dancing angels—he'd never,
ever said I wasn't physically up to the job.

"I'll be fine." I put the Mini in gear. "Are you positive we're going
to be okay with the helicopter stirring up all the air and that pesticide
next door in the new fields?"

"Of course I am." He sounded annoyed. "I told you already.
We're in no danger. The guy from Lambert Chemical even called his
head office in Roanoke to double-check. We've got tarps on the
fields and we're more than three hundred feet away from them.
Technically we're safe at anything beyond a hundred feet."

"I hope you're right."

"I know I'm right. He'll be back Monday to haul away his equipment. You can talk to him yourself."

"I thought he took everything today."

"Nah, by the time he finished it was late. So I told him he could
leave it out by the fields. No one will go near it. His next job is in
Haymarket, so since he's saving money on gas he cut me a break on
our price."

"Really? That's good."

"I knew you'd be happy." Quinn got in his share of jabs about my
Scottish thriftiness. Or, as he called it, penny-pinching.

Thanks to me, though, the vineyard was now once again running
in the black. I ignored the crack, as usual. "I hear the helicopter. Let's
go."

Chris had told us he'd only be flying fifteen to twenty feet above
the vines, so if we valued our heads, we needed to stay well away
when the helicopter hovered over the fields. Under normal circumstances the higher the altitude, the colder the air. Sometimes, though,
the opposite situation—known as an inversion—occurred and the
cold air sat next to the ground with a layer of warm air above it. That's
what we had tonight and why we needed Chris. The helicopter could
push the warm air down so it was next to the vines where we needed
it to keep the fruit from freezing.

For the next few hours, as the cold seeped into my fingertips and toes, Quinn and I grimly hopscotched across the fields, calling to Chris, who trained the helicopter's large searchlight on us, tracking us like a couple of fugitives on the run, as we led him to the places where beeping sensors indicated the temperature had again slipped into the danger zone. Once every hour Chris set the helicopter down to reorient himself. Twice he and his partner refueled.

"Why can't you use your instruments?" I asked during one of the breaks.

"Because we're flying too low. It has to be all visual," he said. "The problem is I can't see anything, and in the dark your worst nightmare is losing the horizon line. Then you don't know whether you're right side up or upside down. That's why I need to get back on land every so often to get my bearings again."

"My God, how scary," I said. "How much longer do you think you need to stay up there?"

"Another hour. Until dawn. Then the sun will take over and warm things up."

True to his word, Chris set the chopper down for the last time just after six a.m. I handed him a check, which he stuck in the pocket of his leather jacket without looking at it. "Call me if you need me again," he said.

"I think this was a onetime deal," I said. "According to the National Weather Service."

"I hope so, for your sake. Sometimes I think those guys use a dartboard to make their forecasts."

Quinn hitched a ride back to the vineyard parking lot with Chris's partner, who needed to retrieve a backpack he'd left at Quinn's place. The two of them took the pickup with the now-empty fuel trailer rattling behind them as it bumped down the dirt road. Then the helicopter lifted off and Chris waved, heading east.

The sunless sky, milk-white a while ago, had turned ash-colored. I collected the flashlights, leaving the sensors so we could continue to monitor the temperature. When I was done, I took the south service road in order to get a look at the new fields. In the distance Randy's neon-orange "Danger—Keep Out" signs looked almost gay—bright splashes of color against the plastic tarps, which shone like dull mirrors.

I did not see the parked car, which was partially screened by a grove of bushes, until I was only a few yards from it. Actually what I spotted was the vanity license plate—"IXMN"—through a break in the foliage. "I examine." Ross Greenwood's license plate. Then I saw his black Ford Explorer.

What was he doing here? Cold as it was, I started to sweat.

I reached for my cane and got out of the Mini. The body was on the driver's side, on the ground. I nearly tripped over it, since I'd been peering through the frost-covered windows instead of watching my feet. Still wearing the mint-green jersey evening gown and mink jacket from last night's fund-raiser, Georgia Greenwood lay facedown in a pool of frozen vomit congealed near an outstretched arm.

Whatever had made her sick like that, it was clear she was beyond medical help.

She was dead.

CHAPTER 2

A single bar on the battery display of my mobile phone after a long day—and night—of use meant I didn't have much juice left. It survived the call to 911 and then another brief call to Quinn. His comment was, fortunately, succinct and to the point.

"Shit," he said. "Where are you? Don't move. I'm coming."

The hardest call came next. I dialed Ross's home number. Their answering machine picked up—his voice, not Georgia's—and I disconnected. You didn't leave a message about something like this. I managed to get a call through to his mobile phone. He answered immediately.

"Lucie!" He sounded tired, but I could tell I hadn't woken him up. "What are you doing calling at this hour? Is everything okay?"

"Ross, I'm so sorry. I'm at the vineyard. I just found the Explorer when I was driving down the south service road. Did you and Georgia switch cars last night? I mean . . . she's lying beside it . . . I'm so sorry." I swallowed. "Ross, I think she had a seizure or something. She's dead."

For a moment I thought the phone had finally died, because of his silence. Then he said in a soft, stunned voice, "Oh, God. You found Georgia?" After that, more silence.

"Ross? Are you there? My phone battery is going. Look, I called 911 and they're on their way." The phone beeped in my ear. "Where are you?"

"Heading home," he said. "I've been out all night. One of my patients had twins. I'll be right there. Give me five minutes . . ."

Another beep and the display went black. I flung the phone on the passenger seat as Quinn's metallic green El Camino came down the road from the opposite direction. He pulled up next to me and got out.

"You all right?" he asked. "Where is she?"

"Over there." I pointed. "Next to the door by the driver's side."

"You're sure she's dead and not passed out?"

"She looked pretty dead to me." My voice shook.

"Stay here." When he came back, his face was somber. "I didn't touch her, but she's dead, all right. Looks like she puked her guts up. God, does Ross know yet?"

"He's on his way. I got him on his mobile. On his way home after delivering twins all night." In the distance, the sound of more tires on gravel. "I bet that's him."

A moment later Georgia's burgundy Mercedes Roadster came into view. Ross, behind the wheel, looked grim.

"Where are the cops?" Quinn asked quietly. "I thought you told me you called 911 right before you called me."

"I did. They should be here any minute."

Ross got out of the Roadster and ran to the Explorer.

"He shouldn't be alone with her," I said. "I'm going to him."

I'd gotten to within ten feet of where Ross knelt over his wife when I felt Quinn's restraining hand on my shoulder. "Leave him, Lucie." He kept his voice low.

As Quinn spoke, Ross gently turned Georgia over and took her in his arms.

"Oh, my God!" I cried softly. "What happened to her face? All those blisters and burn marks. How did they get there?"

"Jesus, Mary, and Joseph." Quinn sounded shaken. "Exposure to methyl bromide can do that."

I stared at him, not wanting to believe what he'd just said. "You don't think she got too near the fields?" His eyes connected with mine and then I got it. "Oh, my God. Someone did this deliberately?"

"Unless she crawled under one of the tarps—which I seriously doubt—then, yeah, it was deliberate. Christ, who would do that?"

I swallowed. "We better get Ross away from her."

"It's a gas. There's nothing left. We should tell him, though." Quinn sounded tense.

In the distance, sirens wailed. "The sheriff's here," I said.

"Sounds like they're heading toward the winery," Quinn muttered. "Didn't you tell them where to come?"

"I think so. I don't remember. My battery was dying, so I made it quick."

He gave me his phone. "Call them. And this time tell them to get the hazmat guys here, too."

"Looks like we can tell them in person." The first tan and gold cruisers from the sheriff's department seemed to change direction and now screamed down the service road toward us. "Looks like they found us after all."

As the crow flies, Loudoun County, Virginia, is only about fifty miles from Washington, D.C.—a city that vies annually for the dubious honor of murder capital of the U.S. Here, though, in the rural affluent heart of horse and hunt country, the crimes are minor— mostly juvenile in nature, pranks gone awry. Toilet-papering someone's house at Halloween. Turning street signs around. Graffiti spray-painted on a wall somewhere. Harmless stuff.

A murder was a big deal. This one was about to be an even bigger deal when we told the police what we suspected. A couple of uniformed officers went straight to Ross, who was cradling Georgia in his lap. Another officer approached Quinn and me.

"What happened?" he said. "Do you know who she is?"

"Georgia Greenwood. That's her husband." My mouth tasted like I'd just chewed sawdust. "I found her and called him. But there's something you need to know right off the bat. We treated some nearby fields with a pesticide called methyl bromide yesterday. It's a gas, but it's highly toxic. We've got tarps over the fields and we posted warning signs." I glanced at Quinn and continued. "But there's still some of the stuff here at the vineyard. We're storing it for the company that applied it for us."

The officer's eyes grew big. "*Where* here?"

"About half a mile away," Quinn said. "But those blisters on her face. They could be from exposure to methyl bromide."

"Holy shit." He turned and called to the other officers. "We got a hot zone here. Methyl bromide. It's a pesticide."

He had their undivided attention.

"Then we better get the fire boys here quick," one of them said. "I heard the hazmat team was looking for volunteers so they could run a drill. Looks like they got lucky. We got the real thing."

I lost track of the number of vehicles and uniformed men and women who showed up, but it looked—from a distance—like every cop, firefighter, and EMT in Loudoun and Fauquier Counties was on the scene. While we waited for the hazmat team to arrive, Quinn, Ross, and I were isolated with the officers and Georgia in the area they'd called the hot zone. Two officers escorted Ross over to where Quinn and I stood, though he hadn't wanted to leave his wife.

Last night he'd been elegant in a tuxedo. Now he looked exhausted in faded jeans, running shoes, and a plaid flannel work shirt over a gray athletic T-shirt. He was sandy-haired, with a fair complexion and pale eyes, and when I first met him as his patient I thought Ross looked like someone who could have been delicate or often sick as a kid—an easy target for bullies. I'd been right, but years of taunting and bullying the child had shaped the man into someone tough as old boots when he needed to be. He'd earned a black belt in karate and ran the Marine Corps marathon every year. And ever since he'd joined the clinic, he'd been tireless in caring for the large local immigrant community. Legal or illegal, insured or uninsured, it didn't matter.

"I don't think we're in any danger ourselves from being exposed to Georgia," Ross was now saying tiredly. "But I guess the hazmat guys will probably err on the side of caution."

"What do you mean?" I asked.

"They may want to decontaminate us, though I doubt it."

A large black man wearing a bright yellow jumpsuit, a mask, an oxygen tank, and salmon-colored rubber boots came over to us. "What do we got, folks?" His voice, through his mask, sounded muffled.

I opened my mouth to explain, but Ross took the lead. "Possible exposure to methyl bromide." He spoke now with a doctor's brisk efficiency. "I've treated a number of farmworkers for it. If any of us have been affected, there'll be signs of respiratory distress, probably in the next four to twelve hours. Otherwise, we're looking for headaches, dizziness, nausea, slurred speech . . . and I don't think we've got any of that here. To be perfectly honest, I don't think you need to keep us in the hot zone."

Something nearby beeped. "What is that?" I asked nervously. "Is something wrong?"

The firefighter shook his helmeted head. "Calm down, miss. Happens when one of us stands still too long. You hear a beep in a burning building and maybe you got a buddy dead or passed out somewhere."

"Oh." My head started to ache, along with my bad foot and just about everything else, but it was probably the lack of sleep and maybe dehydration after drinking so much coffee. And maybe the power of suggestion. Ross said we were in no danger, even if we were being treated as though we might suddenly start glowing.

One of the other yellow-suited men called to our firefighter.

"I gotta look at this. Stay put, folks," he told us, and left.

"How would they decontaminate us? What do they do? And how do you know so much about it?" I asked Ross.

"I've been helping out with the mandatory hazmat training at the hospital," he explained. "We're doing terrorism drills just like the police and the fire department. Like I said, I don't think they're going to put us through it today. But if they did, first we'd have the gross decon, where they'd make us strip and then hose us down."

"Hose us down with what?" My heart began thudding against my ribs.

Ross pointed over to the fire trucks. "Those."

"Oh, my God."

"You mean strip to our underwear?" Quinn asked.

"Nope. Right down to our birthday suits. Then after the hoses, a second shower or lots more water to remove whatever's left."

"I do not need to do this," I said emphatically, leaning on my cane. "I'm fine."

Ross had seen my ugly twisted foot often enough, but I never let anyone else get close enough to look. I'd take my negligible chances of chemical poisoning over parading around naked in front of every firefighter and cop in two counties. Stupid, maybe, but we all have our vanities.

"It's for your own good," Ross said. "And they wouldn't ask, either. But don't worry, it's probably unnecessary in this case." His voice shook a little. "On the other hand, they will decontaminate Georgia."

For a moment I thought he might break down. They would hose Georgia's body down like they were cleaning a fish on a pier. I said, chagrined, "I'm so sorry. Sometimes I should just keep my mouth shut."

Our firefighter returned and led us out of the hot zone through a maze of emergency vehicles. It had been less than two hours since I'd found Georgia alone on this deserted road. Now there were easily a hundred people milling around. Ross, Quinn, and I were separated, each of us accompanied by a police officer.

I lost sight of them in the crowd, but I didn't have much time to speculate where they went before Bobby Noland, carrying a reporter's notebook with a pen clipped to it, stood in front of me looking none too happy. We'd known each other since I was in the second grade and he was in the fourth. Now he was a detective with the sheriff's department and caught criminals. He unclipped the pen and clicked it like he was detonating something.

"Hey, Lucie," he said. "I need to talk to you. First, I'm asking as a formality if we've got your permission to be here so we can process the scene. If you say no, I'll be back with a search warrant."

If it had been anyone else but Bobby, I might have been intimidated. "Of course you have permission. But be careful around the vines, okay? It's easy to knock the grapes off and that's our harvest."

Bobby tapped the pen against his notebook and looked annoyed. "You got a homicide here. Not to mention a serious EPA violation on your hands. From what I hear, that menthol bromite is supposed to be under lock and key."

"Methyl bromide." I said. "I know. It's a long story."

"Well, you'll get to tell it to someone from the EPA soon enough. And speaking of stories, is it true you were here all night with a helicopter flying overhead that had a searchlight on it? And nobody saw anything? Not even that chopper?"

"He was paying attention to a couple of blocks of vines, flying about fifteen feet off the ground. It was all he could do to see them.

Quinn and I wore protective headgear because of the noise. We wouldn't have heard a bomb go off," I said.

In the past hour the mist had rolled in, softening the hard edges of the scene unfolding around us. The earlier cacophony of sirens, walkie-talkies, and shouting voices overlaid with the droning engines of emergency vehicles grew muted as though filtered through gauze.

"You had a party last night, too," he said. "Georgia Greenwood came."

"Along with almost everyone else in Atoka," I said. "We hosted the fund-raiser for the free clinic."

"When's the last time you saw Georgia? Alive."

"When the party ended around eleven."

"What was she doing? Was she with anyone?"

I nodded. "Just saying good night to everyone. Then she left with Hugo Lang."

Bobby rolled his eyes. "He was the last person you saw with her before she got popped? Aw, jeez. A U.S. senator. Just what I need. Where was Ross?"

Popped. I winced. "He got called away early. One of his patients went into labor. He was out all night delivering twins."

Bobby wrote in the notebook. "What time did he leave?"

I tried to remember. Last time I'd seen him he'd been talking to Siri Randstad, the clinic's executive director.

"I think it might have been when the band finished their last set. So around ten-thirty."

"I need a guest list," Bobby said. "Everyone who was there. Also waiters, waitresses. And anyone you got working at the vineyard."

"The guest list is in my office at the winery. Quinn has the information on our workers and the day laborers. Dominique can tell you about the catering staff."

"Anybody else I missed? You have any music or entertainment?"

"Randy Hunter's band played all night."

Bobby looked up from his notes. "You kiddin' me? No offense, but what's a redneck band doing playing for that kind of fancy-dress crowd?"

"Georgia set it up," I said. "Randy did it for free because it was good exposure, plus it was for charity."

"She did, did she? All right. Anything else I should know?" When I hesitated, he added, "Make my job easy, Lucie. If you don't tell me, I'll find out anyway." He tapped his pen on the notebook.

"Harry Dye got drunk and gave Georgia a piece of his mind."

"Talk to me."

"She and Hugo Lang went up onstage during one of the band's breaks so she could announce that he was endorsing her for state senate."

"Harry went with them?"

"No, of course not. Actually . . ." I stopped.

He was right on top of me. "Yeah? What?"

"Harry'd just finished having it out with Randy. Then Georgia started to talk and Harry started in heckling her. Something about, 'Gals like you ought to stay home where you belong instead of trying to mind everybody else's business.'"

"You mean he had words with Georgia *and* Randy? Jeez. What'd he say to Randy?"

"I didn't hear."

"All right. Go on about Georgia."

"It was over pretty quickly. The place went completely quiet, then Georgia told him he'd obviously had one too many drinks and that he wasn't a good advertisement for his own vineyard," I said. "Polite, but you could tell she was ready to rip his insides out and tie them in a knot. Luckily, a couple of the Romeos hauled Harry out of there right away. I think they took him home."

The Romeos were a group of retired businessmen whose name stood for "Retired Old Men Eating Out." Patrons of a grateful network of local restaurants and cafés, they played poker, solved the world's problems, and, along with Thelma Johnson, who owned the general store, were the richly vibrant source of local information otherwise known as gossip. In Atoka the six degrees of separation rapidly compressed to two.

"Which Romeos?" Bobby asked.

"Austin Kendall and Seth Hannah."

He noted that, then said, "You got any idea what Georgia would be doing on your service road in the middle of the night?"

"No. It's not open to the public unless it's apple-picking season. The only people who used it yesterday were the caterers and the people who brought in the tents. The guests came by the main road and parked in the winery parking lot. Then they walked to the Ruins."

"Everybody leave the way they came?"

"I'm not sure, since I took off around midnight. But usually once the guests leave, the staff takes Sycamore Lane. The service road's full of potholes. If you don't know where they are—especially in the dark—it's hard on your alignment."

He shut the notebook. "I'd appreciate having that guest list. My officer will drive you over to the winery."

"Okay if I take my car?" I asked. "It's over by where Georgia . . . The hazmat guys don't need to decontaminate it, do they?"

Bobby eyed me. "I'll ask. Stay here."

He returned about fifteen minutes later. "You can take your car. They don't need to do any decon," he said. "By the way, who uses that old hay barn you got over by the creek?"

"We let Randy's band practice there," I said.

"Practice what?"

"Music. What else would they be practicing?"

Bobby eyed me skeptically. "One of my men just radioed from your barn. He found an open package of condoms in the loft. Some quilts and a sleeping bag, too. You know anything about that?"

I blushed and said, surprised, "No, I did not."

"Any idea what women Randy and his band might have brought there?"

"No." I'm a terrible liar. My face always turns red. Bobby'd been watching it do that since I was eight.

"Lucie?" He waited.

"Just a rumor about Randy. He, uh, might have brought Georgia."

Now it was his turn to look surprised. "Are you kidding me? Randy and Georgia, huh?" He shook his head wonderingly. "You see him leave the party last night?"

"When it was over and the band packed up. About eleven-thirty."

"Was he with anyone?"

"Nope. Alone. The rest of the band left earlier." I leaned on my cane. My throbbing left foot felt like hundreds of pins and needles were stabbing it. "Anything else, or can I go now?"

"As a matter of fact, there is something else," he said. "I got good news and bad news for you. The good news is that considering the location of the crime scene, we're not going to make you temporarily close your winery while we do our investigation."

"I appreciate that. And the bad news?"

"The EPA might not be feeling so generous by the time they get through with you. Those boys could slap a big ole fine on you and take your bonded license away for leaving that menthol stuff out by those new fields." He looked at me severely. "In other words, they could shut you down for good."

CHAPTER 3

After I gave a copy of the guest list to the officer who accompanied me to the villa, I dropped off the flashlights at the equipment barn. Another tan and gold cruiser was parked in front of the barn door. Two uniformed officers came out as I pulled up.

"Can I help you?" I asked. Hardly necessary. They'd already helped themselves.

"No, thanks, miss," one of them said. "That door usually unlocked?"

"No, but we were working last night so we didn't lock it."

"And what brings you here now?"

I said evenly, "I'm dropping off a couple of boxes of flashlights we were using to mark the fields so the helicopter knew where to go."

My answer seemed to satisfy him and they got in the Crown Victoria and drove off. I left the flashlights, locked up, and headed home. Would I find a cruiser there, too? Or maybe someone from the EPA?

Lord, was Bobby right? Could they really shut us down?

No car in the driveway. And no sign that anybody had been here, either. Relieved, I parked the Mini and went inside.

My home, Highland House, had been designed and built by my ancestor, Hamish Montgomery, in the early 1800s after he received five hundred acres from the sixth Lord Fairfax as a reward for distinguished service during the French and Indian War. The house was a pleasing combination of Federal and Georgian architecture, built mostly of locally quarried stone, except for the foundation. Those stones came from Goose Creek, which meandered through two counties—and our property—as it snaked its way to the Potomac River. According to family lore, Hamish had hauled them himself to the highest bluff on our land. There he'd watched the sun set in all its vivid glory behind the low-slung Blue Ridge Mountains, then sited his house so he'd always have that spectacular view.

Last year a fire had destroyed part of the first floor, but from the outside the place looked like it had for the last two centuries, as the fire had miraculously spared the stone façade. The Montgomery clan motto carved over the front door—*Garde bien,* which means protect well, defend well—was grimier, but still quite appropriately intact.

As I walked inside, I heard the answering machine's monotonous chirp. One message. My brother, Eli, sounding garbled. He must have been calling from his mobile phone while he was on the road, because he kept fading in and out.

"It's me. What the hell's going on . . . heard about finding Georgia Greenwood dead at . . . on the news just now and I nearly drove off the . . . on my way to Hilton Head with Brandi and Hope for a week. You know I'd come home, but I don't see what I could . . . were you, I'd be trying to cover my . . . so you really ought . . ."

The message ended there and he hadn't called back to finish telling me what I really ought. As for the offer to change his beach plans and come home, the fake sincerity in that gesture was patented Eli. The way he was now. Since he married Brandi a few years ago, he had changed from the big-hearted brother I could count on no matter what to a self-absorbed stranger who decided what to do after calculating first what was in it for him. Sometimes I wondered what had happened to his conscience. He used to have one.

In fact, he used to care about a lot of things, like this house and the vineyard. Even after the fire, he'd been pretty blasé when I asked his opinion—whether I should restore it as it had always been or change it.

"Do whatever you want, Luce," he'd said. "It's your house now. You wanted it, you got it. I don't have such great memories of growing up there, so you can dynamite it, for all I care."

Eli, an architect, now lived in an eight-thousand-square-foot palace he'd built outside Leesburg for Brandi and their new daughter. My sister-in-law's idea of "old" or "antique" meant anything still hanging in her closet from last season. She and Eli owned the latest-model everything. Clothes. Car. Gadgets. Eli didn't know I'd heard that Brandi called Highland House "a great place, if you like funeral homes."

Our sister, Mia, was equally indifferent. "This house is dead, Lucie. Full of ghosts. Why do you want to live here, anyway?" she asked. "It smells like old people ever since Mom died and really creeps me out. I don't care what you do with it. I'm moving out for good after I graduate."

So I'd hired a young interior designer who did not share my siblings' anathema of the past, though I did decide, finally, that it was time for a change. Last fall I'd returned to Atoka after spending two years living in my mother's family home in the south of France. While there I'd fallen in love with the sun-drenched Provençal colors of earth, sky, sea, and sand, and that's what I wanted around me now. The transformation of Highland House was magical and I loved it.

As for the furniture, my budget wasn't grand enough to replace the antiques destroyed in the fire, but we salvaged what we could, bringing any items that could be restored to my designer's father, a retired carpenter who lived nearby in Culpeper. One by one, the pieces returned, gleaming with a burnished elegance I had not seen for many years.

Though the place was more sparsely furnished, I liked it better this way. It seemed less cluttered and more open. By the time we were finished, the old bones of the house were still evident, but the fustiness and burned smells embedded in the walls and furniture had vanished, replaced by the clean scent of polished wood, freshly cut flowers, and the calming fragrance of dried lavender.

Right now, though, a stiff drink appealed better than aromatherapy and counting to ten. I punched the delete button on the answering machine more savagely than I needed to. No point returning that call. I'd just have to listen to Eli tell me what I was doing wrong, and there'd be plenty of time for that. My watch read just after eleven a.m. Thirty hours with no sleep. I thought about that drink, then I thought about my aching muscles and the gritty tiredness in my eyes. I headed for the stairs and bed.

It had been another miracle that the grand circular staircase that Hamish had designed so it looked as if it were floating in midair had survived the fire structurally intact, when so much around it did not. The only repairs to the carved walnut banister involved replacing the newel post and a few singed balusters, but now it looked as good as new—or rather, as good as old.

When I got upstairs I checked Mia's room, across the hall from mine. Her bed was made. No idea if she'd slept in it last night, since I hadn't been home myself.

My bedroom, the former master bedroom suite, had also been completely transformed since the fire. The walls were painted a warm yellow that reminded me of the sunflower fields in France. I'd bought inexpensive unfinished furniture from a factory in North Carolina, which my designer had whitewashed. The result gave the room a Quaker-like simplicity and clean style. Inexpensive green, yellow, and cream-colored braided oval rugs covered the floor, and my one splurge—an antique wedding-ring quilt in faded sherbet-colored fabrics—lay across the four-poster double bed.

I pulled back the quilt and stripped off my clothes, leaving them on the floor. The moment my head hit the pillow I fell asleep, too tired to think about anything that had just happened. There would be enough time later to deal with all my problems. God knows, I had plenty of them. And they were just beginning.

I don't know when the phone on my nightstand started ringing, but by the time I got to it the caller had given up. Outside my window, the light was dusky. I'd slept all day. A moment later it rang again. This time I answered right away.

"I figured you were there. How come you didn't pick up the first time? I know you don't have caller ID. You ducking calls? I hope you're not avoiding me."

I had known Katherine Eastman since we played together in the sandbox. Avoiding her—then, as now—was like trying to avoid gravity.

I rubbed my eyes. "Why would I be avoiding you? And I'm not ducking calls. At least, not yet."

"I'm writing one of the stories about Georgia. You found her."

Kit, a reporter with the *Washington Tribune,* had been an ascending star on the national desk, destined for the White House beat, until her mother had a stroke. The doctor didn't pull any punches about how much care Faith Eastman would need. The next day Kit put in for a transfer to the rural Loudoun Bureau, the journalistic equivalent of asking to be moved from the express lane to the parking lot. If she minded the free-fall consequences to her career, she never complained or said she regretted her decision to be there for her mother.

"*One* of the stories? How many are you guys writing?"

"It's big news. Jerry Roper covered the crime scene. I'm supposed to write the feature—you know, the human-interest story," she said. "How'd you happen to find her out there? Jerry said she was completely disfigured."

"We'd been out all night with the grapes because of the freeze and I was driving home. Did Jerry see her? God, she looked awful. Her face was covered with open sores and blisters like she'd been burned." I could hear the tap of Kit's computer keys. "Are you writing this down?"

"Of course. What else? Any idea who was with her last night?"

"The whole town was with her last night. Your boyfriend asked for our guest list, along with everyone who was working there." Kit and Bobby Noland had been seeing each other for the last nine months. Any day now I wondered if I'd get the invite to be a bridesmaid. "You get any information out of Bobby?"

"You know he can't talk. You, on the other hand, can. How about dinner? I'll pick you up. We can go to the Inn."

She'd been brusque when she mentioned Bobby. If there was trouble in paradise, it was news to me. "What's up with you lovebirds? Did I say something?"

"Nothing's up." Terse, again.

Which meant there was. "Why don't we eat here? There's not much in the fridge, but you're welcome to what I've got. Besides, don't you have to get home to your mom?"

"My aunt is in town for a visit, so she's looking after her. She thinks my social life is stagnating, so I'm supposed to go out every night while she's here."

"That's a nice offer."

"Yeah, but I can't get in before midnight or she's disappointed. I'm too beat at the end of the day to take myself out to a movie or hit a bar. Some nights I just work later."

"I'm sure that wasn't what she had in mind. And why are you going out by yourself? Did you and Bobby break up and you didn't tell me?"

"Have dinner with me," she pleaded. "We can talk then."

"Come here and I'll cook."

"No offense, but I want more than the rabbit food you usually have on hand. Let's go to the Inn."

"I'm really grimy. I need a shower."

"So take one. I'll book us a table. Pick you up in forty-five minutes."

I got out of bed and retrieved my clothes off the floor. My mobile phone fell out of my jeans pocket, landing on the bed. Dead as a doornail.

I plugged it in to the charger next to the answering machine downstairs as I was on my way out the door. Then I called Ross. A woman answered.

"Greenwood residence."

"Siri?" I should have figured she'd be there looking after him. She was devoted to Ross, in awe of the way he'd been turning the clinic around ever since she'd persuaded him to take the job as chief physician. "It's Lucie."

"Hi, honey." She sounded weary, but relieved. "The press has been calling nonstop, hounding him. Ross is absolutely shattered. He's asleep, so I'm manning the fort."

"What can I do?"

"Nothing, nothing. Thanks for asking. The best thing now is to leave him alone and give him some time to deal with what's happened. He might be better tomorrow, but tonight he's . . . well, it's pretty bad. I'll let you know when he's ready to see friends."

"Sure. I'd appreciate it." I said goodbye and hung up.

Siri had lost her husband to lung cancer three years ago. It had been only a few weeks from the time Karl Randstad was diagnosed, after complaining of chest pains when he returned from his daily three-mile run, until he passed away. He hadn't touched a cigarette a day in his life. No one could believe it.

Karl and I had been patients at Catoctin General Hospital at the same time, though he was in the oncology wing and I was, by then, in a general ward. Siri made a point of stopping by to see me each day for a few minutes when she wasn't keeping vigil at Karl's bedside. We didn't know each other well, but I was Ross's patient and she had just opened the clinic and was in the process of persuading Ross to come work for her.

I suppose I will always remember when Karl died, for the irony of it. He was scheduled to begin chemo the next day. That afternoon Siri stopped by to see me as usual, and for the first time since they found out about the cancer she'd sounded upbeat and hopeful.

I couldn't make it to his funeral, but Ross told me later there wasn't a dry eye in the church. I lost touch with Siri when I moved to France, but when I came home to Atoka, I'd been stunned the first time I saw her. Her once-glossy shoulder-length dark brown hair was prematurely streaked with gray and the worry lines around her eyes and her mouth belonged on someone much older.

Kit's khaki-colored Jeep pulled into the driveway just as I finished dialing Quinn. His phone went to voice mail.

"If you're getting this message, I'm not available. You know what to do. Here comes the beep, so do it."

"Hi. Me. I'm going out to dinner with Kit," I said. "My cell phone's dead, so leave a message at the house if you need me. Otherwise I'll talk to you tomorrow."

Kit pulled a map book and some papers off the dashboard and crumpled a large empty chip bag as I opened the door to the Jeep, tossing it all in the backseat.

"Climb in." She picked up a cloth satchel from the passenger seat and flung it over her shoulder. "I've made room."

The floor was littered with copies of the *Trib,* a battered tissue box, a water bottle, and a greasy bag in a Styrofoam tray that held the remains of a meal. Not today's.

"Where am I going to put my feet? You don't have to keep this stuff in perpetuity, you know. That's why they make garbage cans." I moved the tray with the tip of my cane and sat down. "I just stepped on something squishy."

"So that's where the bubble-wrap mailer went." She sounded cheerful. "Hand it to me, will you? My mom bought something from one of those home shopping channels and I'm sending it back."

I slid an envelope out from under a file folder and gave it to her. "What'd she buy? Must have been tiny, to fit in here."

"A lace teddy. Cost a fortune."

"Good for her. Why can't she keep it? Too expensive?"

"Too small. She thought she ordered a size twenty, but a size two showed up."

"Oh, brother. Hey, do me a favor? Go through the parking lot at the winery and take the south service road. I want to see what the police and the hazmat guys did to the place. We had every cruiser, fire truck, and emergency vehicle in two counties here this morning."

"You don't have to ask me twice. I'm dying to see it." She glanced at me. "You know I didn't mean that."

When we got there, she stopped the Jeep and we got out of the car. The ground where Georgia's body had lain was still waterlogged. Ross hadn't been kidding about the decontamination process.

Kit read my mind. "I heard they had to turn the fire hoses on Georgia to wash that pesticide off her."

I nodded and touched my fingers to my lips.

"You okay, Luce?" Kit squeezed my shoulder. "You look like you're going to lose your cookies."

"I'll be all right."

"What kind of sicko would do something like this?"

"Someone who knew about the methyl bromide being left out in the field. Or saw it when we were setting up for the fund-raiser."

"Well, it had to be premeditated. Man, I heard about that stuff not being locked up. That is such bad news."

"I know." I shivered. "Okay, I've seen enough. Let's get out of here while there's still daylight left. It's getting cold again, too."

Kit drove too fast as usual, one hand on the wheel and the other gesticulating as she talked. By tacit agreement, we avoided discussing Georgia's murder, my EPA woes, or her relationship with Bobby. Instead she asked about Chris Coronado's helicopter and last night's freeze and I answered halfheartedly. I needed food. And a drink.

The Goose Creek Inn sat on a quiet country lane about ten minutes from the center of Middleburg. For anyone who didn't know exactly where it was—meaning the nonlocals—it seemed to material- ize suddenly out of the woods around a sharp bend in the road. A pretty half-timbered ivy-covered building whose silhouette was now outlined by tiny white lights, it glowed softly in the gathering twilight as if plucked out of a fairy tale. Kit pulled into the parking lot as wait- ers illuminated electric candles in the arched picture windows. We found a space at the far end of the nearly full lot. When we got out of the Jeep, the cathedral-like canopy of trees overhead hushed all sound except for rushing water where Goose Creek tumbled through a boulder-filled ravine nearby.

"Too bad it's too cold to eat outside. It's nice sitting on the terrace so you can hear the creek," Kit said.

"At least it won't be as cold as last night," I said. "The tempera- ture's supposed to stay above freezing, thank God."

A wreath of dried flowers and rushes hung on the fire-engine-red front door. I pushed against the latch and it swung open. My late godfather, Fitzhugh Pico, had opened the Inn many years ago and it had won every dining award in the metropolitan Washington, D.C., region. My cousin Dominique, Fitz's former business partner, now owned the place and wisely changed nothing when she took over, so guests still felt like they were dropping by for dinner at the home of good friends.

The large foyer was full of dark-suited men and pretty women. Fitz had consulted my French mother on the Inn's décor and as a result, the place resembled a comfortable auberge with its white- washed walls, quarry-tiled floor, and eclectic collection of gaily hued oil paintings and vintage posters advertising French alcohol, ciga- rettes, and travel. At night the staff wore tuxedos, so the three men who hovered near the maître d's stand debating the seating plan reminded me of a small flock of well-groomed penguins.

"Lucie." The head maître d' bussed me on both cheeks. "*Ma pauvre*. Dominique told me what happened. I'm so glad you came to see us. We'll take care of you." He nodded to Kit. "*Bonsoir*, Katherine. Always a pleasure having you here. Your table is nearly ready. Would you like to wait in the bar *un petit instant* while we finish setting it?"

A buzz of conversation above the clatter of dishes and the clinking of silverware seemed vaguely comforting. I could see through the warren of interconnected rooms that all the tables appeared to be taken.

I said, "No, thanks" as Kit said, "Yes."

Kit's eyes narrowed. "Why not? You could use a drink, if you ask me."

"I could, but I just saw a couple of the Romeos in the bar. You know they're going to hit me up for every detail about what happened. I don't think I can handle it right now."

The maître d' swiftly picked up two menus. "I have a table available right now. In the main dining room, not where you usually sit, and not terribly private. Will that be satisfactory? Otherwise . . ."

Kit nodded as I said, "Perfect."

"I'll let your cousin know where you're sitting. Enjoy your dinner."

Kit got her earlier wish—almost—as our table was next to a window overlooking Goose Creek. A necklace of Japanese lanterns strung along its banks shone serenely in the darkness. I could no longer see the water except in places where it glinted, shiny and black as coal in the lantern light, nor hear it above the din of voices.

Our waiter took drink orders, but it was my cousin who showed up with two glasses. Not what we'd asked for.

"Kir Royal. On the house." Dominique set the flutes of raspberry-colored champagne in front of us. "How are you, *ma puce?*" She brushed a spiky strand of auburn hair out of her eyes and leaned down to kiss each of us on both cheeks.

Before Dominique became the full-time owner of the Inn, she ran a catering company that she'd nurtured from a startup when she moved here from France to look after Mia when my mother died. Before long she was putting in Washington-type sixty- and seventy-hour weeks and business was booming. Everyone figured she'd get an assistant once she added the Inn to an overfull plate, but by then she'd been named Loudoun County's businesswoman of the year and you don't stomp on superwoman's cape, to loosely paraphrase the song.

A few months later she came down with pneumonia brought on by exhaustion and finally decided maybe she could use a little help. She went through three assistants in three months and had just hired her fourth. Fortunately, my cousin hadn't been around at the time or she probably would have micromanaged God into taking only five days instead of seven to get the ball rolling creation-wise.

"I'm all right," I said. "Thanks for the Kir."

"I heard about Georgia from Sam Constantine," she said. "*Mon Dieu,* how awful!"

"How did Sam know?" I asked.

"He was with Ross at the sheriff's office."

Sam was one of the Romeos, even though he was still a year or two away from retirement.

"Ross needed a lawyer?" I had been reaching for my champagne glass and nearly knocked it over. Dominique rescued it before it tipped. "Sorry," I apologized. "Ross is home now. I just spoke to Siri Randstad. She's answering his phone and trying to keep the press at bay." I glanced at Kit, who made a face. "I didn't mean you. Anyway, Siri didn't mention that Ross had been charged with anything."

"He wasn't," my cousin said. "Sam was just there making sure nothing happened to Ross's Second Amendment rights."

Dominique was finally getting her U.S. citizenship and was hoping to be sworn in just before Flag Day, after she took a test in civics and American history.

"The Second Amendment," Kit said, fishing a raspberry out of her champagne flute with her finger, "is the right to bear arms."

"*Merde.* One of the other ones, then."

"Ross has the best alibi in the world," I said. "He delivered twins last night. Got the call before the fund-raiser ended. When I reached him this morning to tell him about Georgia, he was just driving home."

"The police always check out whoever is closest to the victim first," Kit said. "You know that."

"I'd better get back to the kitchen." Dominique glanced over her shoulder. "They probably need me there. By the way, the pastry chef made Fitz's Double Chocolate Died-and-Gone-to-Heaven Cheesecake." She glanced at Kit. "In case you're interested."

Kit rolled her eyes. "I couldn't. Okay, I shouldn't."

"Go on back to work, then," I said to my cousin. "We won't keep you. I'll call your assistant in a day or two to go over the plans for Memorial Day."

"What number assistant is this?" Kit asked when we were alone. "Eight?"

"Four. Dominique swears she'll let this one handle the catering business, but for now she's got her on a short leash."

"The only leashes she owns are short. Speaking of which, is she ever going to marry Joe?"

Joe Dawson taught history at a private girls' high school in Middleburg and occasionally helped out at the vineyard. He'd been going out with Dominique for years.

"Who knows? They're engaged, but I think the wedding's on hold for a while. She's too busy to plan anything at the moment."

"You know, it ought to be against the law to make that cheesecake. The diet starts tomorrow. I mean it."

Kit had gained at least twenty-five pounds during the two years I'd been in France. Every day the diet started tomorrow.

I smiled as her mobile phone, which was lying on the table next to her bread plate, started to vibrate. She picked it up and stared at the display. "Well, will you look at that? Quinn Santori. I bet it's for you."

Kit opened the phone and said, "She's right here. Hang on."

I stood up, reaching for my cane. "I'll take this outside. Excuse me."

He was none too happy at waiting on me. When I said hello, he snapped, "I've been chasing you all over two counties. I finally called Faith Eastman and got this number. Where *are* you?"

"You had to track me down through Kit's mother? I'm at the Goose Creek Inn. What's up?"

"Unfortunately, nothing is up. I just checked the sensors in those low-lying fields. The temperature's dropped pretty fast in the past hour. Harry Dye's going to turn on his turbines again tonight. I can't get hold of Chris Coronado, so it's just you, me, Hector, and anyone else we can round up to try to deal with this. You need to get back here right now."

"What are you talking about?" I said, stunned. "It's going below freezing *again*?"

"Yup. Another killing frost. And this time we're not ready."

CHAPTER 4

Kit looked like I'd stabbed her through the heart when I told her I had to leave immediately. She was only slightly mollified when our waiter boxed our meals to go and included an extra-large piece of cheesecake for her. I gave him an outrageous tip and we left.

"No more criticizing me for eating in my car," she said as we got into the Jeep and I pulled the Styrofoam containers out of a large paper bag. "You're doing it, too."

"Dammit. The weather forecast said the temperature would stay above freezing tonight." I drove a plastic fork too aggressively through a piece of roasted eggplant and heard the plastic snap. "Why did I do that? All I've got left is a spoon."

"Take my fork. I'm using my fingers. Don't tell me you believe what those people say. That cute guy on Channel Two is no meteorologist, you know. They just hired him to boost ratings because he's such a hunk. He used to be on a soap opera. I think he played a brain surgeon." She fiddled with the latch of her Styrofoam box. "I can't open this. Can you please hand me a piece of chicken? I'm famished."

"We never had a chance to talk about you and Bobby." I opened the box and passed her the chicken. "Do you have any napkins? I think our waiter forgot them."

"What's to say? He's tied up most evenings and weekends coaching a kids' soccer team with the Special Olympics. Look in the glove compartment. Or on the floor."

"I didn't know he was involved with the Special Olympics. So what happened to the two of you? You were pretty tight."

"We're just in different places right now. Kind of like you and Quinn."

"Me and Quinn! What's that supposed to mean? Quinn works for me. I thought you and Bobby might be getting married." I handed her a napkin. "Of course, Quinn would like it if *I* worked for *him*. Drives me nuts."

"Are the two of you going to be out together again all night?"

"Will you knock it off? It's not a date. And, yes, unfortunately, we are."

"Why 'unfortunately'?"

"Because . . ." I hesitated. "I could kill him for not locking up that methyl bromide. It's completely jeopardized our future. But I can't blame him, either. He was working flat-out, dealing with the freeze and the new fields. In the end, if we lose our license the matter of fault will be moot. We'll still have to close our doors."

"You can't—"

"It's not just about getting in trouble with the EPA, either." I cut her off. "Someone used that stuff to kill Georgia. I feel like I'm partly to blame."

"Don't go there, Luce." This time Kit was firm. "Whoever killed her would have found something else. It wasn't random. You said so yourself. As for the EPA, you might get off with a fine and a slap on the wrist. Maybe they won't pull your license."

"I'll find out, won't I?"

Kit dropped a picked-clean chicken bone into her box. "What are you going to do without a helicopter?"

"Use the smudge pots. We haven't put them out for years."

"Those little stovepipe things that give off toxic black smoke?"

"I definitely won't make it on anybody's do-good environmental list, will I? Come on, you know I can't afford to lose five acres of grapes. It's a lot of money. I don't have any choice."

She signaled for the turn at the main gate of the winery. Her headlights caught the blue and white sign that said "Sycamore Lane. Private Byway."

"I know, I know." She turned at the fork in the road by the two-hundred-year-old sycamore tree that gave the road its name. "But someday we're all going to be sorry when Alaska is a tropical beach resort because of global warming." She pulled into my driveway. "Let's try dinner again. Maybe we'll make it all the way to dessert next time."

After she left, I changed into warm clothes and drove over to the vineyard. The night air was cold and sharp and the cloudless sky was star-spattered. The wind had died down—which was, once again, our problem. With no airflow moving through the vineyard when the temperature went below thirty-two, the dew would freeze the grapes. And no cloud cover meant nothing stopped the heat in the soil from radiating up into that limitless sky.

Quinn and Hector were already in the barrel room when I arrived. Hector smiled at me, but the harshness of the artificial lighting made it look like he was in pain. Normally he wore his years lightly, but tonight his shoulders seemed stooped and his step was more of a shuffle. Had we not needed him so desperately, I would have sent him home and back to bed.

"Who else have we got?" I asked Quinn.

"Manolo, of course. But I can't find Randy anywhere. He's not answering his mobile. We could really use him."

"I bet that boy took off and went fishing," Hector said. "He's done it before. Besides, the brookies are biting."

"The what?" Quinn asked.

"Brook trout," Hector said. "Virginia's state fish."

"You people know what your state fish is?"

"Sure. Been here since the Ice Age," I said. "Why?"

"Nothing," he said. "Look, César and Jesús ought to be back pretty soon with that last load of tires from the garage. They've got Hector's pickup and a dump truck César borrowed from a buddy of his. Hector, Manolo, and I will take the El over to Randy's barn. He said something a while ago about a bunch of old tractor tires being dumped there."

"He's right," I said. "But don't tell me you're thinking of burning tires for heat. The smudge pots give off enough of a smokescreen. Tires are nasty. Plus they smell disgusting."

I was getting to know that look Quinn gave me whenever I questioned his judgment or a decision. Strained patience, fake smile. Incredulous stare like looking into my eyes would be a clear view to the back of my head.

"Tires," he said carefully, "burn really, really hot. We used 'em in California before we installed wind turbines. We can stack piles of three around the perimeter of the Chardonnay and Riesling blocks. The fire's gonna be contained, so it's not like a bonfire. No worries about it getting out of control or the vines catching fire. And it's the only choice we have right now. Unless you got a bunch of pairs of wings stashed somewhere."

"Very funny. But the smoke—" I began.

"Will save the grapes." He unhooked his car keys from a thick lanyard attached to his belt. "Look, sweetheart, nobody burns tires for fun. But you know as well as I do that in agriculture, you can be wiped out in a night. So what do you want to do? Either we can all go to bed or we can save the damn grapes."

I looked at Hector, who was intently fingering the brim of his stained John Deere baseball cap. He had been through every one of our harvests since my parents planted the first vines. Hector adored my mother, whose great instincts, personal charm, and savvy marketing skills had put us on the map as a young vineyard with a promising future. When she died and my father took over, he'd gradually run it up on the rocks, wiping out nearly everything she'd built. I wanted to restore the place and put it back on the path she had charted. Hector knew that and understood the emotions tangled in what I was trying to do in a way that Quinn never would.

Hector pulled on his cap and met my eyes, watching me steadily. My mother would have saved the vines.

"All right," I said. "We'll burn tires, but we are really scraping the bottom of the environmental barrel right now. The rest of Atoka would go nuclear if they knew. And let's not even talk about the EPA."

"Hell, I want to save the earth, too." Quinn sounded mad. "Doesn't everybody? Unfortunately, the choices aren't always black and white. That's why they have those global conferences on the environment so people can figure out ways other countries ought to shape up before they go home and do what they damn well please."

"Well, then Kit's right. Someday Alaska is going to be a tropical beach resort," I said. "So just how many tires are we talking about?"

"If we do this, we better do it right. I'd say a hundred," he said, ignoring my shocked expression. "We also need to create some artificial wind. If we get the two tractors out there with the sprayers and turn the regulators on without opening the nozzles, that ought to work."

I had never actually seen anyone burn tires, though I'd read about them being used as alternative fuel at cement kilns and paper mills. Hector and Manolo took care of the fires, dumping diesel fuel on the tires and then throwing lit books of matches at them. César and Jesús manned the tractors and sprayers, turning on the regulators to create high-pressure fans with enough force to blow your clothes off six rows away. Quinn and I stayed clear in the Mini, monitoring the sensors as we had done the night before.

It didn't take long for everything inside the fire ring—including us—to be coated in a viscous cloud of black smoke. As the orange flames licked the blue-black sky, the tractor headlights cut white swaths through the gritty darkness and silhouetted the rows of nearly bare vines twisted like supplicants. The overpowering stench of burning rubber filled the air as the tires sizzled and dissolved. We could have been in hell, except for the cold.

Funny thing was, tonight I didn't feel the frigid temperature. The urgency of what we were doing, keeping the fires stoked and the sprayers aimed at the vines to prevent the grapes from freezing, crowded out everything else in my mind. We worked feverishly, mostly in silence.

By the end of the night, I had soot in my lungs, my nostrils, and under my eyelids. It penetrated my clothing and coated my skin. Quinn and I looked like a pair of coal miners. We were checking thermometers in the Chardonnay block when he said, "I wonder who else was out here besides us last night."

"Any ideas?" I asked. "Who do you think did it?"

He looked away. Then he said softly, "In a way I feel like I did. I should have made sure that stuff was put away. I'm sorry, Lucie, I really am."

Apologies didn't come easily to him. My anger melted. "It's okay.

It happened. There's nothing we can do about it now. But I feel the same about being responsible. The only time we didn't lock something in the chemical shed . . ."

"Dammit, after I finished talking to Chris when he showed up with the helicopter I should have gone back and moved those canisters. Instead I went home and crashed for a few hours because I knew it would be an all-nighter. I was beat." He sounded beat now, too.

"Kit said whoever killed her would have found another way to do it," I said. "This wasn't an accident. Someone really went after her."

"I didn't like Georgia, but she didn't deserve to die like that. I hope the cops nail whoever did it," he said.

"Me, too."

"Hey," he said after a moment. "Look at this." He shone a flashlight on one of the thermometers.

"Twenty-eight degrees," I said. "Colder than last night."

"I know. But look at the grapes."

I looked. "Nothing's frozen."

He smiled tiredly for the first time all night, his teeth gleaming white against gritty black skin. "At least we got something right. I think we pulled it off."

"Thank God. How much longer do we have to keep the fires going? That smell is revolting and we're almost out of tires."

"Probably another hour. Until around five." He put his arm around my shoulder. "Come on. You've been limping the past hour. You need to get off that foot."

"I have not been limping. I'm fine."

I stumbled and his arm tightened around me. "Don't argue, and get back in the car."

I obeyed while he went to talk to Hector. He was right about my foot. The skin was scraped raw where the deformed bones had rubbed against my heavy mud boots.

As Quinn predicted, we stopped burning tires by five, meaning the small pyres died down well before the sun came up. By six the heavy smoke had become a grimy haze, and by seven-thirty the dirty-gauze filminess—the last vestiges of what we'd done—had evaporated completely. Only the piles of steel belts and a few smoldering ashes gave any clue to what had happened in the dark.

The windshields of Hector's pickup and the dump truck César had borrowed were ice-coated, but inside the firewall perimeter nothing had frozen. Quinn paid Manolo, César, and Jesús double overtime from a thick envelope of cash in the El's glove compartment and they left, tired but slapping-each-other-on-the-back happy.

"Go home and get some rest," I said to Hector. "We'll clean up from the fire tomorrow. I mean, today. I mean, later. God, I'm tired."

"We also got to take the plastic tarps off those new fields," he said. "Ought to be done today."

"Get some sleep first," I said. "You look exhausted. We're all exhausted."

He touched a sooty hand to his heart. "I am old, *chiquita*," he said. "I am worn out. This is work for a young person. It is time for someone else to take my place."

"No one can take your place, Hector. Go on, now," I said gently. "We'll talk about it another time."

Afterward I said to Quinn, "I can't imagine who could possibly replace him. He's the memory of the vineyard. Our living history."

We were in the Mini again, heading over to the north block of Chardonnay, which was near my house. Along with a late-flowering block of Pinot Noir, these were the only other vines on that side of the farm. Last night we had agreed that we would concentrate our efforts on the southern vines.

"We really don't have the manpower or the equipment to cover two locations this time around without the helicopter. Those vines need to be replaced, anyway," Quinn had said. "They're not producing much anymore. If we lose the fruit, then so be it. I know we killed ourselves to save it the night before, but what are you gonna do?"

I pulled off Sycamore Lane onto the north service road. In the distance, the vines glittered and sparkled. It would have been beautiful if it hadn't been frost. I downshifted and stopped next to a row marker, cutting the engine.

For a long moment we stared silently out the window at the frost-covered posts and vines. "Hector's right," he said. "This is work for someone young. It's backbreaking, you know that."

"Maybe we can keep him on somehow—"

He cut me off harshly. "Oh, for God's sake. What is it about you

Virginia folks, anyway? You're always living on your memories. Mosby . . . the damn Civil War . . . you talk about that stuff like it happened yesterday."

"We do *not*—"

He was in no mood to listen. "You do so. Hell, half the Romeos spend their weekends parading around in Civil War uniforms reenacting the battles on the same damned battlegrounds. I hate to break it to you, but you *lost*. The South lost. Why do you have to go over and over and over it, like picking at a scab?"

Either his passion or our body heat was starting to steam up the car windows. He rubbed a small circle in his window with the side of his fist and said without looking at me, "Let Hector go, Lucie. You gotta write your own chapter. Everyone else had their day. Now it's your turn. You changed your house after the fire. Now it's time to change the vineyard. It doesn't have to be preserved as a shrine to your mother."

As speeches go, it was a long one for him, but clearly something that had been festering. With the clinical precision of a surgeon he had just cut open my life to expose my family's proud heritage like it was dead tissue that needed removing. Unlike me, he'd come to Virginia to forget his past. I often thought he was trying to shed his memories as a snake sheds a skin. Mine made me who I was. Eli was right that we hadn't always had an easy time of it after our mother's death, dealing with Leland's gambling habits and his errant ways. But I couldn't stay on at the vineyard without finding a way to fuse the past and present together.

"What you don't understand about me . . . about Virginia . . . the South," I said, "is that we aren't mourning the past, we're honoring it. You make it sound like I've got cobwebs in my hair and roots growing from my feet. It's not like that at all. If you're a Southerner you're not talking about geography. You're talking about a way of life. We're polite, we respect our elders, our families are important. We have values and traditions."

"Yeah, well, I have those things, too," he retorted. "But it doesn't stop me from moving ahead. I want to do things differently. Break some rules. Experiment. I can't do it if you're going to stay mired in keeping everything as it was in your mother's time."

"Do we have to have this conversation now?" I asked. "I'm exhausted and filthy. I need a shower and my bed. Why don't we continue it some other time, okay?"

He shrugged. "Sure. And no point getting out of the car, either. Look." He pointed to grape clusters, lost to the freeze, that hung limp and shriveled on the vine.

"We saved what we could," I said. "That has to be good enough."

I dropped him back at the vineyard parking lot by his El Camino. "See you in the morning," he said, then smiled faintly. "God, I'm beat. See you whenever."

"Thanks for everything," I said.

He reached out and swiped my sooty cheek with a sooty finger. "I've been meaning to tell you," he said. "You look good in black. Suits you."

"Very funny."

I had almost fallen asleep when I realized that perhaps the remark about me wearing black had only been half joking. It was the color of funerals, of death, and of the past. The perfect color for someone who clung to old memories and couldn't let go.

CHAPTER 5

For the second day in a row I woke up late. Though I'd washed my hair twice and stood under the shower for at least half an hour before going to bed, when I smelled my pillow it stank of smoke. Another shower still didn't remove the tarry grime from under my fingernails. I gave up and got dressed. What I really needed was coffee and something to eat.

Through the open door to Mia's room I saw tangled bedsheets and clothes flung everywhere. I'd never heard her come in nor get up, but her purse was on her dresser, so she was still home. I found her in the kitchen, sitting in one of the ladder-back chairs at the old pine table our mother had brought from France after she and Leland were married. Dressed in a gray T-shirt that ended midthigh, my sister's head was bent over a coffee mug in one hand and a cigarette in the other. Her long blond hair screened her face and she didn't look up at the sound of my cane tapping on the tile floor.

"Hey, when did you get in?" I asked. And when had she started smoking again?

Mia raised her head and for a split second it was Leland's eyes looking at me, wary and defensive, the haunted, wasted look he'd worn the mornings after he'd had too many Scotches on poker night with the Romeos.

"You're hung over," I said, then wished I hadn't. All I'd done was antagonize her. But seeing her eyes, dark and hooded like two bruises, shocked me the same as if someone actually had hit her. I knew she drank at college like all kids did, and she certainly had access to alcohol at home. She looked like she'd tied one on in a big way last night. I stared again at her eyes. It wasn't the first time, either.

"No, I'm not."

I sat down across from her, hooking my cane on the back of another chair. "How much did you drink?"

She sucked hard on her cigarette. "A few beers."

"Yeah, and I'm going to run the Marine Corps Marathon. Did you drive home drunk?"

She exhaled smoke out of the side of her mouth and stubbed the cigarette in the ashtray. "Will you lay off, for God's sake? What business is it of yours what I do?"

"You're my sister."

She shoved her chair back and stood up. "When did that ever matter?"

I had set that up perfectly. "I'm worried about you. You're under-age. If you get caught—" I sounded too defensive.

"I can vote and join the army and get married. So I'm not legal to drink. Big goddam deal. I will be, in a few months."

Mia had been fourteen the day she went riding with our mother when Orion, Mom's horse, threw her as they took a jump over one of the many dry-stacked stone walls that ringed the perimeter of the farm. Mercifully she didn't suffer long, dying later that day of internal injuries. Mia never spoke about what happened, nor explained why my mother, good enough to qualify as an alternate to France's Olympic equestrian team, had stumbled over a hurdle so low anyone could have stepped over it without breaking stride. I always wondered if they'd been quarreling and Mom was distracted when it happened. Even back then, Mia had been headstrong and temperamental.

After Mom's death it was as if something came unmoored inside my sister or she lost any compass she'd once possessed, because she seemed dead set on taking the swiftest passage down the road to hell, without the good intentions. She had always possessed the stunning good looks and the waiflike fragility of a runway model and, as a little girl, her gossamer hair and angelic features had turned heads. Some-time during her short life, though, she'd managed to acquire the sulky, jaded apathy of an old soul who has seen it all before. It was that bored vulnerability that attracted her to the wrong people, and vice versa. The guys she dated ran the bad boy gamut from A to Z. They always had cars that were hot and fast—and that about summed up the boyfriends, too.

"You better be careful," I said.

"Butt out of my business."

The grooves of our arguments were so deeply etched over the years they had become ruts we could no longer climb out of, even if we wanted to. It would end as it always did, with her storming out of the room after we shouted at each other. If there was any way to reach her or change things, I no longer knew what it was.

"Look," I said, more quietly, "I did the same thing when I was your age, so it's not that. But I'm worried about you. Don't get into binge drinking. That's really bad news. Plus if you get caught trying to buy stuff—"

"I won't get caught. Nobody else is underage. Abby's twenty-one already, so it's perfectly legal for her to buy booze."

"Abby?"

"Lang."

"You're hanging around drinking with Senator Lang's daughter?"

"Where've you been, Lucie? We're in the same sorority. We live in the same house. Don't you listen to anything I say?"

"I do. I just forgot."

"I gotta go." She dumped her coffee in the sink. "Abby's coming for me."

"Where are you going?"

"I don't know. Brad and them are deciding." She scooped up the pack of cigarettes and a book of matches. "We'll figure it out."

I watched her slide the matches inside the plastic wrapping. "Who's 'Brad and them'?"

She stood in front of me, her long tanned legs crossed over each other, arms folded, looking remote and unreachable as a stranger. "Abby's boyfriend. And some friend of his."

"Promise me you'll watch it. Don't get drunk again."

"Lucie," she said, "leave me alone. I know what I'm doing. I'll see you sometime."

"Are you coming home tonight?"

"I don't know." She fiddled with a strand of hair, twirling it around one finger. "I might sleep at Abby's. I don't like sleeping here ever since Georgia—" She didn't finish the sentence.

"Whoever killed Georgia probably knew her, Mia," I said. "There's not some killer on the loose stalking women in their homes."

"How can you be sure? How do you know it wasn't, like, random or something?"

"The police don't think it was. Look, call me and let me know what you're doing later. Just so I know you're all right."

"Let's just leave it that no news is good news, okay? I'll call you if there's a problem. Otherwise, you should figure that everything's fine."

She left the room and I sat down again at the pine table. At least this time we hadn't ended the conversation shouting at each other, but everything was a long way from fine.

Siri Randstad phoned while I was fixing bacon and eggs. "Can I ask a favor, Lucie?"

"Anything."

"I'm driving to Dulles this afternoon to pick up a friend of Ross's who's coming in for the . . . uh, for Georgia's funeral. Could you come over and stay here while I'm at the airport?"

"Sure," I said, surprised. "Are you worried about Ross being alone?"

"Good Lord! I don't think he's suicidal, if that's what you mean. He's just so bereft that I think it would be best if he had company."

"I'll come," I said. "What time?"

"Mick's plane gets in from Miami around four-thirty," she said. "So I'll probably leave here at three-thirty."

"You'll be stuck in rush-hour traffic on the way back. You won't get to Middleburg until well past six. What if I pick up a few things and fix dinner for everyone?"

She sounded relieved. "That would be great. The past two nights we got Chinese takeout. I'm up to here with moo goo gai pan."

"I'll see you when you get back from the airport."

Before I went to the grocery store, I stopped off at the winery to check in with Quinn. The design for the compound, which was based around an ivy-covered villa, had come from a sketch my mother had done. She'd hired an architect who added the semi-underground barrel room, connecting the two buildings by a horseshoe-shaped courtyard with a porticoed loggia and graceful arched stone entrance. A large tasting room and our offices were located in the villa; we made and stored wine in the barrel room. The place still looked much as it had when my mother was alive, except the trees and bushes she'd planted twenty years ago were now fully mature and the ivy that branched gracefully over the windows was full and thick. I parked my car in the gravel parking lot alongside Quinn's El Camino.

Even after all these years, I still sensed my mother's spirit every time I opened the front door to the villa. Across the room, late afternoon sunshine streamed in through four large sets of French doors that opened onto a cantilevered deck and a view of braided hills covered in vines. The sunlight made gold stripes on the tile floor and picked out some of the colored stones in the grapevine mosaic on the front of the bar so they glowed like jewels. Someone had left a pretty bouquet of red roses on the carved oak table we used for wine tastings. Sera, no doubt. She must have cut the flowers from her garden to keep them from freezing.

Quinn and I had our offices off a small wine library that adjoined the tasting room. The wrought-iron door that led to the library had been one of my mother's treasured finds from an architectural salvage shop. The library itself had evolved from our previous winemaker's interest in Virginia's four-hundred-year effort to develop a wine industry, dating from the Jamestown settlement. At first Jacques left the books he'd read scattered throughout the villa so visitors could read or borrow them. But when the piles grew too high, my practical mother had bookshelves built in the alcove, adding two leather barrel chairs and a reading lamp on an old wine cask.

Beyond the library, a short photo-lined corridor led to the offices and a back door to a small kitchenette. I walked by the vineyard's lone award—the Governor's Cup, won twelve years ago by my mother and Jacques. If Quinn and I agreed on anything, it was our determination that one day this wall would be covered from floor to ceiling with awards.

I found him bouncing a tennis ball off a wall in his office.

"What are you doing?" I asked. "Besides making scuff marks on that wall." When it had been Jacques's office, the room had looked like a small museum. Now it reminded me of a locker room.

"I'm not making scuff marks. I'm thinking."

"About what?"

"The Chardonnay. It's driving me nuts. I'm going back to the lab to do some more blending. Want to come?"

"*More* blending? There won't be anything left to bottle if you keep experimenting. I thought we agreed on that sample last week."

He made a face. "Nah. Too fruity. I've got some new ideas."

Last year at harvest we put some of our Chardonnay into oak barrels and left the rest in stainless-steel tanks. Barrel-fermented wine gains an added complexity from the taste of the oak—like adding spice to a sauce—though too much oak will overwhelm, or even dominate, the flavor. On the other hand, wine fermented in refrigerated steel tanks tastes fruitier and brighter. What he was trying to do now was figure out the ratio of oak and steel that would produce a wine we both liked. From this point on—now that the fermentation process had ended—everything we did was about taste and aroma. And the only way to get the perfect blend that suited us was to experiment, tasting the results.

"Look, you know in Virginia we don't like it too oaked or too sweet," I said. "So I hope that's not what you've got in mind. I'm not trying to rush you, but don't you think we'd better get it bottled soon? We can't afford any spoilage, especially after losing the grapes from the old vines last night."

"We *won't* have any spoilage," he said, "so stop worrying. And I'm still going to do some more sampling."

"Well, use the two-hundred-fifty mil beakers, then. Surely you don't need to make a half liter of everything you try."

"You know, Dom Pérignon used to start blending before the grapes were even pressed. Grapes, not juice. He got 'em from everywhere, too. Different blocks. Other vineyards. So it wasn't the *goût du terroir* that made his wines world-class. It was the grapes themselves. I'll bet the Benedictine abbot at Hautvillers didn't jerk a knot in his chain when he needed more time for blending."

The *goût du terroir* literally means "the taste of the land" and it is that indefinable *x* factor that gives a wine its distinct taste. But Quinn was right. Dom Pérignon knew some magic the rest of us hadn't figured out. And he used his own rule book.

I reached out with the hooked end of my cane and swatted at his tennis ball as it sailed past me. The cane connected with the ball and sent it back at him so it hit his arm and bounced under his desk. He grinned and ducked to look for it.

"My mother told me that as a bedtime story," I said. "Dom Pérignon also had a very delicate palate. All he ate was cheese and fruit. He didn't even drink. You still need to use the two-hundred-fifty mil beakers or we'll have nothing left."

"Why don't I get those little mouthwash cups the dentist uses? They're even smaller. Man, you are really tight with a buck, you know that?" He looked disgusted and held up a sheaf of papers. "The order for the new rootstock. I need a certified check for fifty percent so they'll ship it. We ought to start planting next week."

"We've got to get the tarps off the new fields first."

"It's done. Crew took care of it after lunch. Tomorrow they're going to clean up those steel belts from the tires when we're sure they're good and cold."

"That was fast." I took the papers. "Can I get you the check tomorrow? I'm going to the bank anyway to pick up the cash to pay the crew."

"Sure, fine. But I have to have it tomorrow."

I flipped through the papers he'd handed me. "I forgot how many new varietals you wanted to grow. Petit Verdot, Syrah, Malbec, Seyval, Viognier, Cabernet Franc, and Norton." I glanced up. "You sure this isn't too ambitious?"

He threw the tennis ball up in the air and caught it. "I told you I'm going to put this place on the map. You gotta be bold, Lucie. Take a few risks."

"It might be too much—" I began.

"Look," he interrupted, "I did the soil samples and we talked about all this. Don't get cold feet on me now."

"After what happened last night I'm wondering if we shouldn't be more cautious. There's not a single grape on this list that we've grown before. What if none of them take, despite the soil samples?

Why couldn't we put in more Pinot Noir? We know that does well. Or more Riesling?"

"Look, if you're going to second-guess me . . ."

"I'm *not*! You say that every time I have a different opinion from yours."

"Let me run this place, Lucie. I'm good. I know what I'm doing. If we stay with the safe wines you've always made, we'll be stuck in a rut. I can't work like that. I'm talking about wines with different labels, wines we market more aggressively. Wines that will win awards."

"You want to change our labels?"

"Honey, I want to change everything."

"I can't let you have carte blanche. We have to work together."

He pointed to the papers. "I want to order all of this. Yes or no?"

I have never liked ultimatums and I can be stubborn, too. "I guess so," I said stiffly. "I'm late. I'd better get going."

"Yeah, and I'm heading down to the lab." He stood up and added sarcastically, "By the way, thanks for the vote of confidence."

I left without responding.

With the June primary election only two weeks away, you couldn't swing a cat in Loudoun and Fauquier Counties without whacking someone's vote-for-me roadside campaign sign. Actually, you'd be more likely to take out a few dozen, since they were either clustered together in an ugly clump at intersections or else placed along the roadside so close they reminded me of dominoes ready to fall. I drove to Ross's house after picking up groceries at the Middleburg Safeway and counted the number of signs for Georgia Greenwood that still littered Mosby's Highway. Now that she was dead, I wondered who would have the task of removing them.

Though Ross had settled in Virginia more than twenty years ago after a residency in Washington, D.C., he was still known around town as "the new doctor." He had family money and didn't need to work a day in his life if he didn't want to, but he'd put in long hours at Catoctin General and also joined with two other doctors in a family practice until he took the low-paying job as senior physician at the free clinic.

I once asked him why he put in such grueling hours when he

could have taken life easier. After all, how many doctors still made house calls? His answer surprised me.

"I suppose it's because I see something that's broken and I want to fix it." He'd smiled ruefully. "Though you don't have to look too far to figure out where that came from. I'm an only child. Grew up in boarding schools and on summer trips with other rich kids because my parents were too busy with their own lives to spend time with me. So I had no one and because I was small I got picked on a lot. I guess I'm what you call a 'wounded healer.'"

When he came to the region with his first wife, Ross had bought an old plantation house in Fauquier County that Stephanie kept as part of the divorce settlement. Georgia was already in the picture as "the other woman" so the split with Stephanie had been acrimonious. Shortly before they got married, Ross and Georgia bought a large estate in Middleburg. This one had an even richer provenance, since it had been built by a descendant of Rawleigh Chinn, the first settler on the land that later become the town of Middleburg. The place was known simply as "Ashby" because it was located on Ashby's Gap Turnpike, the colonial name for Mosby's Highway. Generations of owners had added somewhat haphazardly on to the main house so it now resembled a sprawling country manor.

In the midst of renovating the place to suit Ross and Georgia's extravagant taste, a construction worker uncovered a cache of Civil War documents concealed in the brick fireplace wall in the library, including a letter from Robert E. Lee to Stonewall Jackson, written just after the local battle at Goose Creek Bridge and a few days before Gettysburg. Though Ross had offers from collectors and museums who wanted to buy the letter, he decided to keep it.

Now it hung in a special archival frame next to its former hiding place—the first document in what grew to be a substantial collection of Civil War papers impressive enough to attract the interest of major museums and historians. Increasingly Ross spent his free time haunting estate sales and auctions, often turning up a significant find.

"He'd rather be with a bunch of dead soldiers than with me," Georgia had complained morosely to Kit and me one night when we'd accidentally run into her alone at the Goose Creek Inn bar. "They're so goddam dull."

"Yeah, but they're a lot lower-maintenance than she is," Kit murmured after we excused ourselves and went to our table. "I hear she drops a bundle every month at Lord & Taylor and Nordstrom's and he never says a word, just pays the bill."

Georgia's flashy Mercedes Roadster was the only car in the drive when I pulled in to Ashby. Ross opened the front door when I rang the bell, looking haggard but composed.

"What have you brought?" He smiled tiredly as he kissed me. "Here, give me those. You wearing perfume? Smells kind of musky."

"It's probably 'eau de burned tire,'" I said. "We had another hard freeze last night in the vineyard. And this is dinner. Siri says you've been eating Chinese food for two days. Time for a change."

I followed him into the pristine kitchen and put the perishable items in the refrigerator. There was plenty of room. Nothing else in there except a bottle of Oregon Chardonnay, four beers, and some moldy cheese.

"You went to too much trouble," he protested.

"I went to Safeway. It isn't much, really. I got strawberries for dessert and asparagus to go with the steaks since they're both in season. Are you growing your own penicillin in here?"

He smiled that tired smile again. "Georgia and I didn't eat at home much lately. She was always out campaigning and I . . ." He trailed off and looked at his hands. "I still can't believe it."

"I have an idea," I said briskly. "Why don't I fix us a cup of tea?"

"I have a better idea. Why don't I fix us a drink? Come on. Stuff's in the library."

The "stuff" looked like he'd gone to the state-run ABC store and bought one of everything. "What would you like?" he asked.

"If it's not too much trouble, a glass of that Chardonnay that was in the fridge. I'll get it."

"I'll get it," he said. "You're limping more than usual. I've been meaning to talk to you about a brace for that foot. Sit down and make yourself comfortable. And prop your foot up."

"I'm not limping," I said. "And I don't need a brace. Thanks, but I manage just fine."

He shook his head. "When you make up your mind about something, there's no changing it, you know? I'll get your wine."

Georgia had decorated the library, which doubled as Ross's office, completely in black and white, including a faux zebra rug on the floor. The lone exception was the mahogany desk, which had a silver-framed cover-model photo of Georgia on one corner and an intriguing modern sculpture of a caduceus on the other. The rest of the desk was piled with medical journals, file folders, brochures from pharmaceutical companies, a stack of publicity announcements for the fundraiser, and half a dozen dusty-looking books whose titles all related to the assassination of Abraham Lincoln. In the middle of the desk blotter was a plastic-encased piece of paper. Another Civil War document?

I walked around and sat in his desk chair. The plastic sleeve contained a letter, written in pencil, but with the characteristic flourishes and swirls that belonged to a bygone era. One short paragraph on thick cream-colored paper, dated April 14, 1865.

Dear Judah,
I do not know when this will reach you, but I have only today learned from Surratt's emissary that Harney was captured before his mission could be carried out. I have no reason to believe that our friend J. Wilkes Booth will not persevere in the manner of Ulrich Dahlgren.
                                                                    J. Davis

Ross walked into the library with the opened bottle of Chardonnay while I was still at his desk.

"I-I'm sorry," I stammered, and stood up. "I couldn't help reading it. Is this really a letter from Jefferson Davis?"

He looked exasperated, but he didn't seem too surprised that I'd snooped. "Yes, it is. Now go sit on the sofa and put that foot up. Here's your wine."

He handed me the glass, then started fixing himself a martini at the bar. I had a feeling it wasn't the first one today. Normally Ross wasn't much of a drinker, but he'd been through a lot. Maybe if I got him talking about the letter it would get his mind off Georgia for a while.

"Do you think 'Judah' is Judah Benjamin?" I asked. "Jeff Davis's Secretary of War? I know Dahlgren was the Yankee who tried to blow up Richmond. I forget who Harney was except I think he was on our side."

Ross's mouth twitched. His ancestors hadn't been on our side.

"Even after all these years I'm still impressed by how well Virginians know their history," he said. "You're mostly right, but by the time Judah Benjamin received that note, he was no longer the Confederate Secretary of War." Ross emphasized the word "Confederate" ever so slightly. "He was Secretary of State. And Thomas Harney was a Confederate explosives agent sent to Washington to bomb the White House."

"Not until *after* the Yankees tried to destroy Richmond," I said, "now that you mention it."

He picked up the cocktail shaker that he'd filled with vodka and a splash of vermouth, a wry expression on his face. "Supposedly Harney was following direct orders from Davis and Benjamin. By then Richmond had fallen, Davis had fled to Mexico, and Lee had already surrendered to Grant at Appomattox. The war was officially over." He paused to shake his concoction. "Unfortunately for Harney, he was caught before he got near the White House. John Wilkes Booth heard about it and that's supposedly what tipped him over the edge and made him decide to kill Lincoln himself."

"What about Dahlgren? Where does he fit in? He was already dead."

"Exactly. Killed while trying to stage that attack on Richmond." Ross strained his martini into a glass, then dropped an olive into it. "But he had papers on him when they found his body. Orders to kill Davis and his entire cabinet, then burn the city. The Confederates knew Lincoln was so desperate to end the war he'd try anything. So they figured these were direct orders from Old Abe himself."

"I've heard that story," I said. "That Lincoln had something to do with a plot to assassinate Jefferson Davis."

Ross sat down next to me and clinked his glass against mine. "Until now nobody's ever been sure Davis didn't want an eye for an eye. There's always been speculation that he might have been involved in Lincoln's assassination. This letter proves that he was. Especially if he got the news from Mary Surratt."

It was a major historical coup. If it were genuine.

"No way," I said. "Jeff Davis would never be involved in something like that. He wasn't that kind of man."

"Lucie," Ross said firmly, "he was."

I got up and went over to his desk, staring at the penciled note written on fine, thick paper. It looked old, all right. But it couldn't be authentic. Could it?

"I thought they had ink in those days."

"Of course they did. But Davis liked pencil."

"Look," I said. "Mary Surratt was hanged for her role in Lincoln's assassination. She had every reason in the world to confess that there was a plot. But she didn't. Neither did anyone else who was hanged along with her. Same goes for John Wilkes Booth, who could have made a deathbed confession after those Union soldiers shot him at Garrett's farm."

Ross fished the olive out of his glass. "None of that negates the fact that the letter proves Davis knew about the plot. At the very least."

"Have you told any of the Romeos about it? You're really going to stir up a hornet's nest, you know? Especially since a lot of them are Sons of Confederate Veterans or historical reenactors."

"Not yet," he said. "Except for Siri and me, you're the only other person who's seen it. I'm sorry you're so upset. But this is quite a historical find, you know."

I knew. "Where did you get it?"

"An estate sale in Manassas. Behind a framed photograph of Mosby. I bought the photo and when I got home, I took out the picture to clean the glass. There it was. That's why the paper looks so pristine. It obviously hasn't been exposed to light for years."

"Ross," I said, "are you absolutely positive that it's the real thing? Jeff Davis was a good man who was just trying to do right by the South. Heck, when they came to his house to tell him that he'd been elected president of the Confederacy, he was pruning bushes in his rose garden. He didn't want the job, but he did it for the South."

He said brusquely, "I know you don't want Davis's image tarnished, but there's always been speculation about this. Just no concrete proof, one way or the other. Now there is. I'll get it authenticated by a third party, of course. But I know I'm right."

Maybe it hadn't been such a good idea to get him talking about this. I tried to shift the conversation to safer ground. "What are you going to do with it?"

"I haven't decided." He still sounded annoyed. "Like you said, it's bound to stir up a lot of controversy and right now . . ." He lifted his martini glass and drained what was left. "I've got to start planning Georgia's funeral."

I went back to the sofa and sat next to him, laying my hand on his arm. "I'm sorry. I shouldn't have upset you more than you already are. I know you know what you're talking about." My voice grew unsteady. "Ross, I am so . . . so terribly sorry about what happened. I feel like it's partially my fault that Georgia's dead because we left that methyl bromide out where her killer could get to it."

For a long moment he played with the stem of his glass, twirling it between his fingers. "Thank you for saying that," he said, finally. "But I don't blame you for anything. You shouldn't blame yourself, either."

"I want to know who did it," I said. "I want to know what happened."

"We all want to know."

"Do you have any ideas?"

"A lot of people aren't sorry Georgia's dead," he said. "I'm under no illusion about that. She was a controversial and complicated woman. But as a matter of fact, I may know who killed her. I think he wrote her a letter. It arrived about an hour ago."

CHAPTER 6

I watched him, stunned, as he walked over to a large bay window overlooking the swimming pool and the impeccably manicured gardens beyond. The underwater light in the pool had been turned on. Against the dusky blues of the twilit garden and the darker-hued sky, the brilliant turquoise water shimmered like a tropical jewel.

"What do you mean, the killer wrote her a letter?" I asked.

"Sometimes it's the stupidest things." He looked at me musingly. "I loved Georgia very much. As different as we were, I adored her."

"I know." I knew better than to rush him. Ross took his time with his stories.

He gestured to the Jefferson Davis letter. "Sometimes I get too caught up in my work. If I'm not at the clinic, I'm chasing down papers at an estate sale or on the phone with a historian or an auction house . . . you know how I can be." He smiled ruefully. "I think Georgia got the idea to run for state senator because she wanted a project, a crusade . . . something to do since I wasn't around that much. At first I was all for it. But then it turned out that we really never saw each other. And I think she was . . ." He paused, searching for words. "I think she was seeing someone else. It may not have been the first time, either."

I held the bowl of my wineglass with both hands. It would be good to have a drink to get through what was turning into an auto-da-fé. As though he read my thoughts, he walked over to the bar and picked up the Chardonnay bottle and held it up.

"Yes, please." I lifted my glass. "Do you know who it was?"

He poured my wine and strained what was left in the cocktail shaker into his own glass. "I do now," he said. "The delivery boy from the dry cleaner's just dropped her clothes off. There was a plastic bag attached to one of the hangars because they'd found some personal effects in one of her pockets. Including this."

He pulled a small folded paper out of his pocket and passed it to me.

Darling—I'm sorry about what happened and I know your mad. You know I didn't mean it and I would never do anything to hurt you. Meet me Saturday night at our special place after the party. I can explain everything.

No signature. I turned it over. Nothing written on the back.

"Do you know who wrote it?"

"My guess is Randy Hunter." He looked deep into his martini glass as if he'd found the answer there. Then he raised his eyes and said steadily, "I, ah, had a pretty good idea that they were having an affair. All of a sudden we were getting groceries from that new store in Middleburg. All the time. I think Randy delivered them. And stuck around for his tip."

"Oh."

I thought of the box of condoms at the barn. If the police had told Ross about them, he wasn't saying—and I didn't want to bring that up.

He added, "At least it gives somebody besides me a motive for killing her."

"You?" I said, startled. "What are you talking about? You were at the hospital delivering twins. That's a rock-solid alibi."

"Unfortunately not." He returned to the sofa and sipped his martini. "My patient wouldn't go to the hospital, so I went to her boyfriend's place. Marta Juarez and Emilio Mendez. Illegal and scared, the pair of them. Especially after Marta's teenage son got involved in a gang fight a few days ago. The cops showed up, but the kid managed to get away, so he didn't get picked up. Marta was afraid they might be looking for the boy, so after I delivered the twins, they bolted. I have no idea where they went."

"What are you going to do?" I asked.

"Find them," he said. "I have to or I'm in trouble." He cocked his head. "I hear a car. That's Siri . . . and Mick. Excuse me. I'd better get the door."

I heard Siri's musical voice, caroling, "Here he is!" followed by a deep, well-bred British voice saying Ross's name, then a murmured exchange. A few minutes later, the three of them walked into the study.

"I'd like you to meet someone, Mick," Ross was saying. "Lucie's one of my patients, but she's also a good friend. Lucie, meet Michael Dunne."

I'd met Ross's friends before. Most of them were just like he was—low-key, reserved, a bit scholarly. Not Michael Dunne, who walked into the library like he owned the place—occupants included. His frank stare was unnerving. I stared back. Well dressed, sophisticated, urbane. And he knew it.

I am always leery of spending much time in the company of men like that. You feel like a third wheel because you're dealing with the life-sized ego that goes everywhere with Mr. Wonderful. Still, there was something arresting about those startling green eyes and the way they held mine.

"It's Mick," he was saying. "I've heard so much about you, Lucie. Nice to finally meet you." He took my hand in both of his.

I'd never heard anything about him. I pulled my eyes and my hand away and glanced inquiringly at Ross. He wore the stricken expression of a deer in the headlights. Great, just great. What, exactly, had he told Casanova here?

"Nice to meet you, too," I said neutrally to Mick.

"How about a drink, everyone? Mick? Siri? Lucie, there's still some more wine left." Ross didn't fool anybody with the fake heartiness, but at least it worked as a subject-changer.

"Lovely," Mick was saying. "Great idea."

After two glasses of wine I did not want—or need—more alcohol. Mick Dunne unbalanced me and it seemed like a good idea to keep my wits about me. Or what was left of them.

"How about if I start dinner and let you all have your cocktails?" I said. "If I have another glass of wine, we'll never eat, and I'm sure Mick must be hungry after that flight."

I could tell, without looking, that he was still studying me.

"I'll help," Siri volunteered immediately. "Let the boys talk."

"Who is he?" I asked when we were alone in the kitchen. "I never heard anything about him. He comes at you like a freight train. And it felt like he was mentally undressing me, the way he kept staring."

Siri blushed and ran a hand self-consciously through her hair. So he'd done it to her, too. "Yeah, he does give that impression, doesn't he? He and Ross went to boarding school together. They were room-mates for a year. Lost touch, then hooked up again at some medical convention in Florida."

"Roommates? They're like night and day."

"Ross says Mick used to be really shy."

"He's not shy anymore," I said. "When he walked into Ross's office it felt like he sucked all the oxygen out of the room."

"I know what you mean, but he I think he's harmless. The rich playboy act is part of his charm. Besides"— she raised an eyebrow— "he's really good-looking."

"In a kind of aging-rock-star way, I suppose," I said, "with that longish hair and too-perfect tan. Nice eyes, though. But I've kind of had it being around men who got shot with the testosterone gun too many times."

Siri grinned. "You mean Quinn?"

"Quinn owns his own gun. Uses it daily."

It didn't take long to get dinner ready. We ate in the dining room because the wind had picked up, making it too cool to eat on the ter-race, though thankfully there were no freeze warnings tonight. I lit new candles in the silver candelabra and everyone helped bring the food and dishes to the table. Ross opened the dinner wine, a Califor-nia Cabernet Sauvignon.

"No Virginia wine tonight?" Mick asked, surprised.

"Lucie brought the wine," Ross said. "In fact, she brought the whole dinner."

"Why California?" Mick persisted. "Don't you drink your own vintage?"

"Of course," I said, "but drinking too much of your own wine gives you what's called a 'cellar palate.' We try a lot of different wines. We're always analyzing bottles from other vineyards."

He picked up his glass and looked at it. "You'd analyze this?"

"Sure. Test it, compare it to other Cabs. If I were home, I'd probably take the rest of the bottle to our lab so we could figure out what the winemaker did to it. What yeast was used, how much it was sugared, if anything was added in case the smell had gone funky . . ."

"It's a chemistry experiment?"

I couldn't tell if he was surprised or disappointed. "In the lab, yes. Here, it's the wine to enjoy with our dinner."

Someone's mobile phone rang.

"Mine." Ross twisted around to get it off the sideboard and glanced at the text in the window. "Marty. Excuse me."

I heard him say, "What's up?" as he left the room.

"Who's Marty?" Mick glanced from Siri to me.

"One of the doctors from the clinic," Siri said. "He moonlights for the medical examiner's office. Ross asked Marty to let him know when the autopsy was finished."

"Marty didn't do the autopsy, did he?" I asked.

Siri shook her head. "No, the chief ME did it in Fairfax. But Marty was at the crime scene. Ross asked especially for him. He wanted Marty to take care of her."

"I thought they already determined the cause of death," Mick said.

"Not until they finish the autopsy," Siri told him.

No one spoke after that until Ross walked back into the dining room. He picked up his wineglass and drained it. I'd been watching him this evening and, though I didn't intend to, had been counting how many drinks he'd had. Too many.

"The ME is finished," he said, and this time the alcohol leached through into his speech, which was sounding a bit slurred. "The PERK exam showed she had sex before she died. And whoever killed her knocked her out first. They found a bruise on the back of her head. She was struck with something."

We were all silent. I couldn't bring myself to look at Ross.

Finally Mick cleared his throat. "Any idea what it was she got hit with?" he asked.

"No." Ross glanced around the room and his eyes rested on me. They were dull and cloudy with booze. My heart ached for him. "I'm sorry, Lucie, but you're going to have the sheriff's department at the vineyard tomorrow morning, tearing the place apart. They're going to take another look around since they didn't find whatever it was the first time."

I nodded.

We had five hundred acres of land. A lot of territory. Although it seemed whoever killed Georgia had stayed within the perimeter of the vineyard, rather than venturing into the woods and fields beyond.

Which meant Ross might be right. Randy Hunter, who'd supposedly been having an affair with Georgia, could very well find himself right in the middle of the sheriff's crosshairs. Except for one thing.

He was gone.

As Ross warned, the sheriff's department showed up the next morning in full force. Bobby had called the night before after I got home from Ross's, as a courtesy. "My officers are going to walk the crime scene grid again," he said. "We're going to take a closer look at your equipment buildings, places like that. See you bright and early."

"Do you know what you're looking for?" I asked.

"Sure," he sighed. "A needle in a haystack. We didn't find anything first go-round. We might not find anything this time, either. But we gotta look. And I want to talk to your crew again, too."

A couple of the officers who showed up the next morning spoke Spanish, but Bobby wanted Hector and Quinn to interpret because our crew looked so scared.

Afterward I sat with Quinn on the stone wall in the courtyard staring at the comforting view of the serene Blue Ridge Mountains in the distance and the well-ordered rows of vines in the foreground. The cloudless sky was so sharply blue it hurt my eyes and the air was clear and sweet. Hector's wife, Sera, had just finished planting all the flowers now that the frost danger had passed and the weather had become more springlike. Everywhere I looked, halved wine barrels overflowed with pink, white, and purple petunias, and the mossed baskets, which hung throughout the loggia, spilled over with dark red fuchsia and lacy white geraniums. The courtyard looked lovely.

"The guys were afraid Bobby was going to yank their green cards. They didn't believe he only wanted to know about Georgia." Quinn pulled a cigar out of a shirt pocket. Yet another Hawaiian design, part of the extensive collection that had become his trademark fashion statement. This one, yellow and brown with dancing monkeys and bananas all over it, had to be a favorite, since he wore it so often.

"The police didn't find the murder weapon this time, either," I said. "Maybe Randy took it with him."

Quinn unwrapped his cigar. "You really got Randy pegged for this?"

"Looks like you were right about him and Georgia having an affair. Ross confirmed it. Last night he showed me a note that came back with Georgia's dry cleaning. Someone asked her to meet up at 'the usual place' after the fund-raiser," I said. "Ross is pretty sure Randy wrote the note. Apparently he came by all the time to deliver groceries. That's when Ross reckoned it started. The note said something about an apology. I bet it all went south and maybe Randy lost his temper."

"Ross has a note from Randy?" Quinn lit the cigar and puffed on it. "Pretty convenient, don't you think? Deflects suspicion from the husband."

"Ross did not kill Georgia," I snapped. "He was delivering twins that night. Look, I like Randy and I don't want to believe it, either, but Georgia's dead and he's gone."

"I thought you told me this morning the medical examiner said she had sex with someone before she died. Not the thing you do before you kill somebody, is it? At least, I don't." He tugged on a thick gold chain he wore around his neck. I used to think it was odd he wore more jewelry than I did, but I'd finally gotten used to it.

I blushed and reached down to pick up a handful of stones from the gravel courtyard, and let them sift through my fingers. "We won't go there. Maybe it wasn't consensual. Or maybe it wasn't Randy and he found out about it and lost his temper."

"The fact that she had sex with somebody other than Ross still gives him the strongest motive for killing her."

"Then explain why Randy disappeared right after Georgia was murdered," I countered.

Quinn shrugged. "Maybe he did go fishing."

"Oh, come on."

"All right, then you explain the methyl bromide. Why not just kill her with whatever she got hit with?" he asked.

"Because the blow didn't kill her, so he had to use something else to finish the job. The methyl bromide canisters were right there. Those fields aren't that far from the barn. Randy knew where to find everything, and besides, he could have kept the protective gear he wore when he put up the warning signs."

Quinn shook his head. "Doesn't sound like Randy, all that premeditated stuff."

"You mean the same Randy who told us he was using the barn for band practice and then set it up as a little hideaway for trysts with a married woman?"

He blew a perfect smoke ring, then watched it vanish. "There's a big difference between lust and murder."

"I don't know about that. With either one, you get caught up in something that makes you lose your head." I reached for my cane and stood up. "I'd better get over to Middleburg. We need the payroll money and you want that check for the rootstock. Maybe I'll stop by Mac's antique store as long as I'm in town."

"And do what?" Quinn stood up, too. "See if Mac knows anything about where Randy's gone? Honey, I got news for you. Bobby sent somebody to talk to Mac first thing this morning. I heard him. You better not get in the way of a murder investigation, playing amateur detective."

"Give me a little credit," I said. "I'm trying to help a friend."

"I take it you mean Ross," he said, "and that boy is going to need all the help he can get. With no alibi and a damn good motive for murder—better than Randy's, if you ask me—it doesn't look so good for him."

"I know that," I said. "Believe me, I know."

CHAPTER 7

———❦———

I took care of my banking at Blue Ridge Federal and accepted the offer of an unnaturally bright blue lollipop from the septuagenarian teller.

"What flavor is this?" I pulled off the wrapper.

"Blue," she said. "Enjoy."

I finished it before I got to Mac's store. He meant it about no eating or drinking around his antiques. I'd once watched him ask a customer to leave because she was chewing gum.

Macdonald's Antiques was located in a graceful old Federal building on the corner of Washington and Jay Streets in the center of downtown Middleburg. The town, founded in the mid-1700s, had once been the midway stop on the main stagecoach road between Alexandria and Winchester—which was how it got its name. Long before that, the area had been the hunting ground of the Sioux Indians.

More than three centuries later, hunting was still popular, though it was now the gentleman's sport of fox-hunting. In the early 1900s wealthy Northerners had rescued our sleepy little region from the severe economic hardship we suffered during the Civil War. As more and more people moved to the area, we were back on the map, but this time as the wealthy heart of Virginia's horse and hunt country.

A small bell on the front door tinkled as I walked into Mac's store. He was sitting at the large partner's desk where he did all his

paperwork, talking on the phone. I got a wave, then he twirled a finger to indicate that he'd only be a moment and I should have a look
around.

I could look to my heart's content, but I already knew everything in
the place was way out of my price range, since it had probably belonged
to a famous Virginian like Washington, Jefferson, or Stonewall—or one
of their kin. I ran my hand across the silky wood of a burled walnut end
table with mother-of-pearl inlay, then propped my cane against a
chair with a pretty back that resembled a lyre. The price of the table
was on the reverse side of a tag decorated with Mac's familiar hand-
stenciled pineapple logo, the colonial symbol for "welcome." I turned
it over.

"Good Lord."

"You interested in that table, Lucie?" Mac asked. I hadn't heard
him hang up the phone, nor come up behind me. He shifted my
cane so it rested against the wall instead of his expensive chair.

"Didn't mean to scare you, sugar," he continued. "I can come
down a bit on that price. It's a beautiful piece. Belonged to the Lee
family. Wonderful provenance."

"Robert E. Lee?"

"No, not Robert. Someone who was kin to an earlier Lee. Francis
Lightfoot Lee. Friend to Thomas Jefferson and Patrick Henry."

Off by nearly a century. Which explained the sum he was asking
for it. I turned the price tag back over. "It's beautiful, Mac. Too rich
for my blood, unfortunately."

"What brings you here, then? Social visit?"

"Randy hasn't shown up at the vineyard the past two days. I was
wondering if he said anything to you about taking off for a while."

Mac was one of the Romeos, white-haired and somewhat stooped,
with a beaky nose and keen eyes, reminding me of a well-dressed
crane, since he always wore a suit. He folded his arms and tapped his
fingers on his forearms. "I just finished answering that very same
question for a nice young fellow from the sheriff's office. Why are you
asking, honey? What's going on? I assume this is about Georgia
Greenwood. You know something, don't you?"

The second fastest way to spread news besides telling Thelma

Johnson at the general store was to mention something to one of the Romeos.

I never play poker. My face gives me away every time.

"I thought you might." He nodded wisely. "I talked to Sammy Constantine over at the Inn yesterday. He was with Ross when the sheriff's boys were questioning him. Is Randy a suspect, too? Nice young fellow. I find it hard to believe that he'd be involved with that woman."

"You didn't like Georgia, did you?"

"I don't like anybody engages in character assassination to further their own ambitions." He rapped his knuckles sharply on the walnut table. "The things she said about Noah Seely were hateful."

"Harry Dye got pretty upset with her at the fund-raiser the other night, too."

"I heard about that," he acknowledged. "Good for Harry. Georgia lied about Noah being endorsed by that gay rights magazine, the one with those extreme ideas about marriage and legalizing drugs. Sure they supported Noah. Fifteen years ago when he was trying to get Virginia wildflowers planted along highways and roadsides. A whole different ball game."

"I remember that wildflower project," I said. "My mother designed the poster for it."

"So she did," Mac said, "now you mention it. Very classy. Just like your sweet momma, God rest her soul."

He laid a hand on my shoulder. "I'm sorry, Lucie, but I don't know where Randy went. That's what I told the sheriff. Trout are biting, though. Bass, too. He might have just picked up and gone fishing."

"Sure," I said. "Maybe that's just what he did."

"That's all you wanted? Sure I can't interest you in making a little purchase today?"

"If I win the lottery, I'll be back."

He laughed. "Hang on a sec. I got something that might be right up your alley. Just came in, too. Let me show you before you leave." I followed him over to a trestle table where antique prints were arranged by subject in a row of toile-covered boxes. He went directly to the box labeled "Nature" and picked up two prints from the front of the stack.

"Beautiful, aren't they? Fellow just brought them in last week. Native Virginia wildflowers. Just what we were talking about. These two are probably mid-nineteenth century. Look at the colors, though. Still so vivid."

"Virginia bluebells! How pretty," I said softly. "And a columbine! They are beautiful."

"Thought you'd like them," he said. "There was a book, too, but I sold it almost as soon as I bought it."

"A book of prints like these? I wish I could have seen it."

"I can keep an eye out for something like it, if you want."

"I'd appreciate it," I said. "How much for these?"

"One-fifty for the pair. I can have them framed if you like," he offered, adding gently, "I know you lost a lot of your mother's paintings in the fire."

I bit my lip. "We tried to save what we could, but we did lose so much of her work. I think I'll take them like they are, though. Quinn and I are looking for ideas for new wine labels. These prints would be great, as long as I can find a few others from the same era."

Mac looked mournful. "Shame about that book, then. Sounds like just what you needed. I'll see what I can do for you, sugar."

I paid him and as he walked me to the front door, I brought the conversation back to Georgia. "I bet there's a lot of speculation among the Romeos about who killed her."

It was all the opening he needed.

"She riled a lot of people, Lucie. Including you vineyard folks. It sure would take the shine off your shoes if she'd gotten that dang-fool bill passed about vineyards going through wholesalers to sell their wine. I know she's trying to keep kids from getting hold of alcohol so easily but I got one word for that. P-A-R-E-N-T-S." He sounded like a church preacher getting ready to deliver a stem-winder. "Why should she rain on everyone else's parade? You know that would be the death of the little vineyards. They bring in a lot of revenue from tourism and from selling wine. I rely on that kind of traffic. But then you got the other folks who still think it's demon alcohol, or whatever, like Prohibition days. She's talking their language. Or was."

"You think her death could have been politically motivated?"

He folded his arms across his chest once again and drummed his fingers on his forearms. "Honey-child, when this all comes out in the wash, I bet we're going to find that there was a lot more to who killed Georgia Greenwood than meets the eye."

When I got back to the Mini, I checked my phone. One missed call, Dominique's number. I hit the send button and she answered on the first ring.

"Where are you?" she asked.

"Middleburg."

"If you haven't had lunch, come by. I have your menus for Memorial Day."

"I'll come, but I thought your assistant was handling the vineyard catering."

A long moment of silence, then she said, "Well, she would be, but she's busy with other things. I'm taking care of it this time."

"Right. See you in a few minutes." I disconnected.

Dominique couldn't let go of the reins to any of her projects. I wondered how much longer assistant number four would stick around.

The lunch crowd had thinned out by the time I got to the Inn, so today I got a parking place close to the entrance. I drove by the four designated handicapped spots near the front door, all empty. Ross had been after me to get handicapped license plates, but I told him that they belonged to disabled people who really needed them. Not me. I could walk on my own just fine.

Harry Dye came out of the Inn as I crossed the flagstone terrace. He looked up and our eyes met. Just as quickly he looked away.

"Aw, gee, Harry," I muttered. "Let's get this over with. You saw me. I saw you."

On cue, he changed direction and came toward me. Normally he and I were on the phone, or he talked to Quinn, on a regular basis. We shared information, workers, equipment, and advice, since our vineyards were located within a couple miles of each other. He had not called since the party. It would be good to get this awkwardness behind us.

"Lucie! How are you?" Harry leaned over for a kiss, sounding hearty enough, but his eyes slid away from mine. A decorated Marine who'd put in his time on the battlefield, he'd spent the last years of his career at the Pentagon. Quinn liked him, especially because he was so level-headed and matter-of-fact. Something really pushed Harry over the edge, for him to take on Georgia at the fund-raiser. An officer and a gentleman didn't bawl out a lady—as a rule.

"I'm all right. How about you?"

He shook his head regretfully. "Still in the doghouse with Amy. I may never get out. And then Georgia . . . God, Lucie, I can't tell you how bad I feel about that. It must have been awful, finding her the way you did."

"It was. What happened with you and her? I don't get it."

"Too much booze," he said simply. "I can't abide dishonorable people, so I told her what I thought of her. There's no excuse for what I did, but she was just so goddam conceited and cocky about how she was going to bury Noah in the election. Laugh her damned head off all the way to Richmond."

"So this was about Noah?"

"That and the way she was trying to destroy us. Vineyards. Restaurants. This crusade of hers that we're evil because we sell alcohol and we poison kids. People are buying that crap, too. I really let her have it, didn't I?"

"It was quite a performance."

He grinned, still a bit shamefaced, but at least it seemed we had gotten back on our old footing. "Well, I paid for it. The mother of all hangovers and a friendly visit from the sheriff's office, asking where I was for the rest of the night since I apparently threatened her."

"You said she needed a good spanking."

"God." He groaned. "I didn't."

"You really were on a roll." I paused. "You had words with Randy, too."

He turned red. "You saw that, did you?"

"What was that all about?"

He hesitated, then said, "No offense, Lucie, but it's personal. I'd rather not say."

"Harry, I've got the sheriff's department tearing my vineyard apart. If you think you feel bad about this, think how I feel. Randy's missing. Disappeared. Please tell me what happened. Please?"

He blew out a long breath and skimmed the top of his military brush cut with a hand. "I guess it's a good thing Amy and I never had kids," he said finally. "I said a few things to Randy about my god-daughter. Gabriella Manzur. She's visiting us for a few days."

"She knows Randy?"

"Oh, yeah. She knows Randy, all right. Gaby met him a few years ago during beach week in Cancún, God help her." His voice was tight with disapproval. "Lots of drinking, lots of free love on the beach . . . so she gets home and after a few weeks finds out guess what?"

"Pregnant?"

"Yep. She didn't even know his last name. No phone number, no nothing. He'd been pretty cagey about all that. Guess he just showed up looking for a good time. Probably sowed his seed all over the damn place. Anyway, I'm sure you can guess where this is going. Gaby had the baby—her parents are Catholic—and gave it up for adoption. It was a few years ago. Then she came here for a visit."

"And ran into Randy."

It was hard to say if Harry looked more disgusted or upset. "Last Friday at Seely's Garden Center. She and Amy dropped by to pick up some plants to go around the koi pond. Gaby saw Randy talking to Jennifer Seely and started crying. Got all hysterical. She, uh, said a few things she shouldn't have, but what just killed her was that Randy acted like he didn't know who she was."

"Did she tell him about the baby?"

He folded his lips together and shook his head. "She told him a lot of things, but that wasn't one of them. Just couldn't bring herself to let him know they had a daughter out there somewhere when Randy didn't even recognize her."

"Where is Gaby now?"

Harry pulled his car keys out of his pocket and began rubbing the key chain like a talisman. "The sheriff asked her to stay in town for a few more days since neither she nor I have an alibi for the night Georgia was killed."

Startled, I said, "I thought Austin and Seth brought you home."

"Austin and Seth took me to my office to sleep it off," he said. "I spent the rest of the night on my sofa in that old carriage house I use. I didn't want Gaby seeing me like that. So I was alone."

"Why doesn't Gaby have an alibi? Wasn't Amy with her?"

"Amy filled in at the hospital that night for a nurse who helped her out a few times. Kind of a last-minute thing. She left at eleven and didn't get back until the next morning. So Gaby was by herself most of the night, too." He shrugged. "Who knew?"

"Do you think she had anything to do with Georgia—"

He cut me off. "No. I do not. Or with Randy going missing, either."

I looked down at his key ring. "Semper Fi." The Marine Corps motto. Always faithful.

I had only asked about Georgia. Harry was the one who brought up Randy.

Up until now, I'd been thinking Randy killed Georgia, then took off. What Harry just said put things in a whole new light.

What if this wasn't about Georgia?

What if it was really about Randy?

CHAPTER 8

Dominique stood at the maître d's stand, her head bent over paper-work, as I opened the front door to the Inn. She looked up and smiled, then the smile faded.

"What's wrong, *chérie*?" she asked. "You look upset."

"Nothing's wrong," I lied. "I just met Harry Dye in the parking lot. He apologized for what he said to Georgia the other night at the fund-raiser. It was awkward, that's all."

I skipped mentioning his altercation with Randy. So far, I didn't think it was common knowledge.

"I heard about that scene with Georgia," Dominique said. "I guess Harry bit off more of his foot than he could chew."

"Something like that."

"Are you hungry? I've made *une salade niçoise* for us."

The place was empty, since lunch was over and dinner wouldn't be served for a few more hours. Though I couldn't see the bar from where I sat, I heard voices coming from that direction.

"Who's here?" I asked.

"The Romeos. Who else?" Dominique led me to a corner table in the main dining room. She placed a folder on the table as we sat down. "They're meeting about some letter Ross Greenwood found. Something to do with the man who killed Abraham Lincoln. Aaron Burr."

"You mean John Wilkes Booth."

"That's the one. Weren't they friends?" A waitress brought our salads and two iced teas almost immediately. "No, wait. Now I remember. They fought a duel."

"Booth and Burr? Not with each other they didn't. You're mixing up your American wars. What kind of meeting?"

"The kind involving pitchforks, tar, and feathers." Joe Dawson, Dominique's sometime-fiancé, said as he walked into the dining room. He hooked a thumb in the direction of the bar and said to my cousin, "You ought to think about removing the knives from the tables in that room. Those boys mean business."

Tall, dark-haired, and rangy, Joe had the kind of wholesome good looks that made him the perennial heartthrob among the sixteen-year-old girls he taught. He smiled, flashing boyish dimples. One more asset that charmed the socks off his adoring fan club.

"They're that upset over Ross's letter?" I asked.

"Hell, yeah. As far as they're concerned, he just committed treason. Of course they're that upset." He came over to our table and kissed Dominique's hair. "Can I join you or am I interrupting something?"

"A discussion of the vineyard menus for Memorial Day weekend," Dominique said. "Have a seat."

He picked up a fork and stabbed an olive off her plate, then sat down. She looked at me and rolled her eyes.

"Shall I ask the waitress to bring you a salad, Joe?"

He set the fork down and grinned at her. "No, thanks. I'm not hungry."

Dominique opened her folder and passed me several sheets of paper. "I thought we should do simple, traditional summer menus. So a barbecue Sunday evening and on Monday, an old-fashioned picnic before the fireworks."

I looked over the pages. "These are pretty elaborate."

"A form of avoidance," Joe said, reading over my shoulder. "Keeps her from worrying about her citizenship test."

"Please," she said gloomily, "I'm like a tiger at the end of my chair, studying for that test."

"I shouldn't tease you, sweetheart. You're going to do just fine,"

Joe told her. "If I can go back to school after ten years and get my doctorate, you can pass a civics test."

"Joe's right. You just need to brush up on a few things," I added.

"I hope so." She still sounded tragic.

Joe picked up his fork again and speared a piece of tuna. "I know so."

"What are the Romeos saying about Ross's letter?" I asked.

"That it's as authentic as a three-dollar bill," he said, through a mouthful of tuna. "It's odd, though. Ross knows his stuff and he's found some amazing documents in the past. I'm surprised he'd stake his reputation on something as contentious as this letter."

"Why?" Dominique asked.

"Because Lincoln's assassination will always be one of the great American mysteries." He skewered an anchovy. "Just like JFK. Did John Wilkes Booth act alone or did someone hire him to kill Lincoln? And if Booth was hired, then who was he working for? Jeff Davis and Judah Benjamin? Edward Stanton, Lincoln's Secretary of War? Hell, one theory says the Catholics did it because Mary Surratt was a Catholic."

"That sounds pretty fringy," I said.

"Um-hum." He chewed a tomato. "Including the notion that it might not even have been John Wilkes Booth who was shot at Garrett's farm."

Dominique shoved her plate in front of Joe and rolled her eyes at me again. "Then who was it?" she asked.

"A look-alike named James William Boyd. Booth survived his wounds and fled to Japan. So they say."

"Oh, come on," I said. "That's ridiculous."

"I happen to agree with you. But there are people who believe it's true." He looked around hopefully. "Any bread around here to mop up that vinaigrette?"

"I'll get some. You're impossible, you know that?" Dominique stood up and headed for the kitchen.

He grinned. "That's why I love her so much and she loves me."

"Marry her and make an honest woman out of her."

"I keep trying to get her to set a date, but she's always got a reason why the time's not right."

Dominique returned with a basket of rolls. "Time for what?"
"Nothing," he said.

"So the Romeos are mad at Ross because he might have found a fake letter?" Dominique took a *petit pain* and passed the basket.

"The Romeos are mad at Ross because they don't believe that Jefferson Davis, who was a good and decent man, would be part of a conspiracy to assassinate Abraham Lincoln as that letter implies," Joe said. "They see Ross as one more Yankee taking a potshot at the South. Doesn't matter whether the letter is real or forged. Either way it's going to stir up a hell of a debate and open old wounds. He's turned into a modern-day Benedict Arnold as far as they're concerned."

"'Give me liberty or give me death,'" Dominique quoted.

Joe and I exchanged glances. "That was Patrick Henry, honey," he told her. Then to me he added, "One or two more study sessions and I'm sure she'll have this nailed."

When Atoka was founded in 1838 it was known as Rector's Crossroads, probably in honor of the Rector family, who, more than one hundred years earlier, received one of the last British land grants for acreage along the banks of Goose Creek. What put our town on the map was the meeting held here on June 10, 1863, when Colonel John Singleton Mosby met in the woods near the old schoolhouse with the men who would become Company A of the 43rd Battalion, better known as Mosby's Partisan Rangers.

In the 1890s, the U.S. postal service decided that "Rector's X Roads" was too similar in name to nearby Rectortown—and they were founded first. So postal officials handed the town fathers a book of three- to five-letter place names they'd helpfully prepared for other towns in the same predicament. After some discussion, the town settled on Atoka. Although that name had already been picked, the place was in Oklahoma Indian Territory. With minimal concern about a mix-up in the mail delivery, Atoka was approved.

Less than twenty years later our post office had gone the way of the dodo bird, although the general store still rented out mailboxes for anyone who wanted Thelma Johnson to take care of their mail. Randy Hunter had one of those mailboxes.

I pulled in next to a postage-stamp-sized piece of asphalt Thelma called the "parking lot" on my way back to the vineyard. If Randy left town for a few days, his mail would still be there. And Thelma, who had a photographic memory when it came to her customers' personal business, would probably remember down to the minute the last time he'd been in to pick up his mail.

The general store, a small single-story building whose white-painted wooden exterior could have used some sprucing up, sat at the junction of Mosby's Highway and Atoka Road. The red neon "OPEN" sign in the store's front window had said "OPE" for so long, it was now a landmark by which people gave directions. The two old-fashioned, low-tech gas pumps out front still required paying Thelma at the cash register after you got your gas. Though she could have modernized and gone electronic years ago, "pay and go" meant a lost opportunity to chat up her customers.

If the Romeos had their collective fingers on the pulse of Atoka and Middleburg life, Thelma—in the nicest possible way—had her hand wrapped gently but firmly around its throat. Even if you swore on the graves of ancestors to keep a bit of gossip or news confidential, she had an almost hypnotic ability to wrangle it out of you.

She was leaning on the counter by the cash register, engrossed in a magazine, when I walked in. The silver sleigh bells on the door jingled and she looked up and smiled. Dressed in baby pink from head to toe, she even wore matching pink bows in hair a shade of coppery red that God never intended any person to have naturally. She wore the usual tonnage of eye makeup behind enormous trifocals that always made her look slightly bug-eyed.

"Why, Lucille! What a pleasant surprise! I haven't seen you for ages. Come and sit a spell." She closed the magazine and clutched it to her chest so I could see the cover. A heartthrob with an unbuttoned shirt, tanning-salon tan, bedroom eyes, and the kind of heavy gold jewelry around his neck that Quinn favored. It had to be one of her soap opera stars. Thelma—who was pushing seventy-five—loved 'em young and virile.

"I think there's still some coffee in the one of the urns," she said. "Can I pour you a cup? I got a cranberry muffin left, too." The stiletto heels of her pink mules clacked like the keys on Leland's old typewriter as she crossed the room. I followed her, the rubber tip of my cane a muted echo.

She gestured to two wooden rocking chairs next to the glass case that held the fresh-baked muffins and donuts she had delivered every morning. Three coffee urns with signs that read "Regular," "Decaf," and "Fancy" sat on an adjacent table next to the bank of glass and gilt mailboxes.

"Thanks, but I just had a late lunch at the Inn. I'm fine, Thelma."

"Now, you sit. That foot looks like it's botherin' you, Lucille. You're limping more 'n usual. The Inn, huh? That's interesting."

I blushed and sat down.

She sat across from me and leaned forward, elbows resting on her knees. "Now tell me *everything*."

"Uh . . ."

"Why, Georgia, child! What did you think I meant? You're the one who found her."

"I'm sure you've heard everything already, Thelma."

"Well"—she touched her hand to the back of her hair like she was primping—"I do like to keep up on what goes on. A person's got to stay informed, Lucille. Especially in this day and age with all those terrorists running around here, there, and the other place."

"Maybe there and the other place, but I doubt we've got too many terrorists in Atoka."

"I wouldn't be too sure, missy." She sounded severe. "We get for-eigners here all the time. Just today I met a nice young man who told me he originally came from the United Kingdom. That's in England."

"Young" in Thelma's book was anyone under sixty.

"You mean Mick Dunne?"

"Why, yes. Ross Greenwood's friend. Did you know he was best man at Ross's first wedding? Apparently they go way back together. Roommates at some boarding school in Connecticut. Lordy, Stephanie took it so terribly hard when Ross left her for Georgia. I swear she still hasn't gotten over it." Thelma leaned closer. "And talking of Georgia, I heard tell she might have been having carnival relations with another man."

"Pardon?"

"You heard me. Extracurricular s-e-x."

I didn't know whether to assume she knew about the autopsy or if she was referring to Randy's affair with Georgia.

I feigned surprise. "I'm not sure what you're talking about."

She smiled like a satisfied weasel. "Oho! So it is true! Your face is the color of a Big Boy tomato, Lucille. Who was it?"

"I don't know." She wouldn't believe that, either.

She didn't. "Sure you do. Georgia was carrying on with Randy Hunter, wasn't she?" Thelma sat back in her chair, rocking gently and watching me, head nodding like a bobble-head doll. "I thought so. I sure hope he doesn't turn out to be the one who killed her. Even if he does know how to handle those chemicals you use at the vineyard. The ones with the ozone in them. That stuff's terrible."

"I heard about Randy and Georgia, too," I admitted. "Even though I don't get why someone like Georgia would have an affair with someone like Randy."

Thelma took off her glasses and cleaned them carefully on a tissue she'd tucked in the sleeve of her pink sweater. When she looked up, the Norma Desmond forever-young vamping was gone. Instead her eyes were full of the wisdom of a seventy-five-year-old woman who understood her mortality. "Honey, you're too young to know what happens when a woman feels her age. All of a sudden you got this young, good-lookin' hunk of a boy who's passionate in bed and probably has a heck of a romp with her. So she feels like a sexy young girl again because he finds that flame burnin' low in her and he knows how to kindle it into a blazing fire. Takes years off a woman, having a young man like that worshipping you."

She spoke with such passion and longing that I wondered when the last time had been that some young man had ignited her flame into a blaze. I opened my mouth to speak when she put her glasses on and the old Thelma, with her va-va-voom persona, was back.

She cleared her throat. "Randy reminds me a little of my Tré."

"Who?" Maybe she did have a boyfriend.

"Tré. He plays Dr. Lance Tarantino on *Tomorrow Ever After.* Such a nice young man, even if he does have to pretend he's a serial killer.

Even so, he's got all the women in Silver Ridge just throwing them-selves at him. You ought to watch that show, Lucille. It's just so *real*. These people are like family to me."

"I'm sure they are," I said gently. "Did you ever talk to Randy about Georgia?"

"I have my way of finding things out, but I never asked Randy direct, you understand. And Georgia . . . well." She pursed her lips. "My store's not classy enough for someone wears those Manolo Blanket shoes. She almost never came by."

"When's the last time Randy came in to pick up his mail?"

"Saturday morning," she said promptly.

"We haven't seen him at the vineyard since the fund-raiser Satur-day night. Some people think he might have gone fishing." Like I was doing right now.

Thelma rocked some more in her chair and regarded me thoughtfully. "Why, no, he hasn't."

"How do you know?"

"Because he would have told me. He gets all those catalogs and such about guitars and music and what have you. I swear that boy's on more mailing lists than I am. Fills that itty-bitty mailbox right up, so I put everything in a special place for him. He's right regular about collectin' it, too. If he's not coming in for a few days, he's pretty considerate about letting me know."

"So where do you think he is?"

She stood up and began polishing imaginary spots off the spotless glass cabinet. "I wish I knew," she said. "I really wish I knew."

"If you hear from him, will you let me know? I'm concerned about him, too."

"I'll do some pokin' around," she said, "and see what I can find out. Everyone just seems to bare their souls to me, Lucille, so if there's any news, you can be sure I'll know about it." She paused and added, "Now, keep me posted on that nice Mr. Dunne."

"Mick Dunne? The English terrorist? I doubt I'll see him except at Georgia's funeral. He'll be gone in a few days."

Thelma put her hands on her hips. "Don't you go mocking me, child. And you'll see plenty of him, believe you me. Told me he's planning on movin' here. He's looking to buy a nice piece of property. A vineyard."

"A *vineyard*? Are you sure?"

"'Course I'm sure. I have a memory like a steel-trap door."

"He seems to have confided in you quite a lot."

"I told you. It's my God-given way with people." She grinned, raising one painted-on eyebrow flirtatiously. "I happen to have a particularly good repertory with men." She glanced at the clock above the cash register. "Lordy, will you look at the time? I missed the first five minutes of my show. I gotta scoot, honey. Be seein' you."

She was gone before I got to the front door. When I climbed back in the Mini and picked up my mobile phone from the console, I saw three missed calls and a message. I punched a button. All of the missed calls—within minutes of each other—were from Quinn.

I listened to the message. He was shouting. "Where in the hell are you? As soon as you get this, get over to Catoctin General. Hector just left here in an ambulance. He had a heart attack. It doesn't look good. I'm on my way there now and I hope I'm not too late."

CHAPTER 9

On the few occasions since my accident when I have walked through the entrance to a hospital—especially Catoctin General—I get a lump in my throat as though I'm trying hard not to cry. When the door hisses shut behind me, my heart starts to hammer in my rib cage and my breath comes short. It is in these moments of panic laced with dread that I understand that I am not done grieving for what might have been.

Ninety-nine-point-nine percent of the time, I am perfectly fine dealing with my physical disability. But I have not been able to confront my invisible injury—that it is impossible for me ever to have children. I do not speak about it. Most people know me well enough not to ask. But something about being in a hospital brings it all back up, like bile.

I went straight to the emergency room. Obviously I wasn't too far behind Quinn because I could see him, oddly refracted through multiple glass doors, talking to someone at the reception desk. I came up and touched his arm.

He turned to me. "The ambulance just got here. They're bringing him inside. We have to wait."

The receptionist, a large man wearing a pale yellow shirt and blue jean overalls, looked over the top of his glasses at us. "Yes, miss?"

"We're here to see Hector Cruz," I said.

"Only family members allowed in the ER," he said.

"She's his niece." Quinn hooked a thumb in my direction. "I'm his nephew."

The man's face never changed expression. "That'll be fine. I'll call you. Please have a seat."

The waiting room had the cozy warmth and appeal of all institutional places—it could as easily have been an airport or the DMV. Molded plastic chairs locked together in rows with an aisle down the middle, all facing an enormous television set that blared the latest news from CNN. Two magazines. *Sports Illustrated* predicting who was going to win last year's Super Bowl and a well-thumbed copy of *Car and Driver.*

Quinn and I sat next to each other in two of the plastic chairs. "Niece and nephew?" I said.

"Well, we aren't his kids. What's left?"

"Nothing, I guess. So how did it happen?" I propped my cane against the chair next to mine.

"We were in the barrel room getting ready to top off the Pinot Noir. All of a sudden he grabbed his chest. I called 911 right away and Manolo went to get Sera. She looked like the world just ended when she saw Hector, but she kept it all together and never stopped talking to him until the ambulance came. They let her ride with him."

"How long did it take to show up?"

"Too long." He ran a hand through his long, unruly hair so I could see the furrow lines in his forehead, deep as canyons. His face was pinched with worry. When I first met him he'd worn his salt-and-pepper hair in a military brush cut. Then his girlfriend—now ex-girlfriend—decided she liked it long when she found out he had naturally curly hair. So he'd let it grow out into an untidy mop that always made me think of an unmade bed. After she moved out I figured he'd cut it again, but he hadn't. Frankly, I liked it better long, too, though I'd never told him.

"Thank God I had some aspirin in the lab," he added. "We got him to take that and maybe it helped."

"He's been working too hard. I told you he didn't look too good the other day. I wish we hadn't needed him to help out the night of the second freeze."

"Yeah, then he insisted on taking those tarps off the new fields yesterday."

I sat up straight. "He did *what*? I thought that was Manolo and César and the others. How could you let him do that?"

His voice rose. "What do you think, he asked my permission? You know him. He does what he wants."

"Well he *can't*. And you should have stopped him!"

He sat forward and steepled his hands like he was praying, resting his forehead against them. "I know. Lay off, will you? I feel bad enough."

"We never should have used methyl bromide on those fields to begin with."

"Oh, God. Don't even go there."

I ignored him. "Besides everything else, it depletes the ozone. I don't want to use anything that toxic ever again. There's got to be something more environmentally friendly that we can use instead."

"Look, I heard about your tree-hugging days, so I know where this is going." He sat up and glared at me. I knew he was talking about the work I'd done for an environmental group in Washington after I graduated from college. Back then—before my accident—I'd been law-school-bound. My life changed forever that rain-wrecked night the car slammed into the wall at the entrance to the vineyard.

Quinn turned toward me and smacked the side of one hand into the palm of the other to emphasize his words. "There is no alternative that works as well or we would have used it. I hate to break it to you, but we live in a chemical world. Look at Hector. You think a group hug and chanting prayers with lighted candles is going to save him? I don't know about you, but I'm praying like hell they give him every goddam drug in the hospital pharmacy."

"That's not the point—"

"If you don't like the way I run things, then hire another vintner." The iciness in his voice meant I'd hit the trip wire that put us in dangerous territory. "I'm sure you'll have no trouble finding someone who thinks it's not moronic to put soap shavings and human hair all over the fields to keep away deer and crows. And I can probably find myself a vineyard where the owner is a realist who wants—someday—to turn a profit." He sat back in his plastic seat with such force the row of chairs jumped and my cane bounced and landed on the Astroturf carpet.

It had been a long time since we'd had an argument this bad. If we kept it up—especially in the taut emotional setting of the ER waiting room—we'd cross lines we never meant to cross. And knowing the two of us, we'd leave no path that led back to compromise or reason.

He'd just thrown down the gauntlet with that threat to leave. Again. It would be stupid for me to pick it up, especially with Hector here in the hospital. I needed him right now. We couldn't leave things like this between us.

"I'm sorry," I said quietly. "I'm upset about Hector, so I'm probably overreacting to everything. It wasn't fair what I said about you trying to keep Hector from removing those tarps. I apologize."

I didn't expect him to say "Me, too," but I did think he would at least be gracious enough to acknowledge an olive branch. Instead, he got up and went over to the television, punching buttons until a baseball game appeared on the screen. After that, we sat together in stony silence and watched the Nationals slug it out with the Mets.

I leaned back and closed my eyes. Someone tapped me on the shoulder and I jerked upright in the cramped seat. Sera stood behind me, pale and anxious. "Lucie," she said. "Sorry to wake you, but the doctor said you can see him for a few minutes. He wants to talk to you."

I rubbed my eyes. The television set now showed talking heads and the logo of a sports network. The baseball game was over. "What time is it? Where's Quinn?"

She looked around. "I don't know. Maybe he went to get a cup of coffee or probably he went for a smoke. And it's seven o'clock. I'm sorry you had to wait so long."

"Don't be silly. How is he?"

"Resting. He needs to stay here for at least two days, maybe more. The doctor told him he was lucky this time. But his heart is not good. Come. He is anxious to see you."

The receptionist pressed a buzzer from somewhere below his desk and a set of double doors swung open. My hands were clammy and my chest felt tight. The door to Hector's room, just off the main nurses' station, was ajar. Sera went in first and gestured for me to follow. Hector was breathing through an oxygen mask, and some kind of intravenous drip hung next to him with multiple tubes that were taped, with lots of gauze, to one of his hands. The display on his EKG was turned toward us and to me it looked like his heart was now doing all the right things. My breathing grew more normal.

"Hey," I said softly. "How are you? You gave us a bad scare, you know? Why don't you take it easy here for a few days and get some rest? You'll be home in no time."

He moved his head from side to side. "No." His voice sounded weak and far away.

"Sure you will . . ." I smiled hopefully.

"My heart is worn out, *chiquita*. The doctor told me I cannot work anymore with the vines."

"I know that," I said. "But you can be the *jefe* like you've always been, and keep an eye on the men. Manolo will do all the heavy physical work from now on. If you just coach him, he knows . . ."

"Not Manolo." As weak as he was, there was a steeliness in his voice.

I said, surprised, "César? I'm not sure he's—"

"No. Bonita. I want her to take my place. She just turned twenty-one. She's ready. Promise me."

His only daughter. I hadn't seen it coming.

Bonita was supposed to be getting her degree in enology from the University of California at Davis, probably the top place in the country to study the business of wine making and growing grapes. But I'd heard differently about what she was really studying.

Another time or place and I would have made a plausible case why I couldn't do this, why I shouldn't do it. Though I loved him more than I'd loved my own father, I was stunned that he would wrap that devotion around my neck like a noose, but maybe I should have known that blood was blood. I glanced at Sera, whose expression was benignly inscrutable. They had discussed this already, right before she asked me to come see him.

I shot her a miserable look, then took a deep breath and made myself say calmly, "I thought she was going to stay in California after she graduated and work out there. Besides, she's only finished her junior year. She has another year to go."

"She dropped out last semester. Said school was boring. You know kids. So she's been working as a waitress out in Collyfornia. We told her we want her to come home." He glanced at Sera, who nodded. "We think it will be good to have her here again where we can keep an eye on her. She will pull her weight, *mi hija.*" For a man on oxygen and a heart monitor, he suddenly sounded pretty tenacious.

"I would really prefer someone with a degree, Hector . . ."

"I left school when I was eleven years old, Lucita. Bonita is smart. She will learn."

"Maybe she doesn't want the job."

"I will take care of that. But first I want your word."

"Why?" I picked at the sheet on his hospital cot, fiddling with it so I didn't have to look into those dark brown eyes and let him see in mine the betrayal I felt. "Why are you making me promise this? It's not going to work. I need someone who can do all the physical—"

"Yes or no? Give her one year. If it doesn't go well, then let her go."

"One year?"

"Yes."

"Okay," I said dully. "She has one year."

"You won't regret it, Lucita." He grasped my hand.

I already did. But I just held his tightly and said nothing.

It did not go down well when I told Quinn.

"So now I've got to take care of her, too?" He sounded disgusted as we left the hospital, heading for the parking lot. "Come on, Lucie. I can't believe you agreed to do this."

I ignored the "too." "I didn't have any choice. He and Sera ambushed me when I walked into his hospital room," I said. "He was lying there on oxygen with tubes coming out of him and that damn machine beeping every few seconds. What could I do? Say no and then he'd have another heart attack? Let's talk about it in the morning, okay? Why don't we go home? It's been a horrible day."

"You go home." He was curt. "I need a drink."

"Where are you going?"

"Mom's. See you tomorrow."

He wasn't talking about visiting his mother. Mom's Place was a nightclub on the way to Bluemont, run by Vinnie Carbone, a guy I'd gone to high school with. Vinnie ran a low-budget, low-life operation, particularly when it came to the nearly nonexistent costumes for his waitresses and the dancers who swung around poles onstage. The joke about that particular strip joint was that all the men who hung out there told their wives or girlfriends they were going to "Mom's," which sounded fine. The first time.

A few seconds later the headlights of the El slashed my rearview mirror as he sped out of the parking lot.

I drove home and had my own mad-at-the-world drink.

It didn't help.

Kit called the next morning as I was leaving the house for the winery. "Want to meet me for lunch?" she asked. "Got a couple of things I want to run by you about Randy Hunter."

"Has he turned up?"

"Nope. Bobby says he's now a person of interest in Georgia's murder investigation."

"So they're not focusing on Ross anymore?"

"Ross isn't off the hook, either, sweetie. Pick me up at my office. How about lunch at Tuskie's at twelve-thirty?" she said. "And I heard about Hector. I'm so sorry."

The El Camino was already in the parking lot when I pulled in. Next to it was a black Corvette with a license plate that read "Boneeta."

Less than twelve hours after Hector twisted my arm to hire his daughter, she showed up ready to start work. How come Hector forgot to mention that she was already back from California?

And what was she doing here so fast? Alone with Quinn, who probably wasn't giving her the newcomer's welcome speech, either. I walked as quickly as I could through the courtyard to the barrel room.

If the airy light-filled villa was the yang of the vineyard, then the semi-underground cave where we made wine was the yin. About the length of an Olympic-sized swimming pool, it had thirty-foot ceilings, fieldstone walls, and four deep interconnected bays where most of our oak barrels lay undisturbed in cool darkness. As always, it smelled of the tangy, slightly acrid odor of fermenting wine.

In my mother's day it had been a somewhat utilitarian place, reserved strictly for the serious business of making wine. But a few months ago I told Quinn I thought we should have a more elegant, atmospheric setting for the place and maybe start using the barrel room to host small private dinners. Quinn was the kind of guy who thought elegant meant you went all out and removed the wrapper from the butter before putting it on the table or actually used a glass when you wanted to drink anything besides wine or Scotch. He didn't have a problem with pushing together a couple of unused wine casks and setting some folding chairs around them, so finally I told him I'd handle this.

A shop in Middleburg sold me an extra-long rectangular Scandinavian table with twenty matching chairs and our electrician hung swags of pinpoint spotlights so they cast overlapping arcs of white light above each seat. To keep it from looking too stark, Dominique designed centerpieces of gilded grapes and twining silk ivy meant to replicate our logo. Finally I hung my mother's cross-stitched sampler with a quote from Plato—"No thing more excellent nor more valuable than wine was ever granted mankind by God"—on one of the arches between the bays. Quinn teased me that it looked like an operating room, but I ignored him. If my mother had seen it, I think she would have been happy.

I saw Quinn and Bonita through the large lab window at the far end of the barrel room as I let myself in the side door. Neither glanced up when it shut with a heavy metal clank, but with the hum and whir of fans, air-conditioning, and refrigeration equipment, they wouldn't have heard Lee's army arrive.

It had been three years since I last saw Bonita, just before she left for her freshman year of school and a few weeks prior to my accident. Back then she'd been all soft curves and baby fat, dressing in a way that Hector once described to me with some anger and disgust as *llamativa*. I figured out pretty fast that the loose English translation was "what are you waiting for?" followed by "you bet I will."

Now, from what I could see, the softness had turned to angles and she looked well muscled as though she worked out regularly. The cocky confidence in the tilt of her head said she'd been around the block with the boys since she left home. Definitely more than once. She sat perched on a barstool, wearing shorts that matched the color of her car and a low-cut white tank top that set off her golden brown skin and glossy black hair. She was leaning toward Quinn, who was holding a beaker—probably more Chardonnay sampling—as he gestured to its contents a little too expansively, the way I'd seen him do when there was an attractive woman around who needed impressing. Judging by their body language, they were hitting it off just fine for a first meeting. In fact, maybe better than fine.

They both turned toward me when I walked through the door. Bonita's eyes went immediately to my cane.

I cannot bear pity, even when it's involuntary. She slid off her barstool and stammered hello. "You look great, Lucie. I mean, like, really great. I mean, not that you didn't look great before and all . . ." Her eyes never left my cane.

"Thanks." I cut her off before she could say "great" one more time. "Your father didn't say you were back from school. Welcome home."

Bonita brushed her shoulder-length hair off her face and I saw the dark circles under her eyes. She still looked embarrassed, but she was no longer staring at the cane. "I just got in on the red-eye a few hours ago. I'm still, you know, real punchy."

"Have you been to the hospital yet?" I asked.

She tugged on the hem of her ultra-short shorts. "No. I'm on my way there now. My mom told me to stop by here first and, like, talk to you about work. I hope it's okay."

I caught Quinn's eye. "Why don't we talk about it some other time? Go see your dad and get some sleep. There's no rush."

She blushed. "I know Pop. He, like, probably twisted your arm to give me this job. He's gonna ask me about it when I show up at the hospital. You know what a *cabeza dura* he is. So bull-headed."

I couldn't help smiling. "Tell him you're not running the place just yet."

Her color deepened. "Oh, God. That bad, huh? So, like, what did he ask you to do for me?"

"He wasn't that specific," I said.

"Look, honey, here's the deal," Quinn said, and I glanced at him warningly. "We're giving your dad's job to Manolo. He'll take care of the equipment and the crew from now on. We haven't exactly worked out what you're going to do here."

Before she could reply, I said, "How much of your studies did you complete at Davis before you dropped out?"

Her eyes flashed. "I didn't drop out! I took some time off. I did good in the enology classes. I like making wine. It's really cool. But, like, viticulture's not really my thing. I just suck at pests and diseases and working out in the field."

"Let her help out in the barrel room," Quinn said to me.

"That would be awesome."

"It's not always awesome," I told her. "You know what hard work it is. Cleaning the tanks, sterilizing the barrels. It can get pretty boring at times."

"I don't care." She smiled for the first time, an incandescent light-up-a-room smile that reminded me of her father. "Grapes, yes. But not bugs. God, I, like, hate bugs." She pulled a car key out of a pocket in her shorts and smiled that thousand-watt smile again. Quinn didn't take his eyes off her. "I better get over to the hospital."

"Tell your dad I'll be by to see him later," I said.

After she left I said to Quinn, "You can reel your tongue in now. She's way too young and she's Hector's daughter."

"She's, like, cute," he said. "And I know she's just a kid."

"Except we're not paying her to be cute. She's got to pull her weight. At least she was up front enough to admit that Hector nearly broke my arm twisting it in the ER last night," I said. "I told him she could stay for a year and he was okay with that. She and Mia used to compete for the hell-raiser of the year award when they were growing up."

He grinned. "I can see that. But, hey, I like a woman with a bit of spirit. It'll come in handy when she's here with the rest of the boys."

"You are such a chauvinist."

"I am not." He paused, then said, "I guess I was kind of hard on you last night."

"You were."

"Angie called." He picked up a beaker and swirled around the straw-colored liquid, watching it intently. "While you were in with Hector."

Angela Stetson was Quinn's ex-girlfriend and a former high
school classmate of mine. They'd met when she was a dancer at
Mom's Place.

"How'd that go?"

He shrugged. "She's getting married. Again. To the guy she was
seeing when she was living with me."

"Oh, God. I'm sorry. She called to tell you that?"

"I think she'd had a few." He set the beaker down and got two
glasses. "She was feeling bad about what she did to me. Wanted to
put things right before she married Bozo."

"What did you say?"

"Nothing."

"Is that why you went back to Mom's last night?"

He looked up. "I never went. I came here instead. To the summerhouse. You're still okay with me setting up my telescope there?"

I watched him fill the glasses. My mother had the little screened-in
summerhouse built as an outdoor retreat, not far from the main
house and behind the rose garden. When I was growing up we used to
have dinner parties there or use it as a hideaway to get lost in a book. It
was now a dumping place for broken or rusted outdoor equipment,
and Quinn had started bringing his telescope there because it was
perched on the edge of a bluff, a great observation site with its
panoramic view of the night sky.

"Be my guest. But I thought you gave up stargazing."

"For a while. Angie didn't like it, so I quit." He handed me a
glass. "Those two nights we were out when it was freezing . . . God,
the skies were so clear you could see clear up to the floor of heaven."
He clinked his glass against mine. "I thought about calling you and
asking if you wanted to join me, but I figured you were probably
dead on your feet."

I drank a large mouthful of wine, then after a moment spat it into
a dump bucket. "Well, one foot, at least."

He spat, too. "Aw, jeez. I didn't mean that. Sorry."

"Don't be. I'm pulling your leg . . . oh, God, now I'm doing it."
We both laughed. "Thanks for the invite. It would have been nice.
Maybe another time?"

"Sure." He held up his glass. "What do you think of this one?"

"I like it, but—"

"I'm sorry, sir, we're closed here," Quinn cut me off. He was addressing someone behind me.

I turned around. Mick Dunne, wearing jeans that had been ironed and an expensive-looking oxford shirt, stood in the doorway.

"I beg your pardon." He was staring at me with the same intensity I remembered from the first time we'd met. "Hello, Lucie. Lovely to see you again. Your assistant in the other building told me I could find you here. I apologize. I didn't realize I'd be interrupting your work." To Quinn he added, "You must be Quinn. Mick Dunne."

Quinn gave me a sharp what's-up look as he shook Mick's hand.

"Mick's a friend of Ross's, Quinn. He's here for Georgia's funeral. And he's in the market for a vineyard," I added. "Or so I've heard."

For an instant, I'd knocked his cocky self-confidence off kilter. Then he grinned. "So I am. News travels fast."

The room was already a nippy sixty degrees thanks to the air-conditioning and the refrigeration equipment. As I watched Quinn take stock of Mick Dunne—who wore brilliantly polished black wing tips along with the pressed jeans and starched shirt—the temperature seemed to plummet nearer to freezing.

Both men looked about the same age, though Mick could have been a few years younger, perhaps in his late thirties. Like Quinn, he had the fit, lean build of an athlete. But where Quinn's sunburned ruggedness came from years of hard physical labor in the vineyard, Mick, who wore a gold signet ring on the pinky finger of his right hand, looked like the type who got his exercise at the country club. Something about the cut of the clothes he'd worn the night I met him said he spent most of his life wearing a suit and tie and working in an office. Wing tips with the jeans pretty much confirmed it.

"This one's not for sale," Quinn said rudely. "Sorry."

"I know it's not," Mick said. "But I'd very much like a tour of your place, Lucie, if it's not too much trouble. I'm particularly keen to see how you laid out your fields and what grapes you've planted." The request sounded like a polite command. Whatever he did for a living, he was used to being in charge.

"Uh . . ." He'd caught me off guard. "You don't mean now?"

"I'm meeting an estate agent this afternoon and I expect I'll make my decision rather quickly," he said. "Right now would be lovely. Thanks very much."

I opened my mouth to explain that wasn't what I'd intended to say when Quinn cut in. "Do you know *anything* about running a vineyard? The English aren't really known as great winemakers, are they?"

When the good angels were handing out the gifts, they went a little light with Quinn in the tact and diplomacy department.

"He meant that there aren't many vineyards in England," I explained.

"No, I didn't."

I frowned at him, but Mick grinned, apparently no offense taken. "Fair enough, but you do remember that when the English arrived in Jamestown, making wine was practically the first thing we did, don't you? England was desperate for its own wine industry in the sixteen hundreds. That's why we made our first wine only two years after we got here. Mind you, it was bloody awful." He was still smiling. "I'm just following in my countrymen's footsteps."

"Why Virginia? Why not California?" Quinn sounded more curious than combative. Mick Dunne had gotten his attention.

"Because they're not experimenting as much in California anymore. Though it's impressive, the world-class wines they produce. But you lot in Virginia seem to enjoy taking risks with your wines, growing some interesting varietals. Didn't Thomas Jefferson try to grow twenty-two kinds of grapes at Monticello?"

"Yes," I said, surprised at the depth of his knowledge, "as a matter of fact, he did."

Though I'd thought he was talking to me, I now wondered if Mick was playing to Quinn, who'd straightened up and was looking at him with new respect, especially after Mick brought up the subjects of experimenting and taking risks in wine making.

"Where are you from?" Quinn asked. "Besides England."

"Florida, for the last eight years."

"What was in Florida?"

"A pharmaceutical company."

"Quinn," I said finally, "give the poor man a break. He just asked for a tour. We don't interview our prospective employees this intensively."

"Yeah, especially the last one we hired," he said.

I turned to Mick. "I'd love to show you around. I'm sure Quinn can spare me for an hour or so."

"I'll manage."

The wall phone in the lab rang. Quinn grabbed it. "Montgomery Estate Vineyard."

"Come on," I said to Mick. "We'll take my car."

"Do you two always get on like that?" Mick asked as we walked outside.

I could have asked, "Like what?" but there was no point trying to con someone as perceptive as he was.

"No," I said. "We're both upset about Hector being hospitalized. And then there's Georgia's death. That pesticide should have been locked up. Maybe if it had been, she'd still be alive. So we're getting on each other's nerves more than usual just now."

We reached the Mini. I'd left the top down because of the glorious weather. As I set my cane on the sun-warmed backseat he said quietly, "Well, the viewing is set for tomorrow evening and her funeral will be on Friday morning. Once the police find her killer, then maybe Ross will have some peace. And so will everyone else."

As we got in the car, my mobile phone rang. Quinn, calling me. I flipped it open. "Miss me already?"

"Like a toothache after it's gone," he replied. "Listen, Mary Sunshine, I've got some news. That call was the EPA. They're coming out to pay us a little courtesy call next week. And the guy I talked to sounded like he's planning on playing hardball."

CHAPTER 10

—oooo—

"What did you tell him?" I asked.

"What do you think I told him?" he retorted. "Your wish is my command. He wants to see all our paperwork, the whole megillah. We got a week to get ready."

"We'll be ready."

"Like we have a choice? Have a nice tour." He hung up.

Mick was watching me. "Everything all right?"

"Just fine," I said, and put the car in gear. "The EPA is going to drop by next week. Come on. I'll take you to see the vines. At least for now, it's still business as usual around here."

It is a truism among winemakers that good wine is made in the vineyard—as opposed to the winery—which means that all the additives in the world won't make a silk-purse wine out of sow's-ear grapes if we've botched things up in the fields. I planned to take Mick through the south vineyard because of its spectacular view of the peaceful, layered Blue Ridge Mountains and because we'd managed to escape any damage from the freezing temperatures among these vines. Here, at least, we still had the promise of a good harvest.

I cut through the parking lot to the south service road and veered off-road at the first opportunity, so we were driving alongside the large orchard.

"Are you going to be all right?" Mick asked. He'd laid his arm across the back of my seat, without touching my shoulder.

"We'll be fine," I said, aware of his arm and the pleasant, masculine cologne he wore. "You know, if you're serious about setting up a vineyard, you really ought to be talking to the people at Virginia Tech or the agricultural extension office. They're the experts."

"Oh, I've rung them," he said. "But I wanted to talk to you, too."

"Why me?"

"Because we're alike, you and I. I heard how you took over this vineyard after your father died and what you're doing to make a go of it," he said. "I also heard about what you went through after your accident."

I could feel the color drain from my face. "Ross told you about *that*?"

"Lucie." His fingers brushed my shoulder. "He didn't violate doctor-patient confidentiality. I didn't mean that at all. But he did tell me about you."

I pulled over and stopped the car by a pale pink clematis that twined through the split-rail fence. I felt, just then, like the Wizard of Oz when Toto pulled back the curtain and the old man stood there in front of Dorothy and the gang, exposed, vulnerable—and feeling like a fool.

"My medical history," I said coldly, "has absolutely nothing to do with running a vineyard."

"On the contrary," he said, "it has everything to do with it."

"Why?"

"Because you're so determined to beat the odds."

"No offense," I said, "but I do know a thing or two about making wine. Unlike you."

"None taken," he replied. "And I didn't mean to upset you. It was the farthest thing from my mind. I'm terribly sorry."

We sat in silence for a while until Mick said, "Those apple trees look quite old."

I appreciated the change of subject, even if it had been anything but subtle. "There have been apple trees on this land since my family settled here after the French and Indian War," I said. "When Lord Fairfax received a land grant from the King of England, he made each of his tenants agree to plant either apple or peach trees as a condition of their tenure."

"Sounds like the English," he said. "Look, if you're not still angry with me, do you think we could take a look at your grapes?"

"I'm not angry," I relented. "But I don't like talking about what happened to me. It's in the past. It's over. I've dealt with it. Now I just want to move on."

"All right," he said. "I'll keep it all business from now on. You have my word."

"Thank you." I noticed he'd removed his arm, along with the easygoing manner.

"Do you sell apples as well as grapes?" The question was crisp and formal.

Maybe he wasn't used to anybody talking back to him. Well, tough.

"Yes. We have two orchards." I matched his tone. "Here we've got all the classic varieties—Winesap, Granny Smith, Macintosh. We let people come and pick them in the fall, then use what's not picked out to make cider. In the other orchard we've got more exotic varieties. Those we sell to the local grocery stores."

"What about your grapes? What do you grow?" He'd pulled a small pad with a slim pen attached to it out of his pocket.

"Right now only *vitis vinifera*. My mother and Jacques, our first winemaker, were French and they wanted to plant the so-called 'noble grapes.' Our whites are Chardonnay, Riesling, Sauvignon Blanc. Reds are Cabernet Sauvignon, Merlot, and Pinot Noir."

He wrote swiftly. "What about the new fields? What's going in there?"

"We just ordered the rootstock." I ticked them off on my fingers. "Norton, which is a native Virginia grape. Also Viognier, Malbec, Seyval, Syrah, Petit Verdot, and Cabernet Franc. The last two are blending grapes."

He noted those as well, then said, "I'm surprised you're going to grow blending grapes, rather than only straight varietals."

I expected a remark like that from a neophyte. Maybe Quinn was right about how much Mick knew about the wine business—or how little.

"Growing blending grapes gives you more options when you produce wine," I explained. "In America a wine can still be called a particular varietal—like Cabernet Sauvignon—as long as it contains at least seventy-five percent of that grape. We're more liberal than the Europeans. They require eighty-five percent of the primary grape."

He nodded like he might have known this, so I continued. "Because we can blend up to twenty-five percent of one or more grapes and still have the varietal, we can experiment until we get a better wine. Something that's more complex and interesting. Basically, the whole can be better than the sum of its parts."

I started the car again. "Let's go over to the established fields so you can see how far along each varietal is. The whites are the first to develop, which is why we harvest them first—but I'm sure you know this."

"Yes." He closed the notepad and stuck it in his shirt pocket.

We motored between blocks of vines as I pointed out the various grapes and gave him a quick history. A light wind blew steadily, rustling the leaves and the garnet-colored bailing ties we used to secure the vines to the wires. The late-morning sunlight filtered through the mostly open canopy, gilding the grapes and transforming the young leaves so they seemed almost transparent.

"You must enjoy coming here," he said unexpectedly. "It's very peaceful."

"It's a good place to come think," I said. "If only you didn't have to spend so much time worrying about the grapes. When they're in bloom, though, and it's just the flowers, it's heaven. It smells sweet, like wild honeysuckle." I glanced at my watch. "We should get over to the new fields."

With the danger signs gone and the tarps removed, it was now merely innocuous-looking red Virginia clay soil. I stopped the car and turned off the engine.

"I'd suggest we go for a walk, but you're not wearing the best shoes."

He laughed. "I saw you staring at them when we were back in your laboratory. Left my trainers at home. I packed in rather a rush." He glanced around. "So why did you choose this place?"

"Because it's high enough that there won't be any frost pockets like the ones that wiped out our fruit the other day," I said. "If you look over there you can see how we cleared out all the trees and vegetation below to maximize cold air drainage." I pointed in the distance.

He nodded, shielding his eyes. "It looks like they face east, judging by the sun."

"As much as possible all vines should face east, north, or northeast," I said. "It's too hot on southern and western exposures. Eastern slopes get the sun first thing in the morning, so dew and rain dry sooner. You get fewer diseases that way."

"Your vines ought to do well here, then. I'm sure you'll have a good harvest."

"Not for another three years. You do know that's how long it takes between planting and the first harvest?" I asked.

"Look, I did read *Wine Making for Idiots* or whatever it's called. And I'm not completely clueless," he said dryly. "Despite what some people think."

I grinned and started the engine. "Have you seen enough?"

When we got back to the parking lot, I pulled up next to his rental car.

"I'd like to take you to dinner," he said, "to thank you for your time and trouble."

"I thought this was going to be all business." I retrieved my cane from the backseat. "And it was no trouble."

"I lied," he said, and pulled me close, kissing my cheek. "I'll give you a ring about that dinner," he murmured in my ear. "I always repay my debts."

My face was still burning as he pulled out of the parking lot.

"Back from the grand tour? Looks like it went just fine. You two certainly hit it off."

I hadn't heard Quinn come up behind me, but managed to say coolly, "The British are very polite. He was just thanking me for showing him around."

"Honey, that was beyond polite. And he was checking out a lot more than the vineyard."

So he'd seen the kiss.

"You have a one-track mind," I told him. "Look, I'm meeting Kit for lunch in Leesburg at twelve-thirty. It's only eleven. Why don't I stop by Seely's and pick up some flowers for Hector? I'll tell him they're from both of us. I should have enough time to get to the hospital before lunch."

"Tell him I'll be by later. And tell him the flowers are from you. He'll know damn well I wouldn't do something like that. Men don't send other men flowers."

"He could have died. You could make an exception, you know? Where are you going now?" We were back on our customary footing, talking about work.

"South vineyard. I want to see how the cleanup of the freeze damage is coming along. You'll be back after lunch, right?" He nudged me. "Hey! Are you listening or are you still playing tour guide?"

"I'm listening."

"No, you're not. I asked if you were coming back after lunch. We've got that reception tonight. Or did you forget that, too?"

"I didn't forget anything, and it's not a reception. It's a private cocktail party. Hors d'oeuvres here, dinner at the Inn."

"Do we know who's coming?"

"Nope. Just that Austin Kendall is paying for it," I said. "And I'll be back after lunch, so why don't we finally settle on the Chardonnay once and for all? That way we can get it in bottles tomorrow, if we work fast enough."

"Or Friday morning."

"Mick just told me Georgia's funeral is Friday morning."

"I can bottle wine without you, you know. I've done it before, believe it or not."

"Very funny."

"Bonita will help," he said. "It'll be awesome."

Seely's Garden Center was a sprawling, beautifully landscaped nursery located at the intersection of Sam Fred Road and the Snickersville Turnpike, not far from where Goose Creek continued its meandering route north toward the Potomac River. The nursery had been founded by Noah's grandfather and it looked as if a fourth generation—Noah's youngest daughter, Jennifer—was ready to carry on the family business when Noah finally retired for good.

Here in Loudoun and Fauquier Counties we take our gardens seriously, not just because we're an agricultural region, but also because of the great natural beauty of the land. The annual Virginia historic garden week tour had taken place at the end of April. The spring farm tour was last week. Both events were great for local tourism and they also gave Seely's an inevitable bump in sales due to the serious garden-lust that resulted from seeing someone else's award-winning roses or heirloom tomatoes. Today the place was crowded as I drove in.

Above the door to the main building was a plaque with a quote from Thomas Jefferson written in calligraphy: "No occupation is so delightful to me as the culture of the earth, and no culture comparable to that of the garden." The building itself was an enormous airy structure that looked like a cross between a log cabin and a barn. On the right was the greenhouse. On the left a warehouse-like store sold garden supplies, lawn care products, small tools, and other gardening essentials. The florist was tucked into a corner of a year-round Christmas shop located just off the main store. I bought a bunch of spring flowers from a pretty teenager wearing a gray polo shirt with "Seely's Garden Center" and the outline of a tree embroidered in green on the pocket.

"Is either Jennifer or Noah around?" I asked as I paid her.

"Noah's in his office behind customer service," she said. "And I think Jen is watering plants outside somewhere. Try the bedding plants under the awning."

"Thanks."

The door to Noah's cluttered office was ajar. He looked up from his paperwork as I knocked, pushing his reading glasses up so they sat on his bald head. For someone whose livelihood came from the outdoors, I often wondered why he chose a room with no windows as the place where he took care of business. The furnishings were spartan and utilitarian except for his thriving African violet collection, which flourished under special lights on a tiered shelf in the corner. Stuck in the pot of the smallest flower, a ceramic sign read "Grow, dammit!"

"Lucie," he said. "Come in, my dear. What can I do for you? What's the occasion for the flowers?"

Noah and my mother had worked closely together when she restored the gardens around our house and later when she decided to undertake more substantial landscaping projects at the villa, the Ruins, the family cemetery, and the pond. As a result we'd spent tens of thousands of dollars at Seely's over the years, which meant there was a gold star next to our name on their ledger. Anyone who showed up from Montgomery Estate Vineyard got VIP treatment.

"Hector's in the hospital," I said. "He had a heart attack yesterday afternoon."

"Good Lord. I hadn't heard. I'm so sorry. How is he?"

"He seems to be doing all right," I said. "They're keeping him for a few days. He's at Catoctin General."

"I'll have to drop by and see him."

"He'd like that. Thanks, Noah."

His desk chair creaked as he sat back in it. "I haven't seen you since that nasty business with Georgia at the vineyard. I was so sorry to hear about it. She wasn't one of my favorite people, as you might imagine, but still. We're all God's creatures. It shouldn't have happened."

"That's very charitable, considering what she did to you."

"It's finished." He picked up a pencil and held it between his index fingers, studying it as if he were gauging its length. "I guess all that's left is for the sheriff to arrest whoever did it."

"They're looking for Randy Hunter," I said.

"So I understand." Noah set the pencil down.

"Were you around when Amy Dye and her goddaughter ran into Randy the other day?"

He shook his head. "No, but Jennifer was. I heard about it, of course. Gabrielle—I think that's her name—apparently has quite a temper on her. Jen and Amy had a job on their hands getting her calmed down."

"It's Gabriella. What did she say?"

Noah pulled his glasses off his forehead and looked through the lenses as if seeing into a crystal ball. "If you really want to know, you should ask Jen, honey. She can fill you in better than I can."

"I think I will." I blew him a kiss. "See you, Noah."

I found Jennifer Seely out in the back watering bedding plants, as I'd been told. She handed off the hose to one of her employees and said, smiling, "What can I do for you, Lucie? You find everything you need today?"

I'd known Jen for most of my life, since she'd been two grades behind me in school. A pretty, quiet-spoken girl with her father's sunny temperament who wore her straight brown hair beguilingly in a long French braid, you could count on her to win a blue ribbon at the county fair each year for something she'd grown in her garden. After high school she went to Virginia Tech to study agriculture, never doubting that her destiny was taking over the nursery one day.

"I just talked to your dad," I said. "Randy Hunter hasn't shown up for work at the vineyard since last Saturday. I heard about what happened here when he ran into Harry Dye's goddaughter the other day. Gaby Manzur."

My unanswered question hung in the air.

Jen's eyes narrowed. "Yeah, it was quite a scene. Thank God Amy dragged her out of here right away. She was hysterical. Screaming and completely out of control. I was afraid she was going to start hitting him or throwing things."

"What did she say?"

"Nothing worth repeating." She seemed uncomfortable. "Called him a bunch of names. Said she hated him for what he'd done to her and that he'd pay for it someday. Poor Randy. I felt so sorry for him. He looked like he had no clue who she was and why she was saying all those horrible things."

"He did?" I found that hard to swallow.

"Well . . . he told me afterwards he remembered meeting her, but he kind of went blank on the details. Uh, there was alcohol involved." We had moved over by the little market packs of petunias and she'd automatically begun deadheading the flowers, avoiding my eyes. Finally she looked up. "Look, he told me he wasn't exactly a saint when he was growing up. But he's changed. He's a good guy now."

"Yes." No point mentioning that, good guy or not, I thought he was the prime suspect in Georgia's murder. "Do you have any idea where he is?"

Jen shook her head. "It's not like him to drop out of sight like this. Even the rest of the band doesn't know where he went."

She held a bunch of dead petunias in one hand. We both stared at the spent flowers.

"I guess you probably heard the rumors about him and Georgia Greenwood," I said. "And now that Georgia's dead—"

"Of course I've heard." She cut me off. "It's a load of crap. Randy told me why he was seeing Georgia. One of her cousins owns a recording company in Nashville. She was going to set up a meeting between her cousin and Randy after he finished cutting his CD. The reason Randy and Georgia were seeing each other was business. Not some stupid affair."

"He said that?"

"He wouldn't lie to me. I know him, Lucie." She was adamant.

Hadn't he lied to her about Gaby Manzur? Or did he really have amnesia about a sexual relationship that produced a child? Either way, Jen sounded pretty defensive.

"So you and Randy are close, then?" I asked.

"We're *friends*. I was dating Josh for a while, so I saw Randy all the time."

"Josh?"

"The drummer in their band. We broke up, but I still hang out with the guys. I go to most of their gigs."

"When's the last time you talked to Randy?"

Her answer was evasive. "I left a couple of messages on his mobile asking him to get in touch."

"Did he?"

She hesitated, then said, "No. The last time I called, his mailbox was full." A walkie-talkie on her hip beeped and she unclipped it. "This is Jennifer."

A garbled voice said something about a customer needing help with plants for a shade garden.

"Tell her I'll be right there." She smiled a tight little smile. "Gotta run, Lucie. Can't keep the customers waiting."

"Before you go," I said, "were you and Randy involved . . . ?"

"I told you already that Randy and I are just friends. So let it go, okay, Lucie?"

She turned and stalked away. I watched her leave and headed for my car. Though the story about Georgia's cousin's recording studio was plausible, it didn't sound right considering how defensive Jen had been when I asked about Randy.

That mobile phone was his lifeline. She admitted he hadn't returned any of her calls and now his voice mailbox was full.

As far as I was concerned, that meant one of two things.

Either Randy was hiding out.

Or he was dead.

CHAPTER 11

Though it would have been faster to take the Snickersville Turn-pike to Aldie and pick up the main roads to Leesburg, I decided to take the long way on the winding back roads. It gave me time to speculate on why Jen might be lying about her relationship with Randy. If he'd killed Georgia and she knew something, then Jen was an accessory to murder. All the reason in the world to tell a few whoppers.

Unless there was something else. Something I hadn't figured out yet.

I followed the turnpike to Mountville, where it made an elbow-shaped turn thanks to Ezekial Mount's decision back in the 1800s to plant a single apple tree in the middle of the road and call it an orchard. In those days the town laws forbade disturbing orchards, so the pike had to be rerouted around the tree. While the tree was long gone, the kink in the road remained.

You could drive for miles without ever running into another car on these bucolic country lanes edged with undulating gray ribbons of low stacked-stone walls dating from Civil War days. Usually I liked the solitude and the serenity as the view opened up each time I rounded one of the many serpentine turns to reveal farmhouses, barns, and stables with their backdrop of sweeping expanses of fields and pastures dotted with placid cattle and expensive thorough-breds—and always the lovely, hazy Blue Ridge Mountains defining the scene. But today I stared at the mountains and wondered where the hell Randy was.

Alive or dead, the answers lay with him.

I pulled into the parking lot at Catoctin Hospital about twenty minutes later and got Hector's flowers from the backseat of the Mini. Hector was asleep, but Sera, who'd been reading in an uncomfortable-looking fake leather chair next to the bed, stood up and came over when I tapped gently on the door. She wore her steel-gray hair in a bun, as neat and tidy as everything else about her. As she got up, she removed her glasses, letting them hang around her neck on a silky black cord. I caught sight of her book. *A Farewell to Arms.* Hemingway.

"Don't disturb him," I whispered. "Let him sleep. Please tell him I stopped by when he wakes up, though."

"These are beautiful, Lucie." She set the book down so she could take the flowers with both hands. "Thank you so much."

She looked tired, though she seemed less tense than the night Hector had been brought to the emergency room. I watched as she took an empty vase next to the small sink in his room and filled it with water. She set it on a window ledge and began arranging the flowers.

"You're welcome," I said, as her hands worked their magic. "Before I forget, I wanted to tell you how lovely the courtyard looks. Thank you for planting all those flowers and for the roses from your garden. I don't know when you found the time."

"I was glad to do it. Kept my mind off worrying. Besides, I've done it every year since your mother asked me. I can't quit now." She finished with the vase, turning it so the arrangement pleased her, and regarded me. "What roses?"

"The vase of red roses you left in the villa," I said. "It was very thoughtful."

She looked surprised. "They weren't from my garden. Though I wish they had been. They came in the shipment from Seely's."

"Really? That's funny," I said. "Although maybe Noah sent them to say thanks for our business. He's done that before, though usually it's a plant. By the way, he sends his best and says he'll try to come by later."

"He's a good man. Hector will like that." She picked up her book again. "Thank you for coming. And for what you did for Bonita. We are grateful."

I blushed. "What about you? Is there anything you need?"

Sera's eyes grew misty and she held Hemingway against her chest like a shield. "Everything I need," she said softly but deliberately, "is here in this room."

I kissed her cheek, my own eyes brimming with tears. "I know that. But call me. In case there's something else."

I stopped in a bathroom on the way out and splashed cold water on my face, wiping my eyes. Then I drove the few blocks to Kit's office, parking outside the small gray clapboard building with "Washington Tribune, Loudoun Bureau" stenciled in elegant gold script on the plate-glass front door. Kit's office manager looked up from her crossword puzzle when I walked in.

"She's expecting you," she said. "Go on back."

I found her staring out the window. "Knock-knock."

"Hiya," she said. "Let's get out of here. I'm starved."

We walked half a block to Tuscarora Mill, a nineteenth-century grain mill that had been converted to a restaurant. The bar was full and the restaurant buzzed pleasantly with the noise of the Leesburg lunch crowd. If the Romeos weren't at the Inn, they ate at Tuskie's. Kit's table was in the main dining room, which still had the original broad timbers, belts, pulleys, and scales from the days when it had been a working mill.

The hostess seated us and our waitress took drink orders. Kit wanted a glass of Pinot Noir. I asked for unsweetened iced tea.

"What, no wine?" Kit said.

"I've been sampling Chardonnays for the last few days. I need a break."

"On the subject of drinking"—Kit folded her hands and leaned toward me, lowering her voice—"there's something you ought to know. It's about Mia."

This wasn't going to be good. "What about Mia?"

"Sorry, Luce, it's going to be in the *Trib* police blotter tomorrow. She got charged with public drunkenness. Not a criminal offense, just a misdemeanor. She has to pay a fine. This time. I asked Bobby about it. He said she was with a bunch of kids who've taken to drinking—of all places—in that old field where they used to have temperance picnics during Prohibition."

"I'll kill her," I said. "I told her to knock it off. She had a monster hangover the other morning when I found her in the kitchen. And it wasn't the first time, either."

The waitress returned with our drinks and we ordered, a chef's salad for me and the meatloaf for Kit.

"I know we weren't saints," Kit said after she left, "snitching bottles from your wine cellar and drinking them down at Goose Creek Bridge, but jeez. Bobby said they were drunk off their asses. He said Abby Lang gave the patrol officer who caught them a lot of lip and the do-you-know-who-my-father-is routine. Bobby said his officer told Abby her old man could be the next face they were putting on Mount Rushmore, but if it happened again he wouldn't cut them any slack. They'd be spending the night in the drunk tank."

I clamped my lips together and shook my head, visualizing the scene she'd described. "Ever since my mother died, Mia's been out of control. It's almost like she has a death wish sometimes, you know?"

"Or she's wearing the superhero suit so she's invincible. Lot of that going around with those kids. Did you know they drag-race late at night on Route Fifteen? All the way from Leesburg to Gilbert's Corner. Sometimes when I'm coming home from work really late, I'll see a lot of parked cars in one of the lay-bys. Someone's gonna get killed."

"God, Kit, what am I going to do?"

She shrugged. "Talk to her."

"She won't listen."

"What about Eli? She listens to him and Miss Apple Blossom, doesn't she?" My sister-in-law had once been the queen of the Winchester apple festival. She'd also been the woman who stole Eli away from Kit. It still rankled.

Our food arrived. Kit doused her meatloaf with salt, then ketchup. She bit into a piece. "I love their meatloaf."

"Why didn't you taste it before you put salt on it?"

"Because it needed salt." She picked up the saltshaker again. "So, get Eli to shoulder some responsibility for a change and talk to her. Unless he's too busy arranging his tie collection by color. Or maybe he does it by designer."

"Miaow."

Kit smiled, unrepentant. "I'm allowed. He's turned into such a wimp ever since he married the Queen Bee."

"No comment. I'll talk to him, although he's at the beach right now. Hilton Head." I pushed a tomato around on my plate.

"What did he do? Rob a bank? How can he afford Hilton Head on the salary he makes?"

"I guess with his share of the money from selling my mom's diamond necklace. Plus I bought out his interest in the vineyard."

"When he gets back, tell him you need him to pull his weight and help out with your sister." Kit poured gravy on her mashed potatoes. "Especially since she's not hanging around the best crowd. Abby Lang is trouble."

"I know. I wonder if her father knows what she's up to."

"He's got his mind on other things, if you ask me. Like the vice presidential nomination. Pass the rolls, please?"

I passed them. "He left the fund-raiser with Georgia. That was the last time I saw her alive."

"Hugo Lang is the Mr. Clean of the U.S. Senate. Hell, of the entire Congress," Kit said. "I can't think of a single reason he'd have for killing Georgia, if that's what you're getting at."

"Do you think they might have been romantically involved? Not that I do, but it would explain things. Like why he endorsed her."

"No, I don't." She was definite. "Come on, Luce. He still wears his wedding ring. There's something kind of heartbreaking about a man who does that when his wife's been dead that long. He could have gotten married again loads of times."

"I know." I watched her slab butter on a roll. "Okay, next subject. What did you want to say about Randy? Bobby tell you something?"

"Just that they're looking for him," she said. "I was hoping you might have some news."

"Only that Jennifer Seely's been leaving messages on his mobile phone voice mail. She said his mailbox is full," I said. "Randy can't go five minutes, never mind five days, without talking on that phone."

"Meaning what?" Kit asked.

I set my fork on my plate. "Either he's dead or on the run."

She considered the options. "My money's on him being on the

lam. Otherwise someone would have found him . . . his body . . . by now."

"Not necessarily. We have five hundred acres. A lot of it's woods and underbrush. Say he was leaving the barn and someone confronted him. It wouldn't be hard to ditch a body someplace where it might not get found for a long time."

She shuddered. "So if Randy's dead, are you thinking his killer is the same person who killed Georgia? Someone had a busy night."

"I don't know. But what if that person was really after Randy— and Georgia was in the wrong place at the wrong time?"

"I need a scorecard. Who wants Randy dead?"

"Harry Dye's goddaughter," I said. "Gaby Manzur. She's one possibility. I heard about her yesterday. Randy got her pregnant at beach week in Cancún awhile back. She ran into him at Seely's when she was visiting Harry and Amy. Jen said she went nuts. Told him he'd pay for what he did to her. Jen said Randy didn't recognize her and that really sent her over the edge."

"Jeez. You think she was mad enough to kill Randy?"

"Mad enough, yes. Capable, I don't know. But she was alone at the Dyes' place the night Georgia was killed. And then Randy disappeared."

Kit looked puzzled. "So who killed Georgia? You think she did that, too?"

"Maybe Gaby knew Georgia was with Randy in the barn, then waited until she left. Or it could be that Randy killed Georgia like we've been thinking all along. The note said he wanted to make up for something, but maybe she wasn't buying it."

"I don't know. Sounds pretty sketchy to me."

"Fair enough. But I still wonder if we've got this the wrong way around. Instead of looking for who killed Georgia, maybe we need to figure out who was after Randy. And that goes down a completely different road with a completely different pool of suspects."

Kit finished her meatloaf and sopped her roll in gravy. "You know, kiddo, you're overlooking the one obvious person who would have wanted them both dead. I heard Ross still can't produce the parents of the babies he supposedly delivered that night."

"Ross didn't *supposedly* deliver twins," I said. "If he says he did, then he did."

"Why are you so defensive? He's got a motive and no alibi. Why does that make him any different than Randy's Cancún girlfriend?"

"He's a doctor. He saves lives. He saved me."

Kit shook her head slowly. "Aw, Luce."

Our waitress showed up and offered us dessert menus.

"No, thanks. Just coffee for me." I glanced at Kit. "You having dessert?"

"I shouldn't." She scanned the menu. "Oh, God. Strawberry shortcake with fresh strawberries in season. I'll take one of those, please, with extra whipped cream. And we'll have two forks."

I rolled my eyes. "No way."

"You eat like a bird. You're pushing yourself awfully hard," she said. "When's the last time you had a physical?"

"What are you, my keeper? I'm fine."

"It seems like that foot of yours is bothering you more and more. You ought to have it looked at."

"I talked to Ross about it," I said. "I'm telling you, I'm *fine*."

After lunch, she walked me to my car.

"Are you coming to any of our Memorial Day events this weekend?" I asked.

"I'm on duty Sunday, but Bobby and I are coming to the concert Saturday night." She fished in her purse and pulled out lipstick and a mirror.

"Everything back on track with you two?"

"It's a date to a concert. We're trying to figure things out. So stop looking at me like that."

"Why don't you both come to the barbecue on Monday, too? I'll put your names on the list."

"Thanks, but I'm working all day Monday." She opened the mirror and applied a bright red mouth.

"You really did pull the short straw on a holiday weekend, didn't you? At least come to the fireworks Monday night."

"I'll ask Bobby. We'll try. Though it seems to me," she said as I

got into the Mini, "for the past week you've had nothing but fireworks at your place."

"Don't I know it," I told her.

Unlike Middleburg, which was a main-street town, Leesburg, the
county seat, was more spread out. It had once served as the temporary
capital of the United States when the Declaration of Independence
and the Constitution were moved there for safekeeping during the
War of 1812. During the Civil War, the town changed sides between
the Union and the Confederacy so many times—depending on
whose army was there—that folks lost count.

The Patowmack Free Clinic was only a few blocks from Tuskie's,
still within the boundaries of what was known as "historic Leesburg."
A pretty one-story wooden structure, it looked more like someone's
home than a business. Half a dozen rocking chairs where patients
could sit and wait were lined up on the veranda, overlooking flower-
filled border gardens maintained by the local garden club. A plastic
box with patient forms in English and Spanish hung next to the door
below a plaque with the schedule and a notice that there were no
drugs on the premises.

Ross and Siri had recently begun locking the front door between
clinic sessions, even when they were in their offices. The reason,
Ross told me, was that they'd had to deal with patients who showed
up at all hours—mostly from the large immigrant community of
Central Americans that now comprised a significant percentage of
Loudoun's population—hoping the doctor could make an exception
and see them for just a *momentito*. The trickle had turned into a flood
and the situation had gotten out of hand.

I went to the staff entrance around the side of the building and
knocked on the door. Though I knew many of the volunteers, Siri
worked tirelessly to recruit new people. The woman who opened
was not a familiar face.

"I'm sorry, dearie," she said, "but you'll have to come back
tomorrow."

"I'm not a patient," I said. "Is Dr. Greenwood around? I'm Lucie
Montgomery. A friend of his."

She opened the door wider. "Montgomery? You're the one who

hosted our party the other night. Come right inside. Dr. Greenwood is at the church, poor man, but Mrs. Randstad is in. I'll let her know you're here."

I could hear Siri's musical voice coming from her office at the end of the hall. Fund-raising. Ross told me it never stopped.

"Would you care to wait in the volunteer room?" the woman asked. "Help yourself to a soda or bottled water in the mini-fridge."

"Thanks, but I just had lunch," I said. "If you don't mind, though, I'd like to look around. Looks like you've redecorated since the last time I was here."

"That nice group of volunteers from the department store in Sterling was in yesterday. They really go to town fixing the place up, don't they?"

She smiled and left. The old floorboards creaked as I walked down the hallway, peering into each room. Walls and windows were cheerily decorated with flags, bunting, and summer beach paraphernalia. A life-sized skeleton in the volunteer room wore a hula skirt, sunglasses, and sandals. Someone had hung a different-colored flip-flop on each of the examination room doors.

I went into the kitchen, which doubled as their storage room. Siri accepted donations from anyone who would contribute. Even if it was of no use to the clinic, she sold it elsewhere and used the cash to buy what they needed. Boxes of gauze, bandages, sterile gloves, and packages of over-the-counter medications were stacked on one counter. Next to the microwave was an open container that resembled a toolbox. I glanced inside.

I knew all of the painkillers by heart. In fact, I knew many of them firsthand. Weaning myself after my surgeries had been hell, but I'd done it. When I was through, I swore I'd never be dependent on drugs like that again. I picked up a couple of the dark brown plastic bottles. All controlled substances. When had Siri and Ross started stocking them? It didn't jibe with the "No Drugs on the Premises" sign by the front door.

"Lucie?" Siri called.

"In the pink flip-flop room."

She stood in the doorway, her gray-streaked dark brown hair cascading around her shoulders, classically elegant in a white sweater and navy skirt. "I thought you were in the volunteers' lounge," she said smiling. "You were supposed to be offered a cold drink."

"I wanted to see the latest décor. And I did get offered a drink."

Her eyes fell on the toolbox. "Lord," she said. "Those meds should be in Ross's office or else in mine—when we have them here."

"I didn't know you kept stuff like this around."

"It was Ross's idea. We're pretty discreet about it and we only do it on the days we have clinic sessions. That's why we kept the sign out front about no drugs. Otherwise we'd be robbed all the time."

"Wouldn't it be safer to use a pharmacy?"

"I don't know how to put this," she said, "but not all of those drugs are ours, so to speak. We're so desperate to help our patients that sometimes if someone passes away and has a prescription for a medication that lowers blood pressure or cholesterol or whatever, then the next of kin or the funeral home will let us know."

"You use dead people's pills?"

"They're not going to use them, are they? Lucie, we're desperate!" She sounded reproving. "Most of our patients have no jobs and many of them are here illegally. Ross treats anyone who walks through that front door. And if he has to he goes to them. Just like he did with Emilio and Marta. He doesn't care if they landed here from another planet, frankly. But drugs don't grow on trees. We already beg, borrow, and, well, we don't steal . . . but we do anything we can to get the treatment and medication we need for our patients. Some of those pills cost as much as a dollar each."

"I had no idea."

"It's not something we broadcast." The reproach was still there, but milder. "But you know Ross. He doesn't have much tolerance for following the rule book, if it doesn't make sense. I like that about him."

"I do, too," I said. "I'm sorry if it came out sounding judgmental. Anyway, the real reason I stopped by was to see what I could do to help for the wake or funeral."

"Just be there for him," she said. "He's under so much stress because Marta and Emilio are gone. We've asked around, but no one's talking. Who knows if they're in Salvador or Sterling?"

"Ross didn't kill Georgia, Siri. Even if they're gone, the police will figure it out."

She nodded, eyes dark with worry. "I hope so. By the way, Ross left something for you. It's on his desk. I'll get it."

She returned with a large sealed envelope with my name scrawled in Ross's familiar doctor's chicken scratch. I thanked her and said I'd see her tomorrow. "Tell Ross everything's going to be fine."

Siri smiled thinly. "Sure."

I let myself out and headed to my car, which I'd parked out front. Marty Gamble, the medical examiner who'd taken care of Georgia and volunteered at the clinic part-time, was just sprinting up the stairs to the front porch, sweat-drenched in a T-shirt and running shorts.

I called his name and waved. He came back down the steps.

"Lucie! What are you doing here?"

I liked Marty. He and one other doctor were the only medical examiners the county had. The county paid him the princely sum of fifty dollars a body, so he once said he reckoned he had two volunteer jobs when all was said and done. Fortunately, they had the appropriate gallows humor for their work. "You stab 'em, we slab 'em" was Marty's off-the-record motto.

He said the joking kept him from falling apart on the tough cases—especially children and the tragic deaths. Georgia must have been one of the tough ones, but I hadn't had a chance to ask.

"I was in Leesburg, so I thought I'd stop by and see Ross," I said to him. "I heard he's at the church."

"Yep." He pulled off his shirt and wiped his sweaty face. I tried not to stare. Marty was in great shape. "You're coming tomorrow, of course?"

I knew he meant the wake and funeral. "Of course. How was your run?"

"Not bad. Ross and I are going to do the marathon again this year. Our tenth together. When the funeral is all over and done with, it'll do him good to get back to training."

"Does the sheriff still think he did it? Siri just told me he's a basket case because he can't find Marta and Emilio."

"You know I can't talk about this," he said carefully. "But he isn't out of the woods."

"What about that note he found? Someone wanted to meet Georgia the night she died. Ross thinks Randy Hunter wrote it and he was pretty sure he and Georgia were having an affair," I said. "Plus she had sex with someone right before she died."

Marty nodded as the light went out of his eyes. "Yep. She did. No surprise, frankly."

He bent to fix the lace of one of his running shoes. The sudden silence lay heavily between us. He was still fiddling with a lace that needed retying, deliberately avoiding my eyes.

"Why wasn't it a surprise?" I asked quietly. "You know who it is, don't you?"

He straightened up and a muscle twitched in his jaw, as if he were trying to keep some emotional reaction in check. "I withdraw the remark. I shouldn't have said that."

"But you did," I said. "So you knew she was having an affair with Randy?" His eyes answered for him.

"How did you find out?" I persisted. "From Ross?"

"Lucie . . ." he warned. "I don't want to talk about it. I shouldn't be talking about it."

"Did Ross tell you?"

"God, no!"

"Then how did you find out?"

He rubbed his forehead with both hands as if trying to excise something from his mind. "Because I treated her for a little infection she'd picked up. She told me it was Randy. This one was." Now his eyes met mine. "It wasn't the first time I took care of her, either. She came to me for the others."

"Oh, God. The others? Ross has no idea?"

His voice was flat. "Of course not."

I closed my eyes. "Don't tell him now."

"I won't. I can't."

"Why you?" I asked. "She could have gone to a doctor in D.C. and no one would ever have known."

He didn't answer. Just stared at me with eyes filled with sadness. And something else.

Shame. He'd been one of her lovers.

"She wanted you to know?" I asked. "Didn't she?"

He nodded and said, still in that monotone, "Georgia could be a very cruel lover. I broke it off after we slept together a couple of times. I couldn't keep doing it to Ross. Or to Tina." He began twisting his wedding ring, but when he spoke he was bitter. "It seemed like the honorable thing to do, even though I was still so crazy about her. So to punish me, to let me know there were others, she made sure I was her doctor of choice for all her female problems. At least I never had to help her with an abortion. Thank God she couldn't have kids."

"Couldn't or wouldn't?"

"Couldn't. She had the surgery so she'd never have to worry."

"I had no idea."

"Don't repeat this, Lucie. Ever."

"Of course not."

He laid his hand heavily on my shoulder, like he was suddenly weary, and draped his shirt around him like a collar. "I have to live with myself for what I did," he said. "So I figure I've been punished enough. Maybe now I'll get some closure, now that she's dead."

"Sure," I said. "See you tomorrow."

He turned away and headed toward the clinic without looking back. Closure, maybe. But didn't that confession give Marty a motive for murder, too?

CHAPTER 12

I drove slowly back to the vineyard. Sometimes there's nothing worse than being alone with your own thoughts. Marty's secret hung around my neck like a noose.

I called Quinn from the car and asked if he needed me in the barrel room. He sounded surprised. "I thought we were gonna sort out the Chardonnay once and for all. You sound weird. What's going on?"

"Nothing," I lied. "I'll be there." I disconnected before he had another chance to quiz me.

But Quinn, like me, also seemed distracted as we made the final decisions about yeast and sugar content. "There's not going to be enough oak in the finish," he said. "So I think we ought to hang the chips in the tanks for a while."

My mother and Jacques had been purists. They produced our wine based on the grapes God gave us and the decisions they'd made in the barrel room ever since harvest. When it was time to finally bottle it, they believed you worked with what you had. So there was no excessive fiddling or changing the wine they'd ended up with. Hanging a bag of oak chips in one of the stainless-steel tanks was the speed-dial equivalent of making unoaked wine taste like it had just spent the past nine months gracefully aging in oak barrels—in about an hour. Jacques would have thought it was cheating. Quinn thought it was brilliant.

Today I didn't feel like disagreeing with him. "Fine," I said, "we'll do it that way."

"We'll bottle Friday," he said. "I've got to get the bottling equipment in tomorrow. Plus the rootstock is arriving."

"If we're done here I think I'll head back to the house to change before everyone shows up later," I said.

"Shows up?"

"Austin's reception. You reminded me about it this morning."

"Oh, yeah. Sure."

There is a French expression my mother often used when someone was behaving oddly or out of character. *Il n'est pas dans son assiette.* Literally it means, "He's not on his plate." It didn't translate too well in English, but right now it described Quinn and me perfectly. Neither one of us was on our plates.

I had no idea where we were.

I tore Ross's envelope open as I walked through the front door of my house. A brochure from a company that made orthotics. He'd circled one of the models, a clunky affair that wrapped around the ankle and foot like a molded plastic boot. I stared at it. How did you wear shoes—normal shoes—with a contraption like that? I shoved the brochure back in the envelope. No way. If I wore one of those, I'd look crippled.

I started to slowly climb the stairs when Mia appeared at the top of the landing. Dressed in a short blue jean skirt, white camisole, and high-heeled beaded sandals, she looked pretty and fresh. She froze in midstep when she saw me.

"What are you doing here?" she asked.

"I live here. Going somewhere?" I shouldn't have let my anger over what Kit had told me about the police blotter show, but I was tired. This would be another showdown.

"Out."

Might as well get right to it. "I heard about the misdemeanor charge for public drunkenness. Nice going."

She stomped down the stairs until she stood a step above me. It gave her the psychological advantage of looking down on me. "Who told you?"

"Kit gave me a preview of tomorrow's weekly police blotter."

Her face grew pale. "Oh, crap. That's just great. It's going to be in the *newspaper*?"

"Yep."

"It was just a stupid fine. I paid it already. So it's not like I had to go to court or anything."

"Yeah, but next time you *will* go to court and you *will* spend a night in jail."

"No, I won't." She banged down the last few stairs in the high heels and then across the foyer, long-legged as a colt, ponytail bouncing like an angry exclamation mark.

"Hey!" I called. "Are you coming home tonight? Or are you still sleeping over at Abby Lang's?"

She spun around. "I'm not sleeping at Abby's, that's for sure. Neither is she. I don't know what we're doing tonight."

I stared at my sister. That last remark sounded more desperate than threatening. She meant it that she really didn't know what she was doing. Kind of a leitmotif for her life right now. But it would probably be whatever came easiest in the heat of a what-the-hell night.

"Come home, Mimi," I said gently. "Please?"

She seemed to waver. "I don't know. I'll see. Anyway, we've got plenty of places to stay."

"Why isn't Abby sleeping at her house anymore?"

She threw her hands up in the air. "Because her dad is so totally flipped out about the cops showing up and asking him about Georgia Greenwood. And he's, like, going nuts because he wants to get nominated to be vice president. Abby's going to the convention in San Francisco and she might take time off from school to campaign with him. She says it will be so cool." She splayed her feet sideways like a young girl would do and it made her seem infinitely more vulnerable. "But this Georgia stuff could wreck everything if it gets out about him being with her the night she was murdered."

"Are you saying Georgia was sleeping with Abby's dad?"

Mia looked disgusted. "God, no. He didn't even like her."

"Then why did he support her campaign?"

"I dunno. Why don't you ask him?" She pulled out her mobile

phone from a tiny purse and looked at the display. "It's five-thirty already. I gotta go. See you maybe tomorrow."

"Please be careful with the drinking. The next time you get caught—"

"Lucie," she said impatiently, "give it a rest. I have no intention of getting caught again. 'Bye."

The door slammed and I heard her car engine start a moment later.

It wasn't until I was standing in the shower with the water sluicing over me that I thought again about what she meant by that last remark. She wasn't going to stop drinking.

She just wasn't going to get caught when she did.

I was surprised to see Bonita setting wineglasses on the bar when I arrived at the villa. The college-kid outfit she had on this morning when I first saw her had been replaced by an elegant black and white knit top, cropped black pants, and slingbacks. She'd pulled her hair back in a loose knot and wore a light floral scent. Altogether, she looked lovely and very sophisticated.

"Thanks for setting up," I said. "Where's Quinn?"

"At his place. I saw his car as I drove by. I figured I should get here, you know, a little early. Quinn's so busy now that he's working two jobs. You guys need me more than you thought." She smiled, sounding cheerful.

"Pardon?"

"Well, with him working for that British guy." Her smile froze.

"Quinn is working for Mick Dunne?" There was no point trying to act like I knew. My face gave away completely that I had no idea.

"Well, not exactly working for him, I guess," she said uneasily. "But he, like, agreed to help him."

"You mean as a consultant?" When did that happen? This morning Quinn had been as friendly as a Rottweiler toward Mick.

"Yeah. A consultant." She knew now she'd let the cat out of the bag. Maybe a lot of cats and a lot of bags. She added, "You seem pretty mad, Lucie. I shouldn't have opened my big mouth, but I figured you knew."

"Looks like it slipped his mind to tell me."

"Oh, God. Please don't say I did. Could you act surprised when he brings it up?"

"Sure." Me and my telltale face. "I'll do that."

"Thanks. I appreciate it." She sounded relieved. "Because I think he'd, like, kill me."

Not before I, like, killed him. "I wouldn't worry," I said.

I kept my word about not saying anything to Quinn when he finally showed up a few minutes later dressed in khakis and another in his extensive collection of Hawaiian shirts. This one was multiple shades of blue with fish swimming all over it.

"That is such a cool shirt," Bonita said. She went over and fingered the fabric of one of his sleeves. "I totally love it."

Quinn looked down at her and something twisted in my heart as I watched the way he smiled at her. No doubt about it. He was falling under her spell, fascinated by her transformation from college kid to beguilingly sexy woman.

"It's vintage," he said, still smiling. "One way you can tell the quality of a print like this is by the size of the fish's lips. This one is kind of special."

"I didn't know that," she said. "That is so awesome."

"Sorry to interrupt this discussion about fish lips," I said, "but do you think we have enough bottles of wine open? I just heard the Goose Creek Catering truck pulling up."

They both turned around. Bonita let go of Quinn's shirt and blushed. Quinn's dark eyes held mine for a long moment. What was in his made me feel like an overbearing schoolteacher yanking her fun-loving pupils back in line, which wasn't too far off the mark. I don't know what he saw in mine, but I hoped it wasn't wistfulness.

"I think we're fine," he said. "But just in case, I'll get more glasses. They're in the barrel room. Excuse me."

He held the door for Dominique's new assistant and two waitresses. When he came back a few minutes later, we were almost done setting out the hors d'oeuvres. Besides our just-released Cabernet Sauvignon and an older barrel-fermented Chardonnay, Austin had asked for champagne, which we'd bought from Harry Dye since we didn't do any sparkling wines of our own yet.

I checked my watch. "What time are they coming?"

"Now," Quinn said. "Three limos just pulled up."

Austin Kendall had rounded up the region's wealthiest citizens and it was immediately clear why when he walked into the room with his arm clapped around Hugo Lang's shoulder. For a man who'd been questioned by the sheriff so recently, Hugo looked like he didn't have a care in the world as he worked the room, slapping backs, shaking hands, and leaning in for the kind of whispered confidences that implied an inner sanctum aura of power and influence.

The mission tonight was to raise money for the upcoming campaign, so Hugo would have even more to bring to the table in San Francisco with his campaign war chest and platinum-plated connections. A nimble-minded Southern senator who chaired the Foreign Relations Committee and spoke with the charismatic eloquence of Bill Clinton, he'd be a definite asset to the ticket.

Quinn was right that Hugo bore a resemblance to President Kennedy, whose memory still had plenty of cachet around here, especially for the old-timers. People still talked about the Kennedys as neighbors, since they'd once owned a home in Middleburg while JFK was president. Afterward, Jackie returned often to ride with several of the local hunt clubs and a pretty pavilion on Madison Street was dedicated to her memory. Hugo had the same Kennedyesque striking good looks and strong profile—though he was now gray-haired—but his most magnetic feature was an irrepressible boyish smile. He flashed it often and it never failed to dazzle whoever he was with.

"How are you this evening, Lucie?" He came up to me after drinks had been served and Austin had proposed a toast to Hugo and "our worthy cause."

"Fine, thanks, Senator. Congratulations."

He smiled. "That's probably a little premature, but thank you."

"Can I talk to you for a second?" I asked. "I won't take long, but it's important. It's about your daughter and my sister."

Dark clouds replaced the sunshine. He took my elbow. Somehow I didn't think he was going to be surprised by what I had to say. "Why don't we go out on your terrace?" he murmured. "We'll have more privacy there."

"Hugo . . . ?" Austin looked questioningly at both of us. "Going somewhere?"

"Be right back, buddy," Hugo said. "I need a moment."

"Sure, sure."

We walked over to the railing. Hugo leaned against it, his back to the panoramic view and the Technicolor sunset. He was all business. "Let's hear it."

"Abby and Mia spend their nights out drinking. They're drinking pretty heavily, too. Mia got a misdemeanor fine for public drunkenness the other day since she's underage. They're hanging out at the old temperance grounds."

He brushed imaginary lint off the cuff of a beautiful custom-tailored suit. "Abby's over twenty-one," he said. "I've talked to her about this and she said she has everything under control. I believe my daughter. She's a good girl."

"With all due respect, I'm not sure she has it under control, Senator."

His face hardened. Not a man used to someone telling him his business. "I appreciate your concern for Abby's well-being, but I think you're overreacting. Perhaps your sister's the one who needs reining in."

"I'm working on that." The rebuke stung. He was digging in his heels because he didn't want to believe what I was saying. Or maybe the timing was inconvenient. On impulse, I added, "By the way, why did you endorse Georgia Greenwood for state senate if you didn't like her?"

What the hell? I probably wasn't going to get another chance to ask him now that I'd ticked him off.

For a moment his eyes went glassy with shock, but he recovered immediately. "I do a lot of things I don't always want to do or agree with," he said coolly. "It's part of the job description. Georgia was my party's candidate, right here in my backyard. This was one of those situations."

"So it's true you didn't like her?"

"I didn't say that. And frankly, it's none of your business what my personal opinion of her was."

He was right, of course, but I kept going. "I saw the two of you leave the fund-raiser together. You're one of the last people to see her alive, except for whoever had sex with her. And her killer. Unless they were the same person. Then you're probably the next-to-last."

He leaned toward me and poked his right index finger at my chest, jabbing the air as he spoke. "How dare you? I have no idea who she was with that night. And as for your smutty insinuation, I volunteered to give the sheriff a DNA mouth-swab sample. No one had to coerce me. After I left Georgia—*alive*—I was on the phone most of the night making fund-raising calls to the West Coast and talking strategy with my campaign manager in L.A."

He lowered his finger and, instinctively, it seemed, began twisting his wedding ring around and around. But his hands trembled. So he had a verifiable alibi.

"I didn't mean to offend you, Senator. But the sheriff thinks Ross Greenwood killed her and he's innocent, too."

The temperature between us hovered near absolute zero. "Then let the sheriff do his job and mind your own business. I need to get back to my guests. I think we're done here."

After the limousines had gone and Quinn and I were cleaning up, he said to me, "What the hell happened with you and Lang out there on the terrace? What'd you do to him to get him so royally pissed off?"

"I tried to talk to him about his daughter and my sister, who spend their evenings together getting drunk," I said. "He said Abby's over twenty-one and that was the end of the conversation."

"What else?"

"What do you mean?" I was stalling and he knew it.

"Don't make me drag it out of you. Right after he came back in I heard him ask Bonita for a glass of water. He took a pill and I saw his hands shaking so bad he spilled the water. Must have been something you said to him."

"I asked him about Georgia," I said. "So did the sheriff. He said he did one of those DNA swabs proving he didn't have sex with her. I guess talking about it rattled his cage."

Quinn put a cork in a bottle of Cab and set it under the bar. "So he's off the hook, is he?" He looked at me soberly. "You never should have said anything to him. He's right. You were out of line."

"Maybe so, but you know something? I think he's hiding something." I wiped the tile counter with a sponge, then wrung it out like it needed strangling. "Lot of that going around lately." I slapped the sponge down on the edge of the sink.

"Something else bugging you?" he asked. "You've been in a rotten mood all day. Ever since you came back from Leesburg."

"I feel great," I snapped. "See you tomorrow."

Afterward at home neither the novel on my bedside table nor an old movie on television held my interest, so I finally gave up around midnight and went downstairs to the kitchen. An open bottle of California Chardonnay—what else?—in the refrigerator looked pretty good. I poured a glass and drank it sitting in the glider, pushing myself back and forth with my good foot.

I didn't see the faint light coming from beyond the rosebushes until my eyes adjusted to the moonlit darkness. Quinn must have gone to the summerhouse with his telescope. He probably couldn't sleep any more than I could. Maybe the tension between the two of us kept him awake, too.

I picked up my cane and walked across the dew-damp grass. In the stillness, his voice startled me. I was about to call out when I heard the other voice. Female. For a moment I stood there like I'd grown roots, waiting.

Then I heard her giggle. "You are so awesome."

Less than a day and he already made a move for Bonita. Their voices rose and fell, sweet chuckles and gentle teasing. Too quiet to understand what they were saying, but expressive enough to know what they were doing.

He'd asked me to look at the stars with him—but that was before he met her. If I had secretly hoped Quinn's invitation to go stargazing was anything more than a casual offer, then it was my own stupid fault. I walked back to the veranda and threw the rest of the Chardonnay onto the lawn. Halfway up the spiral staircases on my way back to bed, the phone rang.

"Sorry to be calling so late, but I knew you'd want to know." Kit sounded agitated. "Bobby just told me the D.C. police found Randy."

"D.C.?" I said. "What's he doing in Washington?"

"He probably didn't start out in D.C.," she said. "They found his car upstream parked near White's Ferry. The cops fished his body out of the Potomac. He must have floated downstream. You were right. He's dead. Shot himself through the head at point-blank range."

CHAPTER 13

The news about Randy overshadowed everything that was—or wasn't—going on between Quinn and me. I told him first thing the next morning when we got to the villa.

"Christ, that's awful." He was standing in the doorway to my office. "I can't imagine him wading out into the water . . . and bang. How do they know it was suicide? Randy doesn't seem like the kind of guy who'd do something like that, if you ask me."

"Kit told me the police fished his gun out of the water at White's Ferry. He left a note. In his car. All it said was, 'I'm sorry.' It makes me sick thinking about it."

"They have any idea how long he'd been in the Potomac?"

"Long enough to float," I said, "or they wouldn't have found him. His body would have sunk at first. Then . . . the gases . . . so he'd float. Plus there are so many rocks and falls between White's Ferry and T. R. Island that his body could have caught on something and got stuck upstream for a while."

"That's where he washed up? Teddy Roosevelt Island?"

I nodded. "I'm meeting Kit for a drink tonight at the English pub in Upperville before Georgia's wake. I'll get the rest of the story then."

"Damn shame," he said. "Keep me posted."

Yesterday we'd decided he'd spend the day in the barrel room with Bonita and Jesús to finish filtering the Chardonnay and get the bottles washed and sterilized. I'd be in the fields with the rest of the crew, planting rootstock. Today I wasn't sorry we weren't going to be in each other's company. He didn't know about my near-miss viewing of him and Bonita in flagrante delicto. If I heard him asking her to open and close the ball valve in the tank, I know I'd start thinking about other things and my face would probably show it.

Manolo picked me up in front of the entrance to the villa, Spanish music blaring loudly through the open windows of Hector's Superman-blue pickup truck. He turned the music down as I threw my garden gloves and cane on the passenger-side floor and climbed in.

"How many guys have we got?" I pulled on Eli's old New York Mets baseball cap and tucked my hair into it.

"Ten," Manolo said. "César's with a couple of them, digging fence-post holes for the Norton block. The rest are planting."

"Let's try to get all the Viognier done today," I said. "If there's time, we can start the Seyval. Or maybe a few of the men can help César put up trellis wires."

He nodded. "We should finish the Viognier, easy. Then we can see how far along César is."

Manolo had been with us almost since the vineyard opened, though he was a good thirty years younger than Hector. My mother and Hector hired Manolo almost as soon as he arrived from Mexico. He'd told Hector he was eighteen, to which Hector reportedly replied, "Sure you are, and I'm Benito Juárez." We finally found out he was only fifteen. At first he worked for us during the season and washed dishes for local restaurants the rest of the year. Gradually, as we became more established, we were able to keep him on year-round. For the last few years he'd been the unofficial *jefe* when Hector wasn't there and the men respected him. I knew he had a string of girlfriends but no one serious enough to marry. He also liked to hang out in the Hispanic bars around Herndon and Sterling, but what he did on his own time was his business and he never once showed up for work drunk or hungover. Though he wasn't as steady and methodical as Hector, he had good instincts and a sense of humor. I liked him. He would be a good manager.

"Can I ask you something?" I said.

"Sure," he said easily.

"Do you know Emilio Mendez?"

He didn't take his eyes off the road, though he could have driven it with them closed. "I heard the cops are looking for him."

"That wasn't the question," I said quietly. "You know him, then, don't you?"

"No."

"But you could find out where he is?"

"He's laying low, Lucie. His girlfriend's older boy got in with a gang. They don't want trouble."

"The police need Emilio and Marta to say that Dr. Greenwood delivered their babies the night his wife was murdered," I said. "They won't do anything to the boy."

"You don't know that. You're not the cops." The easiness had vanished.

"What if I can get Bobby Noland to come here to the vineyard— alone—and talk to them right here? Then they can leave."

"They'll never believe that." He was adamant.

"Could you get them to talk to me, at least?"

"I don't know. I told you, they're scared."

"An innocent man could get convicted of his wife's murder," I said. "He took care of them when they needed him. Please, Manolo. I'm begging."

He parked the truck next to our two green and yellow Gators. Finally he said, "No promises. I'll do what I can."

He wasn't going to budge. "Thank you," I said.

We both got out of the truck, Manolo giving orders to the crew in staccato Spanish as he pulled on a pair of muddy gloves. "Lucie, you gonna prune the roots, right?" His expression was bland. No more discussing Emilio and Marta.

I nodded and picked up a pair of pruning shears that were lying in the back of one of the Gators, then pulled on my own gloves. Message received.

Until the vines were ready to be planted, we kept them soaking in five-gallon utility buckets filled with water. Between one and two feet long, the vines had thin, straggly roots like a woman's tangled hair. I unthreaded one from the bulky mass in the bucket and lifted it out of the muddy water, trimming the roots until they were even.

Next I handed the vine off to whoever was ready to plant. Slowly the pile of trimmings at my feet grew.

Ever since we'd been in business, we got our rootstock from a nursery near Williamsburg. It was top quality—and we paid for it— because in Virginia we still had a problem with phylloxera. A devastating aphid that fed on the roots and foliage of vines, it changed the world of viticulture forever when, in the mid-1800s, European botanists unknowingly took infected American vine cuttings home with them. The result was a horticultural catastrophe, as millions of acres of European vineyards that lacked the natural resistance of American vines withered and died. Only American rootstock, grafted onto European vines, had saved the industry from obliteration.

As a result, the cuttings we got now were also two different vines grafted together and held in place by a wax nodule—the roots, or rootstock, which was phylloxera-resistant, and the scion, or top of the vine, which in this case was Viognier, the actual vine variety.

Planting vines is the same slow, backbreaking manual labor it's been since Noah supposedly planted the first vineyard on the slopes of Mount Ararat. For a while, the only sound was the metallic chipping of shovels above the gentle whistling of the wind. The men set the plants in holes about a foot deep, keeping two to three feet between each vine. Other vineyards planted their vines farther apart, but we followed the European way, thanks to Jacques, which meant one strong trunk per vine that grew straight up before spreading out along the top wire. Had we left the canes on the lower wires, they'd be stripped by foxes, groundhogs, raccoons, or geese. Even now we had to put grow tubes—pale blue plastic tubing—over the bases of the young vines to protect them from being eaten.

I stayed out in the fields until early afternoon, then took one of the Gators back to the villa. My bad foot ached from standing so long, but I'd die before I'd admit it to the men. Instead I told Manolo I needed to catch up on paperwork.

He nodded. "We're okay here. I'll stop by later and let you know how much we get planted."

I made myself a pot of coffee in the kitchen, then went back to my office and propped my foot up on my wastebasket. Halfway through calculations for the monthly TTB report—the Alcohol and

Tobacco Tax & Trade Bureau—Quinn appeared in the doorway holding an unlit cigar.

"Hey," he said, "how come you didn't let me know you were back? I thought you were going to come by the barrel room when you were done in the fields."

I set down my pen. "Because it's the end of the month and this report is due."

He squinted at me. "What's your problem? I say anything and you bite my head off. Is there something you're trying to tell me?"

"Nothing I'm trying to tell you," I said. "How about you? Is there something you want to tell me?"

At first his expression was blank, then the light dawned in his eyes. "Oh," he said quietly. "I get it. Mick Dunne. You're upset about that."

I exploded. "How come you didn't say anything? Why did I have to hear about it from someone else? I thought you were working for me. Here. At this vineyard."

He held up a hand. "Whoa, sweetheart. Stop right there. You don't own me. I am not your property."

"Of course I don't own you. That's a cheap shot and you know it. But you still could have told me that you're moonlighting . . . or whatever it is you're doing . . . for Mick. The other day you were barely civil to him. Now you're his new best friend."

"He pays well," he said. "And, no offense, but I'm not exactly breaking the bank on the salary I get from you."

His words hit like a bucket of cold water. But he made perfect sense. Money.

"I see. So he was the high bidder. You should have told me it was an auction."

"Look," he said. "I'm sorry. That came out wrong. I'm just giving the guy advice. He's paying me for it. You ought to be flattered he thinks you've got yourself someone good who knows what he's doing. He could have asked anyone. Especially with the money he's throwing around."

"Did he offer you a job as his winemaker?"

"No." He looked at me levelly. "I work here."

"That's good to know, because I wasn't sure. I'd better get back to this report. I'm meeting Kit at six and Georgia's wake is at seven-thirty." I started punching numbers on the calculator again. He didn't move or speak.

Finally he said, "You coming here tomorrow before the funeral?"

"I don't know." I kept making calculations, eyes fixed on the LED display. "I'll call you in the morning and let you know."

"Sure," he said. "Call me. I got those EPA reports to finish getting ready. Sorry for disturbing you."

After he was gone I put my head down on my desk and thought about him working for Mick and what had happened last night when I went out to the summerhouse and heard him with Bonita.

I never did get that report done.

Kit was nursing a beer at a table on the terrace when I got to the pub. In the milky light, her face looked washed out and marionette lines framed her mouth. It took a moment before I realized her pallor was due to the fact that she wasn't wearing any makeup. I wondered if she'd been crying.

"Want a beer?" she said. "Keep me company."

"Sure." I sat down. "Talk to me."

"A Boy Scout troop found Randy. They were working on some merit badge studying woodland sanctuaries."

"Oh, God. Those poor kids."

"He was in awful shape, Luce. At least that's what Bobby said."

"He must have died instantly from that gunshot wound."

Kit nodded. "Looks like it, but they're still doing the autopsy."

"Did they find anything that tied him to Georgia's murder besides the note?"

"A yellow hazmat jumpsuit in the trunk of his car," she said. "And I'm not supposed to know this, but they found a used condom in your barn. A couple of 'em. They're waiting for the results to see if there's a match with what they found on Georgia."

The waitress set down my beer and another for Kit. We clinked glasses.

"Do you believe he killed himself?" Kit swallowed more beer.

"As opposed to what? Someone staged it to make it look like he did?" I asked.

Kit nodded. "There's one person who wanted them both dead." She picked up her beer coaster and began rolling it back and forth like a wheel. "Ross."

"Who couldn't have done it," I said flatly. "He wasn't there. So let's move on. Georgia left the party with Hugo Lang, but he was on the phone all night making calls after he said good night to Georgia. And he gave a cheek swab for DNA. So he wasn't the one who had sex with her, though I think he's nervous about something."

"Hell, yeah. It's called the vice presidential nomination," Kit said. "He needs this kind of tabloid fodder tarnishing his pristine image like a hole in the head. I'm sure he can't wait for the funeral and everything to blow over."

I thought about what she'd said and Hugo's shaking hands. That kind of high-stakes politics—even without all the tawdriness of Georgia's death and now Randy's body being recovered—could account for the strung-out nerves. "I guess you're right."

"Of course I'm right. So eliminate Hugo. You want something to eat? I'm starved." Kit signaled for the waitress and asked for an order of french fries. Then she said, "So who did it, if you're so sure it wasn't Ross?"

"I still think we ought to consider the possibility someone was after Randy, rather than Georgia."

"You mean besides the Cancún girlfriend?" she asked, and I nodded. "Who've you got in mind?"

"Jen Seely seemed too defensive when I asked her about Randy. I think she knows something. Or she's hiding something. Maybe about Randy."

The french fries arrived with two plates. Kit picked up the ketchup bottle and went to town. "Are you serious?" she asked. "Sorry, I can't picture her mixed up in this. She's not the type."

"She used to date the drummer in Randy's band and she's pretty tight with everyone in Southern Comfort."

"Maybe we're knocking ourselves out for no good reason," Kit said. "It could just be a case of Occam's razor."

"What's that?"

"A principle that some guy named William of Occam came up with. Kind of the KISS theory of the fourteenth century. You know,

'Keep it simple, stupid'? Occam was a Franciscan friar, so he lived a really simple, spartan life and that's his theory. Don't make anything more complicated than it is."

"What's the 'razor' part?"

"That you should shave off the assumptions that don't make any difference in the outcome." Kit picked up a french fry and laid it on her plate. "One. Georgia is found dead at the vineyard." Another french fry parallel to Georgia. "Two. Randy's body is pulled out of the Potomac River. Looks like suicide because he left a note." A third french fry across Georgia and Randy. "But we're thinking maybe it's a double homicide faked to be a suicide." She picked up the connecting french fry and bit into it. "According to Occam's razor, it's always the simplest explanation. So it is what it looks like. Randy killed Georgia, then he killed himself. Period."

She picked up the other french fries. "And that's probably what the cops are going to go with, unless something else turns up," she added. "If they can close a case, that's what they'll do. They've got too many others to solve to start asking a million what-ifs once they get all the ducks in a row. Don't forget, it's an election year and the sheriff's running, too."

Her explanation was neat and tidy, tying up all the loose ends. Plus, it meant Ross was no longer a suspect. But what was still nagging at me?

Kit wiped her hands on a paper napkin and set it by her beer glass. "Something else bothering you? You seem kind of preoccupied. Is it that thing with the EPA?"

"That's part of it." I picked up the saltshaker and studied it. "Mick Dunne hired Quinn as a consultant. He's looking for land to buy a vineyard."

Kit traced a pattern in the ketchup on the plate with one of the fries. "That's no big deal, is it? Just some consulting work?"

"I guess." I pulled my wallet out of my purse and made a check-writing gesture to the waitress, who immediately set the bill down next to me. I handed her my credit card right away.

"What else?" she asked shrewdly. "It's not like you to pay without at least looking at the bill."

I blushed and thought about Bonita and Quinn last night in the summerhouse. This I couldn't talk about. "Nothing," I said. "Nothing else."

She didn't ask again.

The sensational nature of Georgia's death and the aura of scandal meant the press was well represented in front of B. F. Hunt & Sons Funeral Home when I arrived shortly after seven-thirty. A couple of cruisers and a handful of officers from the sheriff's department tried to keep them at bay, but it didn't stop one woman with a microphone from sticking it under my nose. She knew who I was, too, thanks to the cane, which not only gave me away but also slowed me down so there was no chance of outrunning her.

"Lucie Montgomery," she said. "The woman who found the mutilated body of Georgia Greenwood on a deserted road on her vineyard. Tell our viewers, Lucie, what you saw and how you felt."

"I saw a dead woman. I felt horrible," I said. "Excuse me."

The carnival-like atmosphere outside had pervaded the funeral home. A crowd already packed the place. I signed the guest book and glanced at the long list of names. Hugo Lang had been one of the first to arrive. Mick Dunne had signed in as well.

Many of my neighbors own farms, so the cycle of life and death is something we live with all the time. But an unnatural death like Georgia's is something you never get used to. Friends and neighbors had come to pay their respects, but everyone was curious, too.

Georgia's closed casket, which I nearly ran into as I rounded the corner to the viewing room, was surrounded by flowers. A heart-catching photo of her and Ross in happier times, arms twined around each other and leaning against what looked like a ship's railing with water and tropical paradise as a backdrop, was propped on a stand next to a large bouquet of white roses. The card, clearly visible, read, "I love you, darling. Ross." A basket of prayer cards sat next to the flowers. Georgia's name and the dates of her birth and death were on one side. I picked up a card and turned it over. Ecclesiastes.

For everything there is a season, and a time for every matter under heaven:
A time to be born, and a time to die;

a time to plant, and a time to pluck up what is planted;
A time to kill, and a time to heal;
a time to break down, and a time to build up;
A time to weep, and a time to laugh;
a time to mourn, and a time to dance;
A time to scatter stones and a time to gather them,
a time to embrace and a time to refrain,
A time to search and a time to give up . . .

I stopped reading. When was it ever a time to kill?

Someone took my elbow.

"I've been waiting for you," Mick Dunne said quietly. He wore an expensive-looking charcoal gray pin-striped suit, a sober tie, and a pale gray shirt. Same wing tips as the other day.

"I just got here. I haven't had a chance to pay my respects to Ross," I said coolly. "I really ought to go find him."

He let go of my arm. "Is something wrong?"

"How did it go with the real estate agent?"

"Brilliant." He looked curiously at me. I'd avoided his question. "I found a place I quite liked."

"Good for you. Did Quinn like it, too?" I asked. "That is, since you're paying him to advise you."

He wore the expression of someone who had just been slapped. "He's not what you're thinking," he said. "Please. Let's get out of this crowd. I'd like to explain."

"That's not necessary."

"Indeed it is." This time the grip on my arm was firm as he maneuvered me to an unoccupied corner of the room next to a large silk schefflera.

"First, I apologize for not telling you sooner, but I wanted to do it in person," he said, his beautiful green eyes gazing down into mine. "I came back to see you after Erica Kendall took me 'round and ran into Quinn, who told me you were out. We started discussing land and vineyards and he gave me some advice." Mick rubbed a silk leaf. It was dusty and left a dark stain on his fingers. "I told him I'd like to pay him for the help and call on him if I need more. That's it. That's how it happened."

"I thought you might be interviewing him for a job."

"No." He removed a handkerchief from his breast pocket and wiped away the dirt. "I would never do that to you."

The crowd parted at that moment, so I could see Hugo Lang embracing Ross. They spoke earnestly, then Hugo clapped Ross on the shoulder and moved away. Then someone blocked my view and I lost sight of both of them.

Mick followed my gaze. "I'm keeping you from seeing Ross, aren't I?"

"Will you excuse me, please?"

He tilted my chin so I had to stare into those depthless eyes. "Only if you tell me that we're okay now."

"Sure," I said finally. "We're fine."

He knew a brush-off when he got one. "Glad to hear it. I need to have a word with Austin Kendall, anyway. I'll be seeing you."

I watched him cross the room and join Austin Kendall, who was with several of the Romeos. Austin's daughter Erica now ran the family real estate business, but Austin still put his oar in when the deal was in the multimillions of dollars. If Mick was talking to Austin, then he must be contemplating buying a significant piece of property.

I threaded my way through the crowd and found Ross. A group of dark-suited men were with him, but he nodded when he caught sight of me. As soon as they left, he pulled me to him and hugged me. Despite the air-conditioning, he was perspiring heavily.

"Are you all right?" I asked. "You don't look too good. Can I get you some water?"

He pulled a handkerchief out of his pocket and mopped his forehead. "The sheriff still thinks I did it, Lucie. He's going to let me get through Georgia's funeral, which is pretty decent, then they want me to come in for more questioning. I think Bobby Noland is behind this. He doesn't seem convinced Randy committed suicide, in spite of that note. Sam's trying to find out what's going down, but it's not looking good."

His voice shook and that's when I saw just how scared Ross really was that he might actually be convicted of killing his wife . . . and maybe her lover, too. All because he had no alibi.

"I talked to Manolo about Emilio and Marta," I told him. "They're hiding. Manolo says they're too frightened to talk to the police."

Ross grabbed my shoulders so hard it hurt. "Manolo knows where they are?"

"No, but he said he'd try to find out."

"You've *got* to find them and talk to them. Tell them this." For the first time since I'd known him, he sounded desperate. "Tell them Dr. Ross says everything will be *fine* if they tell the police that I was there that night delivering the twins. That's all they have to say. Nothing else. I will take care of them and their babies and the older boy. Tell them I give my *palabra de honor.*"

I nodded. "Your word of honor. Okay. I promise. Don't worry."

"Good girl." He kissed my forehead, then pulled back and scanned my face, still apprehensive. "I knew I could count on you. You won't let me down, will you?"

"No," I said. "You saved me once. Now it's my turn."

I left after that, shaken by Ross's palpable fear. He said he didn't do it and I believed him. What evidence did the police have that indicated otherwise? Why weren't they convinced by the suicide note?

Something wasn't right.

Later, when I was home alone, I opened a bottle of Gigondas and brought it out to the veranda. No light from the summerhouse tonight.

I lit the citronella candles and torches and sat there in the gilded darkness. "Wine is a perfect cure for heaviness and sorrow," wrote Seneca, the Roman statesman and philosopher, nearly two millennia ago. Tonight it wasn't doing anything for me.

I thought of the prayer card Ross had made for Georgia and the verse from Ecclesiastes. We'd used the same verse on Leland's memorial card nine months ago—though a different interpretation. The version Ross chose talked about "a time to search and a time to give up."

Maybe it had been prophetic, but I hoped not. As far as I was concerned, it was still a time to search.

It was no time to give up.

CHAPTER 14

The impact of Randy's death on top of Georgia's murder hit Atoka somewhere between seven and eight on the Richter scale. The continuing reverberations eventually reached the tasteless domain of journalist bottom feeders who mined every tawdry detail. Our barn, Ross and Georgia's home, T. R. Island, and White's Ferry all made up what one reporter called "the trail of lust."

"Makes me ashamed of my profession reading crap like this," Kit said to me. She'd called my mobile as I was pulling into the church parking lot for Georgia's funeral.

"We had to throw a reporter off the property this morning," I said. "Quinn said Manolo caught him moving the barrier so he could get access to the south service road."

"Jeez," she said. "Tabloid heaven, but hell for everyone involved."

"I just got coffee at the general store. Thelma's got every newspaper she could get her hands on laid out by the cash register and she's poring over them," I said. "It's better than her soaps."

"Yeah, we get 'em at work. I swear to God, whoever writes those headlines really scrapes the bottom of the barrel. 'All Washed Up Boyfriend Kills Lover, Then Takes the Plunge Himself.' Or 'Country Boy Fell for Sexy Socialite Hook, Line, and Sinker.'"

"My favorite was 'Corked—Vineyard Victim's Slayer Found Dead at Potomac Bottleneck.'"

"I missed that one."

"I'd better go," I said. "I'm at the church. There's a van with a satellite dish out front and reporters crawling all over the place. Even more coverage than her wake. I suppose you guys are here."

"It's not like we have a choice. Jerry Roper's on it."

"Well, so are the cops. This is going to be a three-ring circus."

"Georgia always did like to be the center of attention," Kit said. "Looks like she still is."

The Episcopal church on Mosby's Highway was located just outside the village of Upperville, where it straddled the boundaries of Loudoun and Fauquier Counties. Built in the late nineteenth century from Virginia sandstone and limestone, the church had been constructed by local workers trained as stonecutters, masons, and carpenters, all of whom had made their tools at a forge on the property.

The building could have been transported to twenty-first-century Virginia from twelfth- or thirteenth-century France because of its unusual architectural features—shallow transepts and a narthex that became the base of the bell tower. It was purposely built off-center because of the ancient belief that no matter how people strive, their work is not perfect. So the church, too, needed to have a tangible sign of imperfection. It seemed fitting for Georgia's casket to lie here, in a deliberately flawed place.

Ross had chosen all the traditional readings from *The Book of Common Prayer*—Isaiah, the Book of Revelation, the Gospel of John—and the old, familiar hymns. But despite the beautiful setting, soaring music, masses of flowers, and the well-heeled sober-suited crowd who gathered to pay their final respects, when it was over I felt hollow inside. The place was dry-eyed, no one moved to tears by sorrow or loss. Georgia had not been religious and the rector, who had given an eloquent tribute, knew her only slightly. The homily had been crafted, not heartfelt. Correct, but not quite right.

At the end of the service everyone was invited to a reception in the fellowship hall to pay respects to the family. As the organ postlude ended, I walked outside into the sun-dappled courtyard with Harry and Amy Dye.

Harry glanced in the direction of the throng of reporters, still kept at bay by the Fauquier County Sheriff's Department. "I'll be glad when this is over," he said. "I heard the cops aren't exactly buying it that Randy committed suicide. What if they're right? Maybe the real killer is someone who's here right now at her funeral."

"Harry!" Amy scolded him. "You're still in church. Enough! At least no one thinks it's you anymore. Thank God for that."

He grew serious. "Yeah, I know. Sorry, Ame. I shouldn't joke about it."

"What about Gaby?" I asked. "Is she still a suspect?"

"The sheriff let her go home finally," Amy said. "But they told her they might bring her back for more questions if they need to."

"She didn't do it," Harry said. "Gaby was hysterical when she saw Randy, but she didn't kill him. Or Georgia. Come on, ladies. I'm starved. Let's get something to eat."

"You two go ahead. I'll catch up," I said. "I left something in my car."

"Parking lot's that way," Harry said, as I started to leave.

"I'm taking the long way."

The navy pickup, backed up to the side entrance next to the church thrift shop, looked as if it had just rolled out of the dealer's showroom. The license plate, though, was familiar. "SVANH." Stephanie van Holland. Ross's ex-wife. I found her in the basement, elegant in jodhpurs, boots, and a fitted white shirt, pulling clothes out of a duffel bag and piling them on a table.

As I walked into the room, she stopped folding what looked like a cashmere sweater and held it up against her chest. "Hello, Lucie."

Ross and I hadn't become close until my accident and by then he and Georgia had already been married about a year. Stephanie and I knew each other as passing acquaintances, meeting at local social events or occasionally in Middleburg shops. She was good friends with Dominique, though, and my cousin still considered Ross a cad for divorcing her.

"Hi, Stephanie. I thought I recognized your license plate. New truck?"

"Yes." She finished folding the sweater and set it on top of the other clothes. A tall, patrician blonde, she had the kind of ethereal all-American looks that smoldered rather than sizzled. If Georgia had been fire, Stephanie could be ice, until you got to know her and she trusted you. At least that's what Dominique said.

"Yes, it is new, as a matter of fact." She raised an eyebrow and said with sweet irony, "I assume you're not here to shop or talk cars?"

Guilty as charged. "No. I came for Georgia's funeral."

"Well, this is my volunteer day." She pulled another shirt out of the bag. "How's he doing?" The shirt was badly creased, so she placed it on the table, concentrating on smoothing out the folds.

"Coping."

She paused in her work. "I heard the sheriff thinks he might have had something to do with it."

"At the moment he doesn't have a verifiable alibi for the time of Georgia's death. He delivered twins that night, but the mother was illegal and wouldn't go to the hospital. So he went to her place. Now the whole family's disappeared."

"Tough break." She finished folding the shirt department-store-perfect. It didn't sound like she felt too sorry for Ross. "But he's not the only one dragged into this. The police came to see me, too. I thought he and that woman were out of my life for good." She sounded bitter.

"Really?" I said, startled. "You mean, just because you're—"

"His ex-wife?" She looked down at her long slender fingers and touched the place where a wedding ring would have been. "It's a known secret I didn't want the divorce at the time. And I resented Georgia for breaking up our marriage." She shrugged and pulled another sweater from the bag. "I guess Ross and I have something in common. I don't have an alibi, either."

"What were you doing, if you don't mind my asking?"

She rolled her eyes. "What any God-fearing person is normally doing at two in the morning. I was in bed, asleep. Alone."

"You're not really a suspect, are you?"

"No." She laughed, but there was no mirth in it. "He was really a bastard when it was all over, you know? I felt so betrayed."

"What do you mean?"

"I was devastated when he told me about Georgia. One minute I thought everything was fine, we'd been talking about taking a safari in Kenya in the spring, then, boom. There's another woman. He'd been seeing her for a while. I had no idea. He seems like an open book, but he's not." She twisted the sweater as she talked until it resembled a thick cord. "Oh, God, look at what I'm doing."

"I'm so sorry, Stephanie."

She shrugged again, unraveling the sweater. "Frankly, I'd be more likely to kill him than her."

Some years Memorial Day weekend already feels as if we're well into full-blown summer because the weather has been blisteringly hot since mid-May and the swamplike humidity wrings you out like a damp dishrag. The haze fades the Blue Ridge Mountains until they are as white as the sky, vanishing from the horizon like smoke. Other years, like this one, the humidity stays at bay, the sunshine is pure gold, and the sky so achingly blue that pilots call this kind of weather "severe clear." The air smells clean and fresh and full of the promise of indolent summer days to come.

I had just finished breakfast on the veranda when the doorbell rang, which meant there was a stranger at the front door. Around here everyone knew the door was likely to be unlocked and protocol usually involved banging loudly, then opening it a crack and yelling, "Yoo-hoo, anybody home?"

When I opened the door, Mick Dunne stood there. Definitely not a "yoo-hoo" kind of guy, though he was wearing jeans, a polo shirt, and brand-new blindingly white sneakers. This time the jeans hadn't been ironed.

"Good morning," he said. "I've come to show you my land."

"I thought you might have come to show me your sneakers," I replied.

He laughed and stuck out a foot. "They are rather white, aren't they? Look, Lucie, please say you'll come. We need to straighten things out."

"You mean Quinn?"

"I mean us. It would mean a great deal to me if you'd do this." Suddenly he was serious. "Please?"

There was no graceful way to get out of this—literally or figuratively—because he'd put one of his newly shod feet in the threshold and was standing there, arms folded, waiting me out.

"All right," I said. "I'll come."

We took his car, a shiny black Mercedes convertible with a GPS system. "Where did you get the car?" I asked.

"From a nice chap at the Mercedes dealership. I gave him some money and he let me drive off with it."

We took Atoka Road and at Route 50, Mosby's Highway, the GPS female voice told him to signal right toward Middleburg.

"Where is this land?" I asked. "Can I scroll down the display and see where we're going?"

"Absolutely not. It would ruin the surprise."

"Are we going to Middleburg to pick up Erica or Austin?"

"No, but we are meeting someone."

We drove through Middleburg behind a slow-moving horse trailer, passing Federal Street and the offices of Kendall Properties. By the time we made it through Aldie, stopping at the light at Gilbert's Corner—the turnoff for Route 15 toward Leesburg—I was baffled. The smooth-talking GPS told him to turn right on 15, south toward Haymarket and Gainesville.

"*Where* are you taking me? And who's the real estate agent we're meeting?"

He smiled. "I never said we were meeting a real estate agent. You said that. I told you, it's a surprise. You're going to like it."

He didn't clue me in until the GPS directed him to make another left toward Manassas.

"We're going to Manassas Airport," he said. "I've rung your friend Chris Coronado. He's taking us up in his helicopter so we can get a good view, not just of my place, but of the whole region."

Ever since I fell through the rotted floorboards of an old tree house when I was eight and broke both arms, I've been scared of heights. Even climbing a ladder still frightens me. The thought of getting into a helicopter—a giant glass bubble—was terrifying.

"W-we are?" I stammered.

"What's wrong?"

"I've never been in a helicopter before." Maybe I could talk him out of this without admitting my acrophobia, but he was clearly oblivious to my growing panic.

"That's fantastic," he was saying, "because you're going to love it."

We drove through the entrance of an industrial park, following signs on the narrow twisted road to the small regional airport. A chain-link fence separated us from a series of corrugated metal warehouses belonging to freight and passenger service companies.

"Destination is straight ahead," the disembodied GPS voice announced. "You have arrived."

Mick stopped the car and called Chris on his mobile phone. "Hey, mate," he said. "We're here." He covered my hand with his. "Don't be nervous. I do this all the time."

I nodded wordlessly as Chris drove up in a golf cart, waving a hand over his head by way of greeting. He did something to a panel in the wall and the gate slowly slid open. The Mercedes followed the golf cart onto the tarmac and Chris gestured for Mick to park next to the hangar door of a warehouse with a red and white sign that read "Coronado Aviation. Aerial Photography, Cargo, Observation, Sightseeing, Surveying."

Mick picked up an oversized book of regional road maps from the back seat of the Mercedes as I got my cane. Together we walked through the open hangar door into the warehouse. The helicopter looked more fragile than I remembered.

"We'll take the MD-500," Chris said. "It's fueled and ready for takeoff, if you two are ready."

"Why are we taking a book of road maps?" I asked. "We're going to be in the air. Don't tell me you need to look at a road map to see where we're going. Don't you *know*?"

"She's a bit jumpy," Mick explained to Chris. "Never been in a helicopter before."

"It'll help get your bearings in the air," Chris said, "if we follow the roads."

"You're going to look at a map *and* fly a helicopter at the same time? How can you pay attention to where we're going?"

He smiled and competently patted his head and rubbed his stomach. "I can multitask," he said. "Don't worry, Lucie. If I can fly night-blind in the dark over your vines, flying today with unlimited visibility is a piece of cake."

The men pushed the helicopter outside and moved it to the take-off area. Chris climbed in first, then he and Mick helped me inside.

"Breathe," Mick murmured in my ear. "I haven't heard you breathe since we sat down."

Chris passed us headsets and went through his checklist. Then he switched on the engine and asked for takeoff clearance as the blades began to rotate over my head. I closed my eyes and the helicopter lifted off the ground.

It was noisier than I expected and the only way to communicate was through the headsets.

"You can look now, love." Mick's voice sounded so close it could have come from inside my head. "And if you can unclench your fingers from my wrist for just a second, I'll get the maps."

The view was nothing like what I expected. Chris said we were flying at an altitude of about twelve hundred feet, but it was—at least to me—surprisingly easy to see what was going on below us on the ground.

"Okay, that's Route Fifteen down there." Chris glanced over his shoulder at us and pointed to the road. "The way you would have come. We'll turn left at Gilbert's Corner and head west on Mosby's Highway."

"We really are following the road map, aren't we?" I said.

He nodded as Mick squeezed my hand. "This is where you come in. You've lived here almost all your life. I want to see this place through your eyes." His voice was a caress in my ear. "You know where we are. Show it to me."

And so for the next hour we crisscrossed the land George Washington had once surveyed, following the silver thread of Goose Creek as it meandered through Fauquier and Loudoun Counties. We flew mostly over the region known as the Mosby Heritage Area, the stretch of Route 50 that began in Aldie and ended in the pretty village of Paris on the edge of the eastern side of the Blue Ridge Mountains. The highway acted like a needle on a compass to orient me and gradually my jitters subsided and I grew more confident in pointing out farms and landmarks, explaining their history as we moved steadily west toward the peaceful-looking mountains that dominated our view. Here the land was almost all rolling hills, pastures, and farmland, the boundaries outlined by split-rail fences and divided like a giant checkerboard by stacked-stone walls.

We flew over the old Goose Creek Bridge and I showed Mick where, in June 1863, the forces of Colonel J. E. B. Stuart tried unsuccessfully to hold off the Union cavalry that was pushing toward the Shenandoah Valley. Ten days later the two armies met at Gettysburg.

"You all right?" Mick asked at one point. "You seem calmer. At least you're not digging into my hand and drawing blood anymore."

"Oh, God, was I really?" I asked. "I'm so sorry. You know, we've seen everything but your land. Now it's your turn with the map."

"That won't be necessary. You know where to go, Chris," Mick said. "Let's fly over Lucie's place first."

Chris banked the helicopter and we crossed Mosby's Highway again. I could see our shadow on the ground as we swooped, graceful as a bird, over the bucolic scene below.

We flew over my toy-sized house, the vineyard, and all the buildings and barns. I saw the grove where I'd found Georgia, and from the air, the distance to the barn where Randy's band had practiced seemed like a hop, skip, and a jump.

"So there it is," Mick was saying.

"There what is?"

"Were you woolgathering?" He put an arm around my shoulders and pulled me close. "Look over there. My land. That's our common property line. Yours and mine."

"What are you talking about?" I was stunned. "Did you buy the Studebaker place? That's a stud farm. There's not a vine anywhere on that property. It's completely set up for horses."

"I know. But someday there'll be vines," he said. "The owners and I agreed on a price last night. I'm signing the documents early next week."

"Are you serious? How can you do that so fast?"

He looked pleased with himself. "It's the only way I do things. I like results. Besides, it's a cash deal. It speeded things along."

"Folks, I hate to interrupt, but I just want to let you know it's time to head back," Chris said. "We've been out for about seventy-five minutes."

"Fine," Mick agreed. "We've had our tour. Cheers, Chris."

"Oh, my God, are we running out of fuel?" I sat up and craned my neck to get a view of Chris's gauges. "Is that why we have to go back?"

Chris said, "No," as Mick said, "Of course not."

"You wouldn't lie to me?"

"We're safe as houses," Mick assured me. "There are FAA standards about how little fuel you can have left before you're required to land. Relax, love. We could fly to Richmond with what we've got left."

We touched down, surprisingly gently, about ten minutes later. I refused to get out of the helicopter until the blades stopped turning. Then Mick lifted me into his arms and set me down before retrieving my cane.

After he paid Chris, we drove to the main gate.

"I suppose you could convert those stables into a tasting room," I said as it closed behind us

"The horses would hate it."

"You're planning on raising horses *and* running a vineyard?"

"Not single-handedly. But yes. I guess I didn't get around to telling you that I used to play polo. At university in the U.K., then more recently in Florida."

"So what, exactly, did you do for this pharmaceutical company in Florida?" I asked.

"Ever heard of Dunne Pharmaceuticals?"

"Oh, my God. Yes, of course. That's *you*?"

"Was me. I sold to Merck."

"Why?"

"I got bored." He put his foot on the accelerator and we sped past a pickup truck. "I wanted to do something different."

"Like own a vineyard?"

"Precisely."

We finished the drive back to Atoka in silence with only our GPS friend interrupting occasionally to tell him to turn right or left. When we got to my house, he turned off the engine and came around to open my door.

"That was an extravagant way to see your new property," I said. "Why did you do it?"

"I wanted you to see it that way. I did it for you." He kissed me as

I knew he would. No peck on the cheek this time. "I still owe you dinner," he murmured. "What are you doing tonight?"

I said breathlessly, "Working. A jazz concert and a wine tasting."

"Tomorrow?"

His persistence was making me dizzy. "Can I let you know? We'll be busy all day. I'm not sure when I'll be through."

After he left I went inside and thought about that kiss. Was he trying to start something? And why me? Somehow I didn't think I fit the prototype of the other women he'd been with. I figured him falling for the tall, leggy knockouts who spent their days caring for themselves so they glittered at night for the men who owned them. Rich, exotic, privileged—just like he was. Not someone who got her hands dirty—literally. And whose only experience with pampering was a physical therapist's muscular massages as she rubbed my deformed foot in hopes of discovering even one nerve that wasn't dead.

The phone rang while I was still in the foyer. Siri, sounding distraught.

"Lucie." Her voice shook. "They've arrested Ross. He's been charged with Georgia's murder. He just left the clinic in handcuffs."

CHAPTER 15

I calmed Siri and told her to call Sam Constantine. He'd know what to do. He'd straighten out a horrible mistake. After I hung up with her, I called Manolo.

"Did you have any luck tracking down Emilio and Marta?" I asked. "Please say yes."

"I got an address last night from someone." He didn't sound happy about it. "I don't know if it's still good."

"It's better than nothing."

But when he told me, I didn't recognize the Leesburg address.

"The new place. You know, the toilet bowl?" he asked.

"Pardon?"

"That's what the kids call it," he explained. "The arch over the entrance to the main building's shaped like a toilet bowl. I think it was supposed to be a horseshoe, but that's not what anybody calls it now. When you see it you'll know what I mean."

"Thanks," I said. "I owe you."

"For this," he said, "you do. You don't want to know what I had to do to get it."

My next call was Quinn. Granted, we weren't on the best of terms at the moment. But I trusted him and I knew he wouldn't let me down. Besides, this was for Ross. I'd already gone on my knees to Manolo. I was getting used to the view.

"I might need an interpreter," I told him. "Please, please say you'll come."

"Yeah, I'll come." He sounded just like Manolo, that same hard, flat voice. "I don't want you wandering around there by yourself. Even in daylight."

"You know this place?"

"Everybody knows the toilet bowl," he said ominously. "You can buy anything you want there. Women, drugs. Tough crowd."

"I'll pick you up in ten minutes," I told him.

"You will not. I'm not getting in that windup toy today. I feel like a sissy riding in it, and besides, someone will probably pick it up and carry it off while we're talking to them," he said. "I'll be by to get you. We're taking the El."

On the drive over to Leesburg he asked me about my helicopter ride.

"How did you know about that?"

"Mick stopped by after dropping you off. Wanted to talk some more about siting his vines. Sounds like you two had quite a time. I thought you were scared of heights." He seemed to be concentrating intently on the road, even though we had it to ourselves.

"You know I am," I said. "He told me he wanted me to see his new property. Didn't bother mentioning I'd be looking down at it from twelve hundred feet until we got to the airport. There was no getting out of it then."

"Pretty expensive date. He likes you." He was driving the El with one palm on the steering wheel, his arm extended ramrod-straight, the other arm out the window, fingers tapping out a rhythm on the car door.

"Don't be ridiculous. It wasn't a date. We're going to be sharing a common property line. It's good he likes me. We're neighbors now."

He glanced at me with a face like granite, hard and maybe a little cold. "We're almost there."

Manolo was right. The minute I saw the main building with its oddly shaped pea-green arch, I knew why it was called what it was called.

Emilio and Marta's condo was a walk-up on the third floor of one of the many rabbit-warren complexes built around a series of large interconnected parking lots whose visual focal points were overfull dumpsters. Music, televisions, arguments, children crying. Any language but English. We heard it all as we climbed the stairs. Except in front of the door to Marta and Emilio's place, where there was silence. Quinn leaned forward to listen, then knocked on the door.

No answer.

"Say we're friends of Ross's," I whispered. "Maybe they'll open up. If they're there."

"*¡Emilio, Marta! Somos amigos del doctor Greenwood. Él nos ha enviado. Por favor, abre la puerta.*"

"Ross did what?" I asked quietly.

"Sent us," he hissed. "I said we were Ross's friends and that he sent us. And to open up."

A moment later the door cracked open slightly and a man stared out. In his late thirties, probably. Jet-black bedhead hair, a handlebar mustache, compact and lithely built. He wore the kind of sleeveless scooped-neck undershirt Leland used to refer to as a wife-beater and a pair of faded jeans.

"Emilio?" I asked. "We're friends of Ross Greenwood's. Can we talk to you and Marta, please?"

"*No están,*" he said.

"*¿Quién?*" Quinn asked.

"*Marta y los niños.*"

"He says—" Quinn began.

"That Marta and the kids aren't here," I said. "That much I got. Can we come in and talk to him, at least?"

Quinn translated. Emilio shook his head and my heart sank. Then Quinn said something low and rapid that I didn't catch. Whatever it was, it worked, and Emilio opened the door wide enough to let us inside.

The apartment looked more like a place to camp than a home. A daybed with a faded purple blanket thrown over it, a floor lamp with a torn shade, a Formica table, and two mismatched chairs were the only pieces of furniture. No sign of children anywhere. Nothing. The sink and the kitchen counter were stacked with dirty dishes. They'd been there awhile. Maybe he was living here alone.

Emilio reached for a crushed pack of Marlboros and kicked an overflowing ashtray that was on the floor so it was next to him. He sat on the daybed and lit up. No invitation to Quinn or me to sit, so I stood, leaning on my cane. Quinn spun one of the chairs, facing it backward, and parked himself like he'd mounted a horse.

"Where are Marta and the children?" I asked.

Emilio looked at me warily. *"No están aquí,"* he repeated.

"They're somewhere," I insisted.

"Lucie." Quinn spoke warningly. "Let it go."

"We need both of them to say Ross was with them the night Georgia was killed," I said.

Emilio's eyes darted from Quinn to me. I had a feeling he understood us better than he let on.

"¿Mande?" he asked Quinn, who dutifully interpreted.

Emilio said something rapid-fire.

"He said, okay, fine, Ross was with them that night. All night."

"They've got to tell the police. It's not enough to tell us."

For the first time he spoke English. "No police."

"Please, Emilio," I said. "Ross—Dr. Greenwood—said to tell you that if you do this he will take care of your family. But he can't help you if he's in jail. He said to tell you he gives his *palabra de honor.*"

Emilio blew out a stream of smoke. "He said '*palabra de honor*?'"

"Yes."

"How much?" he asked in English.

I glanced at Quinn, who regarded me placidly.

"How much what?" I said.

Emilio made the universal gesture for money.

"Aw, Emilio . . ." I began.

"Es muy caro vivir aquí," he said.

"He's not gonna talk otherwise, Lucie," Quinn said. "He says the cost of living here's killing him. How much you got on you?"

I opened my purse and pulled out my wallet. "Fifty-five dollars."

"Give it to him."

I handed over the money to Emilio, who pocketed it, then said, "I want more."

"Here's mine," Quinn said. "An even hundred."

I looked at Emilio and tried to keep the contempt out of my eyes. "We'll set up a meeting at the vineyard," I said. "Tomorrow. You and

Marta must come with the babies. I promise there will be only one police officer. A detective. Tell him what you told us. Then you can leave."

"I work. After ten." Emilio exhaled more smoke and bent down to crush his cigarette in the ashtray. "Outside. Not inside. No buildings."

"What about the parking lot?" Quinn said. "Do you have a car, Emilio?"

"No." He lit another cigarette.

"Maybe Manolo can pick them up." I waved away the fug of smoke. My eyes burned.

Quinn negotiated with Emilio in Spanish, then said, "Okay. We're set. Manolo will get him at nine-thirty and bring him to us."

"Marta and the babies, too," I insisted.

Emilio shrugged. "Cost you more I bring them."

"How much more?"

"Five hundred bucks."

I exchanged glances with Quinn, who remained mute. My crusade. My money.

"Okay," I said evenly. "Five hundred. Only if everyone's there."

Emilio looked me up and down. *"Señorita,"* he said. "I know what to do."

He stood up and stubbed out the barely smoked cigarette in a plate that had dark smears and bits of dried food on it. Then he walked over the door and opened it.

"Hasta mañana."

When we were back in the El, I said angrily to Quinn, "What a humanitarian! Ross took care of his family for *free.* He can't stand up and do the right thing for someone who helped him when he needed it? They're not even in the country legally, for God's sake. Maybe he ought to go back where he came from."

Quinn jerked the car in reverse so abruptly I had to put my hand on the dashboard to steady myself as he roared out of the parking lot. When we were back on the main road he said, "I'm surprised you could get the words out of your mouth around that silver spoon, sweetheart. Say we did send Emilio and his family back to the mud hut they call home in Salvador. Then who's gonna clean all the toilets in the restaurants around here? Mow all the rich people's lawns? Wash dishes all night, then jump on the back of the garbage truck first thing in the morning in the pouring rain or freezing cold? You wanna do that?"

We were back on Route 15 now, headed to Gilbert's Corner. I didn't want to look at his speedometer, but we were going well past the limit.

"I'm sorry," I said. "I shouldn't have said what I did. But that was extortion."

"Do you blame him?" Quinn was still mad. "Beats making minimum wage with no benefits, don't you think? Maybe he'll splurge and take the family to McDonald's for a Happy Meal now that he's so rich."

"Okay," I said. "Okay. I said I'm sorry. But we still had to buy Ross's life from him. I would rather have given him a job than hand over cash like that. We could at least pay him a living wage."

Quinn kept staring straight ahead, palm on the steering wheel once again as we hammered down the road. "Doesn't work that way," he said. "We'd have a mutiny on our hands with the rest of the crew who waited their turn and got green cards so they're legit. You know that as well as I do."

"There's something else," I said.

"What?"

"I don't think the speed limit's eighty."

A muscle twitched in his jaw, but at least he let up on the accelerator. When we got back to the vineyard I said as I got out of the car, "Bobby is coming to the concert tonight with Kit. I'm going to ask him to come early so we can talk to him then and set up the meeting for tomorrow. Okay?"

"Fine." He headed toward the steps to the winery, taking them two at a time.

"Hey!" I called.

He stopped and turned around. "What?"

"Are you still mad at me? I'm sorry about what I said. I mean it."

He threw his hands up in the air. "I don't know what I am anymore," he said. "Especially where it involves you. Go call Bobby. I got stuff to do in the barrel room."

I called Kit instead.

"Sure, we can come early," she said. "Why, what's up?"

"I need to talk to Bobby and it's better if I do it face-to-face."

"Uh-oh. Luce, it better not be about Ross. Bobby's been up to his ass in alligators ever since they arrested him at the clinic. Apparently the sheriff department's been getting calls—a lot of 'em on 911—saying Ross didn't do it and the police are a bunch of pigs. Bobby's had about all he can take."

"Please do this favor for me," I said. "Please? You won't be sorry."

"Somehow I think I already am," she said. "The things I do for you. See you at six."

At five-thirty I fixed a tray with four wineglasses, four plates, a basket of crackers, and Dominique's tapenade in the villa's small kitchen. Quinn found me uncorking a bottle of wine at the bar.

"Bobby is gonna smell a setup a mile away." He picked up the bottle and whistled. "Where'd you get a bottle of Angelus? I've never seen that. An eighty-dollar bottle of wine ought to buy you plenty of help."

"Leland's wine cellar," I said. "And it's not a setup. All of us can have drinks on the terrace. It'll be easier to talk that way."

"He's gonna hate this."

Bobby and Kit arrived at six sharp. I smiled and Bobby's eyes grew wary as his eyes slid from Kit to me.

"Told you," Quinn said under his breath.

"Hi," said Kit brightly. "Here we are."

"How about a drink? We can sit on the terrace," I said. "Hey, Bobby. Thanks for coming."

Quinn poured a small amount of wine into his glass, then filled the others before finally topping off his own. I passed the crackers and tapenade.

"What is this stuff?" Bobby asked.

"Tapenade," I said.

Kit spread some liberally on a cracker and took a bite. "Kind of a fancy olive dip," she said, licking a finger. "Try it. It's good."

We clinked glasses and drank, then Bobby said, "What gives, Lucie? You want to talk about Ross Greenwood, don't you?"

I set my wineglass down. "What if we can prove Ross couldn't have killed Georgia?"

"Then you would know more than the Loudoun County Sheriff's Department does."

He spoke with such complete conviction that it rattled me. "What if we get Emilio and Marta to talk to you? And they say Ross was at their place all night delivering their twins?" I folded my hands in my lap and squeezed them tightly together like I was praying. And waited.

"Lucie," Bobby said carefully, "we think we have a strong case or we wouldn't have arrested him."

"You could be wrong! How could he have killed her if he was with them?"

"Bring them to the station," he said, "and we'll talk."

"They won't go to the station," Quinn said. "They're scared they'll be deported."

"That won't happen."

"Marta's son was involved in a gang fight recently. He managed to slope off before he got picked up," Quinn said.

"I know," Bobby said. "Kid's only fourteen. Marta oughta pay more attention to what he's up to or she'll be visiting him in juvie before his next birthday."

"What about meeting her and Emilio here at the vineyard?" I asked.

"Set it up and call me."

"It is set up. Ten o'clock tomorrow night. Here in the parking lot."

Bobby's eyes held mine and his mouth twitched. "What a surprise."

"Will you come?"

"Yeah," he said. "I'll come. And now I got something to ask you."

I sat up straight. "Yes?"

"I've had the day from hell. Your wine's real good, but I'd give anything for a cold beer. You got anything like that around here?"

Our luck with the glorious weather—clear, sharp sunshine, azure sky, tufts of cottonball cumulus clouds—continued on Sunday, the day of our first annual "Memorial Day Weekend Run Through the Vineyard." It had been my idea to raise money for the soup kitchen near Bluemont where we often donated leftover food from our events. As soon as we announced it, Blue Ridge Federal, the *Washington Tribune,* and Kendall Properties offered to sponsor the race, paying for advertising, special T-shirts, and other promotional expenses.

About three hundred people signed up to run. The course started in front of the winery and, for the more serious runners, consisted of a ten-kilometer circuit through the south vineyard along the service road, then down Atoka Road to our main entrance and up Sycamore Lane. For the less intrepid, it was four and a half laps around Sycamore Lane, which was exactly five kilometers. There also was a 2k fun walk-run for anyone who just wanted to stretch their legs.

Quinn had thought we could pace off the course using the odometer in the El.

"Absolutely not," I had said. "We'll get Marty Gamble to come over with a measuring wheel and walk off an accurately measured course. He runs with the Downtown Athletic Club."

"The place that used to give the Heisman Trophy? No fooling?" Quinn rubbed his chin with his thumb.

"No, no. This is a group of guys over in Leesburg. They meet at the Dunkin' Donuts."

"What's the difference between the odometer and that wheel thing?" Quinn asked.

"If you're a runner," I explained, "you're always trying for a personal best. If we're sloppy and it's really an almost-but-not-quite-ten-k, then just imagine what happens when some guy is high-fiving his buddy and whooping and hollering after he crosses the finish line because he's sure he just shaved ten or twenty seconds off his best time. You want to be the one to tell him it's fifty meters short?"

"Okay," he'd said. "I get your point."

So I was surprised when Quinn met me at the villa first thing in the morning wearing running shorts and a T-shirt. There is no time when I am more aware of the limitations of my disability than when it comes to sports. In high school, Kit and I had run cross-country and I'd been pretty competitive, but those days were gone forever. When I was in the hospital, my physical therapist had been an adorable ninety-nine-pound sprite who looked like she'd blow away in a stiff breeze. I found out soon enough that she'd trained with the Marines and their elite "tip of the spear" lead-the-pack aggressiveness had rubbed off on her but good. She ended every one of our sessions with a sweet smile and the promise that she would be back the next day to, as she said, "kick your butt from hell to breakfast."

Besides Ross, she was the best thing that happened to me, accident-wise. Part of kicking my butt meant she never let me feel sorry for myself and, hard-ass that she was, she wasted no pity on me, either. "Listen to me, Lucie," she'd said during one of our sessions, "your disability is a part of who you are now, but it isn't all of who you are. It doesn't define you. Don't make it that way."

I hadn't. But days like this were still hard.

"I didn't know you were going to run," I said now to Quinn. "You never mentioned it."

He looked embarrassed. "Bonita talked me into it."

"Good for you. You doing the ten-k or the five-k?"

"My pride wants to do the ten-k like a hot dog, but my knees are telling me to do the five-k." He grinned, still self-conscious.

I laughed. "Listen to your knees."

Then he turned serious. "Manolo called. He's gonna pick up Emilio tonight after he gets off work. He should be here by ten."

"What about Marta and the babies? I got the money."

"He didn't say one way or the other," Quinn said.

"I'm not sure Bobby will buy this without the children there," I said.

"Then you'd better pray to whoever you pray to that they come."

Almost all of our events at the vineyard—except for apple picking—are geared to adults since they revolve around wine, but the daytime charity race brought families with children. Some of the parents ran with their kids and a few pushed baby strollers as they walked and chatted during the laps around Sycamore Lane. Besides the local Girl Scout troop handing out bottled water along the way, we gave flavored Popsicles to the kids and before long every child had a brightly colored tongue.

Sera surprised us by showing up with Hector, who had just gotten out of the hospital the day before. "I didn't want him to come," she murmured. "But you know him. He insisted."

Hector patted her hand. "This woman worries too much."

But his face was pale and the heartiness seemed forced. I kissed him on the forehead. "Let me know if you need anything."

He waved me away with his hand. "I'm fine, Lucita. You wait and see. Next year I'll be running with all these people."

"Sure you will, *my vida*," Sera said affectionately, mussing his hair. "You'll bring home the blue ribbon, won't you?"

I smiled and left to join the race officials.

It was a folksy down-home kind of event, completely low-tech, with no computerized timers or cars following the runners along the course. Austin Kendall, wearing pink and lime plaid Bermuda shorts, a "Run Through the Vineyard" T-shirt, and a straw boater with small American flags tucked into it, genially yelled, "On your mark, get set, go!" and that started everyone off. Seth Hannah from the bank and Clayton Avery, who owned the *Tribune,* joined him at the finish line. It would be their collective decision as to who broke the tape and got first, second, and third place.

I didn't see Jennifer Seely until after the race was over. She had competed in the 10k, turning in one of the better times among the women. I watched a Girl Scout hand her a bottle of water. Jen unscrewed the top and dumped the bottle so water sluiced over her hair and face, soaking her thin T-shirt, which clung to well-muscled contours. She looked tired but exhilarated. I watched with some envy. That used to be me.

She caught me staring. "Hello, Lucie."

I walked over and leaned on my cane. "Congratulations. Great time you turned in."

"Thanks." She chugged the rest of her water.

"You sticking around for the picnic?" I asked.

She shook her head. "Randy's sister is in town. She's packing his things. I said I'd help."

"You really were close, weren't you?"

She flushed lightly. "I'm just trying to help. His family is devastated. No one can believe he killed himself. Not to mention all that crap about Georgia."

"You know the police found bedding and condoms at our barn, don't you?" I asked.

"I heard." She picked at the label on the water bottle.

"You've been there with him, Jen. You were more than just friends."

She stopped fiddling with the label and looked up. "What if I was? No one knows, Lucie. I'd like it to stay that way. Especially now that he's dead."

"Were you there the night Georgia died?"

"No. Of course not." Her eyes flashed. "I gotta go. See you around."

She sprinted past me and I watched her, long-legged with gazelle-like grace, as she ran down Sycamore Lane toward the parking lot.

She was lying. Too bad I couldn't prove it.

CHAPTER 16

———

Manolo called that evening on his way to pick up Emilio.

"They might be late," he said. "But everyone's coming. Kids, too."

"Good." I patted the pocket of my jeans where I had stuffed a roll of twenties. "This won't work unless they all show up."

The lit tip of Quinn's cigar glowed orange in the soft darkness as I pulled into the parking lot just before ten. He sat on the stone wall by the stairs to the villa, smoking quietly.

"Manolo called," I said as I joined him. "Everyone's coming, but they're running behind."

"At least they're showing up."

"Moon's pretty tonight," I said. "Looks like a harvest moon."

"Nope. It's a blue moon," he said. "The second full moon this month. They're pretty rare."

"That's why they say 'once in a blue moon'?"

"Yep." The cigar glowed again and I heard him expel a breath. "I thought you were going to come out and look at the stars with me at the summerhouse."

I said with a small shock, "I almost did the other night. I was nearly there when I realized you were with Bonita. So I left."

He sounded surprised. "You were? We never heard you."

Fortunately in the darkness he couldn't see my face burn with embarrassment. I never should have brought it up. "The two of you were sort of busy."

"What's that supposed to mean?" he drawled. "Wait a minute. Don't tell me you think—"

I cut him off. "Listen. Someone's coming."

Bobby's tan unmarked Crown Vic pulled into the parking lot and he climbed out, leaving the engine running and the headlights on. Because he was backlit by the strong white glare, all I could see was a dark silhouette, including the bulge on his hip where he carried his gun.

"Evenin', folks," he said. "Where's the happy family?"

"Running a little late," Quinn said. "But they're on their way."

Bobby pulled a pack of bubblegum out of his pocket and held it out. "Gum?"

I said, "No, thanks," as Quinn shook his head.

"How come you had to bring your gun?" I asked. "You'll scare them."

Bobby and Quinn exchanged glances.

"Uh, look, Lucie," Bobby said, "in my job the only time I'm not carrying is in the shower. I didn't do this just for Emilio and Marta."

"Oh."

He stuck a piece of gum in his mouth and joined Quinn and me on the wall. Behind us a chorus of bullfrogs sang loudly, the sound of the beginning of summer.

Another set of headlights cut a swath through the darkness.

"They're here," Bobby said. "Let's do this."

Emilio Mendez and Marta Juarez got out of the backseat of Manolo's Toyota Camry. Each of them carried a small bundle. Manolo followed them. Emilio had plenty of yesterday's swagger in him, but Marta, who looked like a child herself, seemed frightened. Her dark eyes were enormous as she clutched her baby and surveyed the three of us.

I stood up and went to her. "I'm Lucie, Marta. Can I see your baby?" I smiled, hoping showing off the child might help her relax.

Emilio said something low and hoarse in Spanish and Marta lowered the bundle from her shoulder, cradling the baby so I could see.

"A boy or a girl?" I asked.

"Angelina," she murmured.

Emilio showed off the other twin. "My son," he said. "Emilio."
For the first time since I'd met him, he smiled.

"They're beautiful," I said. "You must be very proud."

Behind me, Bobby cleared his throat. "Maybe I could ask them a couple of questions, Lucie, if that's okay with you?"

I turned. "Sure. Sorry."

He pulled out his notebook, positioning himself inside the wedge of light made by his headlights so he could see what he was writing. I held out my arms for baby Emilio and his father obliged. The child smelled sweet as I bent to kiss him. His eyes were closed.

"Okay," Bobby said. "I'd like to ask you both what happened last Saturday night, May twenty-first, and Sunday morning, May twenty-second."

It was pretty straightforward. Emilio did almost all the talking, occasionally in Spanish but often in English.

Marta went into labor early Saturday night. Emilio called Ross around ten-thirty p.m.

"You called his answering service?" Bobby asked.

Emilio glanced at Quinn. *"¿Mande?"*

Quinn interpreted, then Emilio said, "No. I call Dr. Ross. He give his mobile number to Marta."

"What time did he get to your house?"

"Eleven-thirty, about."

"Then what?"

Emilio shrugged. Angelina started to fuss and Marta turned away from us to quiet her. I could hear her crooning softly to her daughter. In my arms, Emilio still slept placidly.

"Then the babies come. First Emilio, then Angelina."

"What time?"

"Four o'clock." He waggled his fingers. "Around. For Emilio. Then maybe half hour and Angelina."

"So they were born Sunday morning," Bobby said.

"Sí."

"What time did Dr. Greenwood leave?"

"A las seis. Six."

"You're sure?" Bobby asked.

"I got Ross on his mobile around six-thirty," I said, looking down at the sleeping child. "He told me he was on his way home after delivering the twins."

"Thanks for that info, Lucie." Bobby glared at me. "I'll just finish with Emilio here, okay?"

"Don't interrupt him," Quinn said in my ear. "Or you'll blow it."

"Did Dr. Greenwood leave your apartment anytime between eleven-thirty and six a.m.?" Bobby asked Emilio.

"No."

"Marta, you agree?"

She looked up when he said her name, her eyes flitting to Emilio, who interpreted. In the darkness I heard her say softly, *"Sí."*

Bobby pulled an overstuffed wallet out of his back pocket and extracted a battered-looking business card. "Call me if you remember something you forgot to tell me. I can get an interpreter for you, easy."

Emilio took the card. "Can we go?"

"Sure."

"I'll help you get the children into the car," I said.

I slipped Emilio the money when I gave him back his son. He took it without a word.

"They're beautiful, Marta," I said, pressing her hand with mine. "Two little Geminis. The twins."

She looked puzzled and glanced at Emilio who said, *"Dice que son gemelos."* He smiled at me. "My son is bull. Very strong. My daughter, too."

"I think she looks very sweet." I smiled back. "Thank you for coming."

"So now Ross has an alibi," I said, as Manolo backed out of the parking lot. "He couldn't have murdered Georgia, since he was delivering those children."

Bobby's eyes narrowed. "I dunno. Something's bothering me still."

"What?"

"The murder weapon would be nice. Whatever was used to whack her on the head and knock her out." He blew a bubble and popped it. "We never found it. You would have figured Randy would have it."

"What are you gonna do now, Bobby?" Quinn asked.

"At the moment we're holding Ross without bail. But he has a preliminary hearing Tuesday morning to determine if there's probable cause and to set the bond," he said. "Under the circumstances, I'd bet it's going to be low enough that he can make bail and we'll kick him loose."

"That's great news," I said. "Why do you have to wait until Tuesday?"

"Tomorrow's Memorial Day. If the magistrate happens to come by the jail, maybe we can move things up. But no guarantees. Anyway, I still think something's off here."

"If you've got hard evidence that he didn't do it," I said, "then what more do you want?"

Bobby blew another bubble. "The truth," he said.

The weather changed on Memorial Day, and not for the better. I had a fitful night's sleep filled with interruptions. Siri had called around midnight to tell me that Sam Constantine was going to try to talk to the magistrate and call in a favor so he could get Ross's hearing moved up to Monday. Even if there was probable cause to accuse him, it had now been weakened by Emilio's statement—and, besides, Ross had such strong ties to the community. She sounded elated, unaware she'd woken me up. Then at three-thirty, I had heard footsteps on the spiral staircase and the sound of Mia's bedroom door closing.

When I finally got up at five-thirty, her door was tightly shut. She'd probably sleep until noon. I went downstairs to fix breakfast and switched on the radio in the kitchen. The forecast called for possible pop-up thunderstorms late in the day, continuing into the evening. We could always move the picnic to the villa if it rained, but you couldn't move fireworks indoors.

I ate on the veranda. The air had thickened and a film of haze settled in, blunting sharp edges so the view looked like a slightly out-of-focus photograph. The outline of the Blue Ridge softened and bled into the skyline. Inside the house, the phone rang. I got to it just before the answering machine kicked in.

"How come you didn't answer your mobile?" Quinn demanded.

"Because it's probably in my car. I don't suppose you have any idea for Plan B if it's pouring rain when we're supposed to have our fireworks tonight?"

"Not really. Maybe we'll catch a break and we can have 'em between storms or something."

"The truck from Boom Town Fireworks ought to be down by the pond setting up," I said. "I'll go talk to Hamp and let you know what he says."

"Call me on your mobile," he said, "because I'm heading over to the new fields to see how the planting is coming." He paused and added, "Unless you forgot to charge your phone again."

"Well, I might have. But it doesn't take long to charge."

"I knew it," he said, and hung up.

I got the phone and connected it to the charger, then drove the Mini down to the pond, parking next to Hampton Weaver's white van. The owner of Boom Town Fireworks spent his days working as a carpenter, building houses. He spent his nights blowing things up.

Hamp was on his knees working over what looked like a large rectangular wooden frame. If I ever got into a barroom brawl, I wanted him on my side. Not because he packed a mean punch, but at six-foot-five, three hundred pounds, and a skin mural of tattoos, all he had to do was show up and he'd intimidate the hell out of everyone else.

"Hey, Hamp," I called. "How's it going?"

"Goin' good, Lucie. Goin' good."

"What are you doing?"

"Putting shells into these tubes," he said. "They go into this here frame and that's your fireworks. Some of them, at least."

"What are we going to do if it rains?" I asked. "They're talking about intermittent thundershowers."

He grunted. "Yeah, I heard. If it's just rain, we can still shoot. I got plastic to cover everything until tonight. But not thunderstorms. You got to worry about the wind in a thunderstorm. It's a safety hazard."

"So you still plan to go ahead?"

"Sure. We might have to be a little flexible about timing. Ain't necessarily a given we have to start at nine sharp. I got three shooters

showing up for you. They'll fire some manually and the rest electron-
ically. If we're pretty sure of twenty, maybe thirty minutes where we
don't get any rain, it should be okay." He picked up a roll of masking
tape and handed it to me. "Tear me off a six-inch piece of that so I can
connect these fuses, will ya, sweetheart?"

I handed him the tape and he stuck one end between his teeth
while he twisted two fuses together. "I can put the rest of this stuff in
my truck unless you got someplace around here I could use for a few
hours." He wound tape around them. "I'm headin' over to The
Plains after this to finish setting up another show."

We did have someplace. Randy's barn.

"I guess you could use the old hay barn," I said. "You know the
one I mean? South vineyard. Over by the big orchard. You can get
there through the visitor parking lot if you take the service road."

"I can find it. That'd probably work good." He pulled a red ban-
danna out of the back pocket of his baggy jeans and wiped his forehead.

"I'll go on over and make sure everything's cleared out. We used
to let Randy use it. I haven't been there since before everything happened."

"Damned shame about that," he said. "What a waste."

I nodded. "If you need me for anything, I'll be in my office after
that."

He promised to call with a weather update around five o'clock.
When I left him, he had more tape hanging out of his mouth, twisting fuses together.

The barn looked like it had been well and thoroughly searched.
Overturned folding chairs and music stands were piled in a corner
and the stall doors were flung wide open. I leaned my cane against
one of the stalls and set about stacking the chairs and righting the
stands. Someone in the band should come get these things. After
what happened here, it no longer seemed like a place to make music.

When I was finished I went to get my cane. It must have slipped,
because it was now wedged in the space between two warped boards.
I had to go inside the stall to pull it through. I knelt and eased it out
so I wouldn't scratch the metal. There was something else there

besides the cane. One of our old yellow flashlights—one of the original eight.

I didn't see the dent on the rim where the glass met the aluminum barrel until I moved back into better light. Caught in the off-on switch were several strands of red hair.

Georgia Greenwood had been a redhead.

No doubt about it. Randy must have had this with him that night in the barn. I'd just found what he'd used to knock Georgia unconscious before he killed her.

CHAPTER 17

I put the flashlight back more or less where I'd found it, then drove to the house to call Bobby.

"Dammit, you moved it," he said when I finally got through to him.

"Of course I moved it. I picked it up."

"Well, don't touch it again. And don't let anybody near that barn. I'll be right there."

He came with another detective and two technicians from the crime lab. By then Quinn had joined me.

"So now we know what Randy used to hit Georgia over the head," I said.

"We won't get his prints off that flashlight," Bobby said. "If that's what you're getting at. You can't lift fingerprints off a ridged surface."

He pulled a pack of gum out of his pocket and offered it around.

"No, thanks," I said.

Quinn shook his head. "What about the switch?" he asked.

"A hundred people could have touched the switch, the two of you included," Bobby said. "Besides, something's off about this. That flashlight wasn't there the other day when we searched this place."

"How can you be sure?" I said. "It was inside a dark stall. I only found it by accident because my cane fell through the space between two warped boards."

"Place isn't locked. Somebody could have walked in and planted it."

"After you searched? That doesn't make sense. Maybe you just overlooked it."

"I don't know." He stuck a piece of gum in his mouth. "Maybe. But I sure as hell don't like this."

It rained long and hard enough to dampen attendance at the Memorial Day picnic and our wine tasting. Only eighty of the nearly two hundred people who bought tickets showed up, even though we'd advertised that in case of rain we'd move indoors to the villa. Unfortunately, the hayrides planned for the rest of the afternoon were a complete washout and the grass was still too wet to set blankets or lawn chairs by the pond to get a good viewing spot for the fireworks. So everyone went home after lunch with most folks promising to return that evening. I talked to Hamp about postponing until the next day, but he'd been checking with the National Weather Service all afternoon. He told me the storms were heading southeast toward the Chesapeake Bay, so we'd have a clear evening.

"You gotta have fireworks on Memorial Day, Lucie," he'd argued. "Unless it's real bad weather and there's wind. Having them the next day is kind of a letdown."

So the fireworks were still on.

"*Merde,*" Dominique said, "I hope we don't end up *avec trois pelés et deux tondus.*"

She, Joe, and I stood on the rain-slicked terrace, watching as heavy cumulonimbus clouds slipped slowly into the distance like freighters leaving port. In their wake, the late-afternoon sky was washed clean and clear.

"Three what and two what?" Joe asked.

"It's an old French expression. Three peeled ones and two shaved ones. It means nobody's coming," I said.

Joe laughed and slipped an arm around Dominique's waist. He kissed her lightly on the mouth and said, "You people say the weirdest things. I think we'll be fine. Birds are singing again, so that's a good sign. I think a lot of people will show up. Peeled, unpeeled, shaved, hairy. Everyone loves fireworks. They'll come." Then he added ruefully, "Though I've got final exams to grade, so I might not make it."

"You've got to!" I said. "It's only half an hour. Can't you leave your papers for later?"

"Graduation's right around the corner," he said. "June tenth. The prom is next week and I'm chaperoning. It's always insane at the end of the school year, plus the kids are so wound up."

"Please come," I said. "It'll be fun."

He smiled. "I know it will. All right, I have a free period tomorrow. The sheriff's bringing the sober-up car over to the school parking lot for the next ten days and the kids will be at a special assembly. I guess I could get to those papers then."

"What is the 'sober-up car'?" Dominique asked.

"Your worst nightmare," Joe said. "We do it every year. The cops bring an honest-to-God wreck from an accident and give a talk to the kids about no drinking and driving on prom night or graduation."

"Does it work?" she asked.

He shrugged. "We hope it does, but I think we really only know for sure when it doesn't. Some kid goes joyriding after knocking back a bunch of beers, then wraps Daddy's Lexus around a telephone pole."

"Mon Dieu." Dominique sounded grim.

I looked at my watch. "I'm sorry to bring this up considering the conversation, but I'm late to get to the cemetery," I said. "I'll see you both tonight."

"Why are you going to the cemetery?" Dominique asked.

"It's Memorial Day."

I had left a note on the kitchen table for Mia and a message on Eli's answering machine saying I wanted to leave flowers and flags at the graves of our family members who served during the wars. Neither my brother nor my sister was sentimental about things like this, so I didn't count on them showing up. I retrieved the white roses I'd picked earlier in the day and a box of small American flags and drove over to the cemetery. My foot, once again, ached from standing on it for so long.

Surprisingly, both of them were waiting next to Eli's Jaguar. Mia, smoking a cigarette, dressed in yet another miniskirt and a cropped top, and Eli, deeply tanned in navy shorts and a new pale yellow "Sea Pines Resort" polo shirt, were talking and laughing as I drove up.

"You're late," Eli called as I got out of the Mini. "You were supposed to be here fourteen minutes ago."

Eli owned an atomic watch that got its signal from someplace in Colorado and the National Institute of Standards and Technology. He lived by its every pulse.

"I was at the villa with Joe and Dominique. Can you take the box of flags while I get the flowers?"

He nodded and reached for them as Mia opened the door to the Jag, stubbing out her cigarette in the ashtray.

"Give me the roses, Lucie," she said. "I'll take them."

"The Jag is a smoke-free zone, kiddo." Eli sounded annoyed. "No cigarettes or butts allowed. Hopie will end up playing with them or putting them in her mouth."

Mia rolled her eyes. "I'll clean it as soon as we get back to the house. Jeez, Eli. That's what ashtrays are *for.* Why are we doing this grave-site thing, anyway? We never did it when Mom was alive."

"I know," I said, "but I've been thinking about it for a while. It's the first Memorial Day since Leland died. And it's just the three of us now. I think it's nice to pay tribute to everyone in the family who served the country. Especially since there was a Montgomery who fought in every war since the Revolution."

"'A martial race, bold, soldier featured and undismay'd,'" Eli quoted in a rich, thick Scottish brogue. "Aye, lassies, that be the fierce Montgomery clan, in the words of the immortal poet Rabbie Burns."

Mia and I smiled. The three of us walked up the hill and Eli opened the wrought-iron gate. At the edge of the horizon, beyond the weather-etched tombstones and the brick wall that enclosed the cemetery, swollen rain clouds still hovered, obscuring the undulating horizon line of the Blue Ridge.

Eli sneezed three times and pulled out a handkerchief. "Oh, God, my allergies," he complained. "There's some plant here that always bothers me. I was fine in Hilton Head. I didn't have any problems at Sea Pines."

"We won't be long," I said. "Thank you both for doing this."

"Some of these markers are falling over," Mia said, threading her way between the oldest graves. "And the grass is still really wet. I'm taking off my sandals. They'll get ruined."

"It's because whoever is buried there is . . . well, ashes to ashes," Eli said cheerfully. "They didn't always have coffins back in the day. And if it was just the body wrapped in a sheet or something and no embalming . . . two hundred years will do that to you. So it's a sink-hole now." He blew his nose again.

"Eli!" I said as Mia said, "That is disgusting."

"But true," he said.

"Okay," I said. "Let's try to show a little respect while we do this."

"I'd like to take care of Pop's grave," Mia said quietly. "If that's okay with you guys."

"Sure, Mimi," I said.

"No problem."

By the time we were done, the cemetery was dotted with flags and a single white rose at more than a dozen headstones.

"Who put the flowers on Mom's grave? They must have really been nice," Eli said. "You, Luce?"

"Yes."

"Aw, jeez. It was her anniversary, wasn't it?" he said. "May second. I don't know how I forgot. Probably crashing on some project."

Eli knew what he did every minute of his life. He hadn't forgot-ten and we both knew it. No point saying anything, though. He was here now. It was good enough.

"I didn't forget," Mia said quietly. "I came by that day to talk to her and saw the flowers. They were pretty."

"They were from all of us," I said. "She knows that."

Eli put an arm around my shoulder. "Thanks, babe. I'm glad you did that. And this was nice, too."

I smiled. "I'm glad we were all together. Either of you two stick-ing around for the fireworks?"

"Hope's too young," Eli said. "They'd scare the daylights out of her. Maybe in a few more years."

"I'm going out," Mia said. "Eli, drive me back to the house, will you? My car is there." She ran down the hill, barefoot, toward the Jaguar.

"Do not even think about getting in my car with those muddy feet," Eli called after her.

"Oh, for God's sake, will you *relax*? I'm putting my sandals on. Your precious Jag will still be pristine." Mia turned around and stuck out her tongue at him.

"She's probably going out with Abby Lang," I said under my breath. "They've been drinking over at the old temperance grounds. She got fined for public drunkenness the other day. It was in the police blotter."

"Yeah, she told me. Said it was no big deal," Eli said in a low voice as we reached the Jaguar.

Mia, impatient in the passenger seat, twisted and untwisted a long strand of golden hair around a finger. "You two take forever," she complained. "Let's get out of here, Eli. I'm going to be late."

"Coming home tonight?" I asked.

"I don't know. Maybe."

"She's fine, Luce. She's a big girl," Eli said soothingly.

Mia made an I-told-you-so face at me as Eli, driving show-off fast, blasted down the road to the house.

The fireworks went off without a hitch shortly after nine. About a hundred and fifty people came along to the vineyard to watch, so it was a good turnout after all. Quinn arrived with Bonita and there was something about the way they acted around each other that made me feel three would be a crowd if I sat with them. Then Kit and Bobby showed up, so I joined them and we listened to the oohs and aahs each time the sky exploded with colors.

I have to say Hamp outdid himself, especially with the finale, which was a deluge of red, white, and blue chrysanthemum fireworks, interspersed with rockets zooming straight up before breaking apart and sending multitiered cascades of filaments showering down on us.

I walked Kit and Bobby back to his car when it was over.

"That was fun," Kit said. "Thanks for the invite. I'm glad we came."

"Yeah, thanks," Bobby said. "Nice change to be here when it's not about business."

"Did your lab find out anything more about the flashlight?" I asked.

"Not on a holiday," he said. "And we're still waiting for the ME's ruling about Randy's death."

"What do you mean? I thought it was suicide."

"Not until he makes the final call," Bobby said. "One of three choices."

"Three?"

"Homicide. Suicide. Or the one I'd go for right now if it was me."

"What's that?" I asked.

"Pending," he said. "I still think we got some loose ends here."

CHAPTER 18

⟨∞⟩

Around one a.m. I gave up on the sheep-counting and got up. Maybe a cup of chamomile tea would bring sleep. I fixed one and went out to the veranda on a warm, star-filled night. Voices floated across the lawn from the direction of the summerhouse, the words inaudible, but obviously Quinn had brought Bonita again. Why couldn't they just go to his place? Why did they have to do it here?

I drank my tea even though it was so hot it burned my mouth, and went back to bed. When Mia came in at three, I was still tossing and turning. I heard her stumbling on the staircase. Then the bathroom door closed unnaturally loudly and I got out of bed. She was throwing up. I knocked on the door, then tried the handle. Locked.

"Let me in," I ordered.

"Go 'way, Lucie. Leave me 'lone."

"You're drunk."

"No'm not."

"Unlock the door or I'll break it down with my cane."

She fumbled with the handle, then finally jerked the door open and lost her balance. I reached out and grabbed her arm. Her eyes had the glazed, dull look of someone who didn't have a clue. No point berating her. She was well and truly pissed.

"All right, cowgirl," I said, "you had yourself enough of a rodeo for one night. I'd give you a couple of aspirins for that killer hangover you're going to have, but I'm afraid you'd choke trying to get them down. So let's just get you straight to bed."

I managed to get her from the bathroom to her bedroom, though she leaned against me so heavily it was like dragging an anchor. She stank of alcohol, cigarettes, and vomit. I eased her down on the bed and pulled off her clothes as if I were undressing a rag doll. She watched, glassy-eyed and silent. Then I laid her down and pulled up the bedsheet.

"Good night," I said. "We'll talk in the morning."

She muttered something unintelligible and turned over. Out cold.

I was alone in my office the next morning when one of the girls who helped out selling wine in the villa stuck her head through the doorway.

"Dr. Greenwood's here to see you," she said. "Shall I send him back or tell him you'll be out?"

"He is? Please tell him I'll be right out."

She raised an eyebrow and smiled. "Wait till you see what he's brought you."

Two dozen gorgeous pink roses in a cut-glass vase.

"How can I ever thank you?" He wore blue hospital scrubs and running shoes, smiling for the first time in a while, though he still looked drawn and tired. "You saved my life. Sam called in some favors and got me released yesterday. God, I'm glad to be out of that place."

"Well, we're even, then." I set the vase on the bar. "There's a fresh pot of coffee in the kitchen. You look like you could use a cup."

"I wish I had time, but I ought to be getting over to the hospital," he said. "I just wanted to say thanks in person."

"You're welcome. And I'm glad you're home again, too."

He said grimly, "It's not over. There might be a trial, though Sammy thinks there isn't enough evidence anymore to convict me."

"Oh, God, Ross. A trial would be horrible."

"Don't worry, I'll survive that, too," he said. "But I've learned a lot the past ten days. I never thought after all the years I've been part of this community, saving lives and helping people, that so many of my so-called friends would believe I'm capable of murder."

I wasn't used to seeing this side of Ross. Angry. Resentful. Bitter. Then again, he'd just spent a few days in jail.

"No one thinks you killed Georgia," I soothed him. "Some of the Romeos are upset about that Jeff Davis letter, but that has nothing to do with Georgia."

I walked him to the door. His hands were jammed in his pockets and his head was down. He was in no mood to be cajoled or comforted.

"Don't get me started on that goddam letter," he said irritably. "I got a letter myself. Signed by several of the boys. They're ready to lynch me. A couple of them offered to buy it off me. Urged me to 'do the right thing.' Don't stir up any trouble. They offered a pittance."

"What did you say?"

"Pass."

"This will blow over," I told him, though I wondered if it would. "You're an important part of the community, Ross. Look at all the good you're doing at the clinic, the people you're helping. None of that's changed. The Romeos will come around and it will be all right again."

He shook his head. "No, they won't. Anyway, it's too late. I'm moving on after this is over. Making a new start somewhere else."

I said, startled, "You'd leave here? The clinic, too? Does Siri know?"

"Not yet," he said. "But I'm thinking about asking her to come with me. We're both free now. I have no children, hers are scattered around the world. My wife is dead. That chapter of my life is over. If I stay here, I'll never get away from Georgia. She'll haunt me."

"Are you sure?" I asked. "Maybe you should think—"

"After what happened to Georgia," he interrupted, "I've learned you never know when your time is up. There are things I still want to do. I'm going to do them, but it won't be here. When I die, I don't want any regrets." He looked at me and added, "If there's anyone who understands what it's like to get a second chance in life, it should be you. So I'm counting on your support, because this won't be easy."

Then he kissed my forehead and left.

*   *   *

The rest of the day did not go well. At noon when I went back to the house, Mia was finally awake, out on the veranda nursing her hangover with an espresso and a cigarette. I expected her to be remorseful or even penitent after last night's performance, but she was hostile and belligerent. So we fought, except this one ended more spectacularly than usual with her telling me to go to hell, before slamming doors as she left for Abby Lang's place.

Then Quinn and I had words when he saw the two floral prints I'd finally propped up on the credenza in my office.

"Where'd you get those?" he asked.

"From Mac Macdonald. They're original prints of native Virginia wildflowers," I said. "I thought we could use them for the labels for our new wines. He's looking for more like these."

"Flowers? You want to use old prints of *flowers* on our wine labels?"

"What's wrong with that?"

"Well, it's kind of hard to be new and edgy when your label is a couple of hundred years old and it's a picture of a flower. I thought we were moving ahead, not backward."

"We're a *Virginia* winery," I snapped. "And these are native wild-flowers. I think they'd make great labels. Unique and very classy."

"Yeah. Thomas Jefferson would love 'em."

"You know, if you don't like it here . . ." I stopped and pressed my lips together.

"What?" His eyes flashed anger.

"Nothing. Sorry. I shouldn't have said that."

"Well, you did."

"Look, we were both up late last night, so we're both tired," I said wearily. "Let's forget this conversation."

"How do you know how late I was up last night?" His eyes were black and depthless.

"Because I went out on the veranda around midnight and I heard you and Bonita in the summerhouse, that's how. I didn't intend to, but you were kind of noisy. Next time, maybe you could find a more private place to conduct your affairs instead of my backyard, okay?"

That made two things I shouldn't have said. "My affairs?" He looked bewildered, then his expression lightened. "Oh, so you're talking about me and Bonita, is that it? Tell you what. How about if I take my telescope out of there so I won't disturb your beauty sleep ever again? Would that suit you?"

"Wait—"

But he'd already left.

A moment later the front door to the villa slammed. I heard his car as it roared out of the parking lot. Probably going right over to the summerhouse.

I laid my head on my desk.

What had I done?

I had just gotten home for the day when my doorbell rang. Mick Dunne held a bottle of Dom Pérignon in one hand and a couple of shopping bags with the logo of an upscale grocery store in the other.

"I brought dinner," he said. "I hope you're hungry."

"Oh . . . gosh . . . I . . ." I had been planning on microwaving anything in the refrigerator that still looked edible and eating dinner while soaking in the tub. Then straight to bed.

"Is that a yes or a no?" he asked. "It's hard to tell with you sometimes."

I opened the door and let him in. "It's a yes. But I really need a shower. I just walked in the door."

"Then show me where your kitchen is," he said, "and go have your shower."

He'd brought filet mignon, baking potatoes with sour cream, and white asparagus. A fabulous bottle of Pétrus to go with the dinner, and fresh local raspberries and blueberries for dessert.

By the time I got back downstairs he was making a vinaigrette for the asparagus. "This is very extravagant," I said. "No offense, but I thought 'British cuisine' was an oxymoron."

"There are a lot of things you don't know about the British, then. Here, try this and tell me if there's too much vinegar in it." He held a spoon to my lips.

"It's perfect."

I didn't have too many illusions and he wasn't subtle. We started kissing in the kitchen and continued throughout dinner, which we ate at dusk on the veranda. I lit the candles and the torches that ringed the porch while he finished grilling the filet mignon.

He came around to my chair to refill my wineglass yet again and kissed my hair. Then he put the bottle down and started to rub my shoulders.

"You're very tense," he said. "Your shoulders feel like they're made of concrete."

"Thanks."

"I'm serious. I'm giving you a massage tonight. You need it."

If he meant what I thought he did, then he would finally see my bad foot, now well hidden under a floor-length halter dress. "Let's take this kind of slow, okay?" I said. "I'm a little overwhelmed."

He went back and sat down, then took my hands in both of his. "I signed the papers the other day so the Studebaker place is mine. I'm not going anywhere. We've got plenty of time."

"When do you move in?"

His mouth twitched. I'd changed the subject and we both knew it. "I'm going back to Florida in a few days to wrap up matters there."

"Are you going to stay with Ross in the meantime?"

Mick shook his head. "I took a room at the Hilton by Dulles Airport the day of the funeral. Ross needs some time on his own."

"He stopped by this morning," I said. "He thinks there might be a trial. Did you know he's planning to leave Atoka once it's over?"

Mick picked up his wineglass and slowly swirled the contents around, watching the long viscous legs slide down the side of the glass. "I'm not surprised. Easier to forget an unhappy chapter of his life. Beginning with his marriage to Georgia."

"What do you mean? He adored her."

"She was miles out of his league. Not financially, of course. He had the dosh she needed to be Madame la Marquise. But she was rather a tart, wasn't she? All those affairs, left, right, and center. Ross put the old blinders on because he loved her so much as you said, but it hurt." He stood up and came around, pulling me to my feet. "And now enough about Ross and Georgia. Right now I want to concentrate on you."

He kissed me again, a long, deep kiss, then murmured, "I assume we've got the place to ourselves? It's nice here under the stars. You're very beautiful by torchlight, you know?" He untied the straps to my dress and moved his hands down my body.

I thought of Quinn's telescope in the summerhouse. He'd removed it this afternoon. I hadn't checked, but I'd figured that's where he'd gone after our argument.

"Mick," I protested, "I'm not sure . . ."

But he wasn't listening. Before I knew it, he'd slipped my dress off and it fell around my feet. He unbuttoned his shirt, then picked me up in his arms and carried me over to the hammock. "I've wanted to do this ever since I met you," he said.

"I thought we were going to wait and take it slow," I whispered into his neck.

"We did wait," he mumbled, laying me down as he finished undressing. He knelt over me and bent to kiss me again. "We finished dinner."

CHAPTER 19

We drank the champagne tangled in each other's arms, then made love again. I got the wedding-ring quilt off my bed and brought it outside. We finally fell asleep and when I opened my eyes as the first streaks of daylight appeared in the sky, he was watching me.

"Morning," I said. "Have you been awake long?"

He reached down and picked up his wristwatch off the wood floor. "Morning, love. No, not long. Since it started getting light."

"How did you sleep?"

"I think I'm going to feel like a contortionist when I stand up, but no regrets. You were wonderful." He kissed me. "I hate to say this, but I've got to go. I have a meeting in Washington in a few hours, so I'd better head back to the hotel for a shower and a change of clothes."

"Want breakfast?" I sat up and held the quilt over my breasts.

He moved to the edge of the hammock and carefully stood up so I didn't go sailing off the other side. "I wish I could."

"How about dessert?"

He turned and looked at me. "That," he said, "is another matter altogether."

Afterward, I walked him to the front door, still wrapped in the quilt like it was a sari. "I'll give you a ring," he said, running a finger down my bare arm.

I shivered, then he kissed me again and left.

I showered, changed, and cleaned up from last night's dinner. Though it was early, I drove to the winery. I'd been at my desk for about half an hour when I heard Quinn arrive. Normally whoever got here first stopped by the other's office. Maybe he didn't think I was in.

I picked up my coffee mug and went next door. "Good morning."

"Good morning." Whatever he was searching for on his desk, it apparently required all of his attention, because he didn't look up.

"Everything okay?"

"Yep."

"I'm sorry about yesterday," I said. "Truce?"

He looked up and said coldly, "No apology needed. I picked up my telescope last night. I won't be bothering you when you're out on the veranda again."

Last night. It was on the tip of my tongue to ask what time he'd been there, but I couldn't. My mouth went completely dry and my throat got a lump in it.

Finally I stammered, "I-it wasn't about the telescope . . ."

"I said I won't be invading your privacy again." He was curt.

He'd been there when Mick and I were out on the veranda. He knew. I nodded. "I understand."

"By the way," he added, "I ran into your sister last night. She'd been drinking again."

"Where? When?"

"At the No-Name. That bar on the Snickersville Turnpike. Obviously they weren't checking for ID. 'Course, those guys wouldn't."

"The shack on the way to Philomont? The biker bar? What was she doing there?"

"Drinking and playing pool."

"Oh, God. What time did you see her?" I asked.

His eyes narrowed and he stared hard at me. "Late," he said. "I walked in around one a.m. and it was last call. She was there with the Lang girl and a couple of guys who were trying too hard to make sure everyone knew they were stinkin' rich but they could go slummin' for a night with the white trash, if you know what I mean."

I leaned against the doorjamb and closed my eyes. "I get the picture," I said. "Thank you for telling me."

"That kid is heading down the road to perdition," he said. "She's going to do herself some real harm. And maybe take somebody down with her."

"I know," I said quietly. "I don't know how to stop her."

"Well, you better figure out something," he said. "Because if you don't, there's going to be hell to pay. It's only a matter of time."

When he left a short while later to join the crew in the fields, the tension between us was still as taut as an overwound clock. Finally, I couldn't stand it anymore. I told one of the girls who'd just arrived for work that she could reach me on my mobile if something came up.

I had an errand in Leesburg.

Eli's office was down the street from the old courthouse on West Market Street. I found a parking space around the corner on Church and walked past the pretty white-columned brick building as the bell in the tower serenely chimed ten o'clock. Out front, a statue of a Confederate soldier, dedicated to the thousands of Rebel soldiers who died fighting for a cause they believed in, stood guard. Elsewhere on the grounds the old stocks and whipping posts memorialized past methods of law enforcement. The way I felt about my sister just now, maybe they knew a thing or two about discipline in those days.

Eli's dark-haired young receptionist was on the telephone as I walked in. She nodded at me and pointed to the stairs, giving me thumbs up to indicate that my brother was in.

He had his back to me, sitting on a high stool hunched over a set of drawings spread across his drafting table. The room was neat as a pin, except for the empty soda cans on top of the filing cabinet— although not surprisingly they were aligned in a perfectly straight row. A scale model of a shopping center occupied another table. Photographs of Brandi and Hope were crowded on top of a credenza, above which hung a corkboard covered with drawings and photos of buildings in various stages of completion. His Filofax, which he practically chained to his wrist, sat on his desk open to today's date. Judging by the amount of writing on the page, he had a full schedule.

"Hey," I said finally. "Sorry to bother you."

He jumped and swung around. "Luce! I didn't know you were there. What are you doing? What's wrong?"

"Why does something have to be wrong for me to drop by?" I asked.

"Nice try," he said. "When your face goes all red like that and you don't blink for a long time, I know it's bad. What's up?"

"Mia," I said. "Quinn saw her at the No-Name last night. That biker bar on the Snickersville Turnpike."

"Oh, jeez. That dump. What was she doing there?"

"What do you think? Drinking. And playing pool. She came in absolutely falling-down drunk the other night. I had to put her to bed."

"It's her age. We were like that, too. I remember when you and Kit used to steal bottles of wine from under Jacques' nose and drink them over at Goose Creek Bridge."

"Kit and I didn't get drunk."

"Sure you didn't."

"You're not helping. She's underage."

"You can count the days until she's not."

"She has a problem, Eli. Binge drinking. God knows what she gets up to when she's at school in that sorority house."

"We can't babysit her. Look, I'll talk to her, okay?"

"Good. She won't listen to me."

He rolled his eyes. "Because you're always on her case."

"What am I supposed to do when she comes home throwing up and I have to take care of her?" I banged my cane on the floor. "Tell her it's okay?"

"Of course not. But why don't you try reasoning with her for a change?"

"I *did* reason with her. Now it's your turn. We have to get her to knock this off. Otherwise she's going to end up an alcoholic. She's already got a head start."

"Okay, okay. I'll call her."

"It needs to be face-to-face, Eli. Why don't you invite her to spend the weekend? You've got, what, ten bedrooms in that palace?"

"Only eight." He sounded miffed. "And ixnay on the weekend thing. Brandi's been getting migraines. She needs to have things kind of quiet."

"How about dinner? Could you have her over to dinner one night?"

He considered the suggestion. "Sure. But not this week. I'm completely slammed with work. Next week sometime."

"When?"

"I dunno. How about Friday?"

"You can't do it before then?"

"Look, most nights I barely make it home for dinner myself. At least Friday I know I'll be there. That's the best I can do."

"Okay. Next Friday. You'll call her, right?"

"Yeah, yeah. I'll call her." Eli reached over and picked up his bulky Filofax, scribbling something on the page. "Jeez. I gotta write everything down these days or I'll forget. Just so damn much stuff going on. I can't keep track anymore."

"Thanks for doing this," I said. "Call me afterwards and let me know how it went, okay?"

He picked up the Filofax again. "Damn. I'd better write that down, too."

Half a block from his office I stopped at a store called Leesburg Little Ones and bought a shopping basket's worth of coloring books, picture books, boxes of crayons, and cases of colored pencils.

"Are you a teacher?" The woman at the cash register smiled as I handed her my credit card.

"No."

"Run a day-care center?"

"Nope," I said. "They're for a friend."

The Patowmack Free Clinic opened for business in half an hour, but already every rocking chair on the front porch was occupied. Children and adults sat on the railing or on the porch floor, and a line, mostly of elderly people and mothers with babies, snaked from the front door down the stairs and around the border gardens into the parking lot.

I threaded my way through the mostly Spanish-speaking crowd and went around the side to the staff entrance. A volunteer let me in.

Ross and Siri kept a large basket of donated children's books near the waiting room. Every child who came to the clinic—either as a patient or accompanying a parent—went home with either a book or a coloring book. While the mothers and fathers might not speak

English, the children did. When I'd been here the other day, the basket had looked like it could do with replenishing.

"Lucie!" Siri came out of the kitchen carrying a small box. "What are you doing here?"

I held up my shopping bags. "Books, coloring books, crayons, colored pencils. Shall I put them in the donation basket?"

"How thoughtful of you! No, I'll take them. Let me just set this down." She placed her box on a table next to the kitchen door. The pink flip-flop still hung on it. "Thanks, honey. I appreciate it."

I glanced in the box she'd just put down as I handed over the shopping bags. "More donated medicine?"

She nodded. "We take what we can get. Thanks for stopping by. I'll get these out right away. They'll be gone in no time."

"Where's Ross? Is he in?"

"Uh-huh. With a patient in his office."

"I thought you didn't open until eleven."

"This is sort of an exception." Siri sounded flustered, then she shrugged. "Well, I guess it doesn't matter if you know. Marta's here with the twins. She's keeping a low profile because of her older boy, but Ross wanted to look at the babies and make sure they're okay."

"I only saw them for a few minutes the other night. In the dark," I said. "Okay if I stick around to see them again?"

"I don't think that would be such a good idea." The request seemed to fluster her even more. "Anyway, Marta just got here, so I think they'll be awhile."

I took the hint. "Tell Ross I stopped by, then, will you?"

"Of course," she said. "And thanks again."

In retrospect it was a good thing I left when I did. Because otherwise I would have missed seeing the car that sped out of the rear parking lot, tires squealing as it took the corner a little too fast onto North King Street. A black substantial something-or-other—I'm hopeless at identifying make and model—but I'm keen-eyed enough to recognize a license plate.

U.S. Senate tags.

They disappeared in a blur.

CHAPTER 20

———— ∞∞∞ ————

It was not a good omen that a white car with Washington, D.C., government vehicle license plates on it was already waiting in the winery parking lot when I showed up for work the next morning. Our appointment with the Environmental Protection Agency inspector wasn't scheduled for another hour.

I got out of my car as he climbed out of his. He carried a clipboard. In his early fifties, a slight build, bad haircut, brown plaid polyester suit.

I smiled, though my heart sank, and held out my hand. "Good morning. You must be from the EPA. We weren't expecting you until nine. I'm Lucie Montgomery. I own the vineyard."

He shook my hand and pulled a card out of his vest pocket. "John Belcher, EPA."

I took the card. He was all business. And he didn't smile back.

I indicated the villa. "Can I offer you a cup of coffee or tea before we go out into the fields, Mr. Belcher?"

Calling him John didn't seem like a good idea.

"No, thanks, Mrs. Montgomery. I've got a thermos and some bottled water in my car. And I've already been out in your fields, thanks."

He caught me off guard and I could tell that had been his intention all along. Already I was on the defensive. There was probably no way we could justify to his satisfaction how the methyl bromide had been left out instead of being locked in the chemical shed. The corner we were painted into just got smaller.

"So you're finished?" I kept my voice steady. "And it's 'Ms.'"

"Oh, no," he said, "I haven't begun. But I always like to get out and see what I'm dealing with before we get into the paperwork. You've got the records for me to look over?"

"Of course. Please come inside and I'll get them for you."

"That'll be fine." He gestured for me to lead the way.

John Belcher refused coffee a second time but, to my surprise, decided to sit at one of the tables on the terrace. I expected him to say that he wanted to review the documents together, but he shooed me off and told me he'd find me when he was done.

"I assume you'll be around?" He smiled without showing any teeth.

My life depended on what he was going to find in those papers. We both knew I wasn't going anywhere.

"I'll be in my office," I said pleasantly. Calling Quinn the second I got there and telling him we got the inspector from hell on our case.

"That'll be fine," Belcher said again. Another pinched smile.

I bit my tongue and left. Dammit. He had all the body language of someone who'd already made up his mind. Showing up today was part of the process, so he did it because he had to. But his judgment had been formed strictly based on rules and regulations, not people and circumstances. Black and white.

I closed my office door, though there was no way he could hear me, and punched in Quinn's mobile number on my phone.

"What's up?" he said.

"He's here."

Silence. Then he said, "Aw, crap. The EPA guy? He came early?"

"He's already been out in the fields. Now he's sitting on the terrace, reviewing the paperwork."

"What's he like?"

"What little bit of bureaucratic power he has means life or death to us and he knows it. I think he's trying to see how badly he can make me squirm."

"Crap," he said again. "I'll be right there."

It was at least another ninety minutes before John Belcher was ready to talk.

"Woodshed time," Quinn muttered, as we both stepped out on the terrace.

I introduced Quinn to Belcher and we sat down across the table. Quinn patted his breast pocket where he usually kept a cigar and I nudged him surreptitiously. We were in enough trouble without adding secondhand smoke to our woes. So instead he began pulling on the gold chain he wore on his left wrist.

Belcher looked up from his clipboard and straightened out the sheaf of papers he'd been studying, aligning the edges perfectly.

"Well," he said, "let's talk."

What he meant was that he would talk and we would listen. Like Quinn had warned, it was the whole megillah.

He began by stating somewhat unctuously that he was sure we were aware that methyl bromide had recently been phased out under the Clean Air Act because of its deleterious impact on the ozone. However, exemptions continued to be granted for certain quarantine and emergency uses. We were one of them.

I did not glance over at Quinn, but I did thank God for small favors.

Then Belcher rattled off with well-practiced fluency the names and numbers of the forms we and Lambert Chemical had been required to fill out. "I've concluded that your restricted materials, recommendation, and fieldwork order appear to be correct. I've also gone over your buffer zone calculations, which were more than adequate."

I gave a silent prayer of thanks. So far, so good. Maybe I'd misjudged him.

"I know. We were careful about that," Quinn said firmly.

I nudged him again with my good foot. Belcher didn't seem like the kind of guy who tolerated interruptions when he was in the midst of handing down the stone tablets. I was right.

Belcher regarded Quinn with renewed annoyance and my heart sank. "Then why were you not careful about locking the canisters in a secure area? The UW regs are clear. Your negligence contributed to the commission of a homicide." He enunciated each word, then sat back and folded his arms.

"We are very aware of that, Mr. Belcher," I assured him. "I'm sorry, but I don't know what 'UW regs' are."

"Universal Waste regulations."

"There were also extenuating circumstances that night." Quinn was not prepared to be so conciliatory.

"If everyone broke the law when it was convenient, Mr. Santara, we'd have anarchy."

This time I kicked him under the table. "Please go on," I said to Belcher. "You were talking about our buffer zone calculations when we got sidetracked, I believe."

"Only in that you are extremely fortunate the homicide occurred in an area that did not impact Goose Creek. Had any methyl bromide seeped into the creek water, I can assure you we would have already revoked your bonded license."

"Yes, sir," I said.

Quinn folded his arms across his chest. He was at least twice Belcher's size. "What's next?"

Belcher picked up his clipboard and stood. "You'll hear back from me in approximately ten business days."

Judging by that tone of voice, we weren't going to like what we heard, either.

"Can you please give us any indication—" I began.

"Ten days," he repeated. "I said you'll know in ten days. And I can show myself out."

"You antagonized him," I said to Quinn when he was gone. "He's really going to throw the book at us now."

"He was going to do it anyway," Quinn retorted. "You said so yourself. His mind was made up before he even got here. Did you see the way he looked around the place? I have no time for petty bureaucrats who abuse their power. That guy was mean. He liked sticking it to us."

"What we did was wrong," I said. "And he's fully justified in holding us accountable. But unlike you, I think honey works better than vinegar. Goading him was not smart."

"Whose side are you on, Lucie?" He sounded incredulous. "Look, I got work to do. I'm going back out in the fields and try to forget about that asshole. I'll talk to you later."

But he didn't come back for lunch, like he often did. Bonita, however, did show up. I found her in the kitchen microwaving a container of Ramen noodles.

"Were you just out with Quinn?" I asked.

"Nope. I was in the barrel room." She gave me an odd look. "Hey, Lucie, is he leaving?"

"Leaving what?"

"The vineyard. I, like, overheard him talking to Mick the other day. Quinn told Mick he was going to think about some offer. Then I saw the box of Cohibas sitting on Quinn's desk and, um, well, I was in there and I happened to see Mick's business card, too. Man, a whole box. Just one of those things costs a fortune."

"Cigars?" I asked.

She nodded. "They're, like, one of the most expensive Cuban cigars in the world. Illegal, too. But you can get 'em if you have connections."

"I see." I picked up the coffeepot and poured myself a cup. "I'd better get back to work. Thanks, Bonita."

"Hey," she said. "You didn't answer my question about him leaving. And that coffee's, like, stone cold. The coffeemaker shut off hours ago. Don't you want to heat it up?"

I dumped it in the sink. "Quinn's not leaving," I said. "And I didn't really want coffee anyway."

It occurred to me later that if Belcher revoked our license Quinn wouldn't have to look far to get another job. He could afford to piss the EPA off.

I couldn't.

Kit called that evening and cajoled me into getting together after she got off work. "I'm lousy company," I said.

"Then you need cheering up," she said. "I'll bring dinner."

She arrived with a couple of white bags. "Two double burgers with cheese and extra fries."

"Fast food? We're eating fast food?"

"Listen, Julia Child, it's *dinner.* How about a bottle of wine to wash it down?"

"I'll see if I can find something to do it justice," I said.

"Great," she said. "Why don't we go down to your pond and take the rowboat out? We haven't done that for ages. The sunset ought to be pretty tonight."

My balance was not what it used to be before the accident, so Kit had to help me climb into the boat. She handed me a basket with the wine, a corkscrew, plastic cups, and our dinner, then got in herself. The boat rocked crazily and I hung on to the basket with one hand and the side of the boat with the other.

"Guess we weighed a little less when we did this as kids, huh?" Kit sat down and faced me. "Or at least I did. You haven't gained an ounce since you were sixteen."

"Maybe not, but plenty of other things have changed."

She picked up the oars. "How about we go out in the middle and just drift around?"

The burgers were now lukewarm, but I'd skipped lunch after that session with Belcher and the talk with Bonita, so now I ate ravenously. Kit watched me with amusement.

"I haven't seen you this hungry for ages. You brought good wine, by the way."

"It's a Chardonnay from a new vineyard down near Charlottesville. I wanted to try it." I uncorked the bottle and poured more wine into plastic cups. "We ought to keep this chilled. Hand me that plastic grocery bag, will you?"

I put the bottle in the bag and tied the handles in a knot, which I looped over one of the oars. Then I lowered it partway into the water. "That ought to do it."

"Great. So how was your day?"

"Lousy. The guy from the EPA showed up."

Kit looked sympathetic. "It didn't go well?"

"He was the kind of person who'd normally blend in with the wallpaper and he knows it, too. So now he's got absolute power over our fate and he means to make the most of it," I said. "I have a feeling he'd made up his mind to throw the book at us before he even set foot on the property. Quinn thinks so, too."

"Jeez. You mean he's going to shut you down?"

I trailed my hand in the water and watched the ripples I made fan out and recede. "We'll know in ten days."

"Maybe you'll only get a fine. Can you hold my cup? It's not very deep here and we'll scrape the bottom of the boat." She gave me her cup and removed the bag with our wine from the oar. Then she grabbed the other oar and rowed us into deeper water while I poured more wine.

"I like this time of day," I said as she reached again for her cup. "The lighting's nice."

We drank in silence.

"What else, Lucie?" Kit said after a while. "Something else is bothering you."

"I think Quinn might be leaving," I blurted out.

Her eyebrows went up. "He told you?"

"No, Bonita did. She thinks she overheard Mick Dunne offering him a job. I got the impression it was for more than just the consulting work Quinn's been doing for him. You know Mick bought the Studebaker place? He wants to start a vineyard."

She whistled. "Boy, he sure didn't waste any time, did he? Mick, I mean. He is one smooth operator. I bet he gets whatever he wants. It's got to be that accent. You can say anything in British and it sounds good. Even if he were robbing a bank, he'd probably sound incredibly polite. I think it's sexy as hell."

"Well, thank you for that honest but shallow opinion," I said as she grinned. "But I doubt Mick's accent was the deciding factor for Quinn. More likely it was the money."

Kit nodded. "Dunne Pharmaceuticals? Yeah, money wouldn't be a problem after what he got when he sold that company."

"If this is your idea of cheering me up . . ."

Kit looked penitent. "Sorry, Luce. Sometimes you ought to tell me to just shut up." She reached for the bottle and topped off our cups.

"It's all right. I'm just feeling sorry for myself."

She tapped her cup against mine. "You think Quinn really might leave on account of money?"

"Is there another reason?"

"Oh, come on. How about whatever is going on between the two of you?" she said. "*That* reason."

"Nothing's going on between Quinn and me. He's seeing Bonita." I drank a large gulp of wine.

Kit stared at the perfect fire-engine-red kiss mark she'd left on the rim of her cup. Then she said, "I wasn't talking about a romantic relationship. But I always did think you two had feelings for each other. What I meant was your working relationship."

"Oh. Well, sure. I knew that's what you meant." My face probably matched the color of her lipstick.

"I see."

"Don't say 'I see' like that, either," I told her crossly. "There's something else you don't know. Mick Dunne came over the other night and made dinner for me."

The eyebrows went up again. "You lucky girl."

"He stayed until breakfast."

"Well, hallelujah and pass the ammunition. About time, if you ask me. I hope it was good."

"Shut up."

She grinned. "So Mick is putting the moves on you *and* Quinn?"

"I think his technique is a little different with Quinn than it is with me," I said. "It's just that he didn't say a word to me about offering Quinn a job."

"So you're just speculating," she said. "Have you talked to either of them about it?"

"No."

"Then ask." She looked at me steadily. "I know you want Quinn to stay, Luce. You should tell him."

"I can't match the salary Mick can offer him."

"Oh, for God's sake. Stop dragging that Scottish pride around like you're hauling the Stone of Scone, will you? It's not always about the money."

I smiled. She knew her Scottish history. "Maybe I should just let this run its course and see what happens. It's not fair to stand in his way."

"Maybe you should tell the man how you feel," she said with heat. "Me, I'd rather regret something I did. You get over that eventually. But to regret something you didn't do . . . that eats at you forever. You wanna keep your mouth shut and let him walk because he thinks it doesn't matter to you?"

"No."

"Okay, then. You know what you gotta do."

We tied up the boat just as the sun dipped behind the Blue Ridge. Kit drove the long way back to Highland House, passing by the winery.

"Quinn's car is still in your parking lot," she said. "He's working late. Perfect opportunity for you to talk to him."

"Not tonight."

"Luce," she warned. "The longer you wait, the harder it will get."

She dropped me at the house. "I'll call you later and find out how it went."

"You're very pushy."

"It's one of my endearing qualities."

The El Camino was still there when I drove to the winery a few minutes later. The villa was dark, so he was probably in the barrel room. I went in through the side door. The lab was dark, so I headed for the alcoves. He was there, all right.

With Bonita.

Both of them mostly undressed, her back against one of the pillars as he leaned into her. Fortunately, the noise of the refrigeration equipment and fans drowned out the sound of the door opening and closing. Anyway they were oblivious of anything but each other. I wanted to leave, but I couldn't. Instead, I watched as his mouth and his hands traveled from her hair to her mouth, her neck, her breasts . . . her eyes were closed, her head thrown back.

Probably not a good time to bring up the subject of whether he was staying or leaving.

I drove back to the house, feeling numb. Maybe I'd lost him already. In more ways than one.

Quinn had been my father's choice as our winemaker, not mine. Would I have hired him if it had been my decision? We got along like oil and water most of the time. And we had completely different philosophies about how we wanted to do the same thing—make great wine. This was about my hurt pride and his big ego. No woman was going to tell him what to do. He wanted to run the show and I wanted a partner. Maybe I was better off without him.

So why did I feel so melancholy?

★   ★   ★

On Friday afternoon Mick called and asked if I wanted to come along to the polo field and watch him play in the twilight games later on.

"We could have dinner afterwards," he said.

"Thanks, but I'm busy."

He was silent, perhaps expecting an explanation or something more polite, but I didn't oblige. Finally he said, "Is something wrong? You're angry with me, aren't you?"

"Yes, I am."

"Would you mind telling me why?" He sounded guarded.

"I guess you're used to more ruthless ways in the world of big industry, but here in Virginia, in the wine-making business, we're still a bit civilized."

"Pardon?"

Was he pulling my leg? He had to know what I was talking about.

"If you wanted to hire Quinn to run your vineyard it would have been common courtesy to at least say something to me. Especially since you practically went straight from my bed to his office to offer him the job."

Another silence, this time from him. "It was a hammock," he said finally. "And that's not what happened."

"What about the cigars? Why the extravagant gift?"

"I see," he said. "Now I understand. Well, I am very sorry indeed, Lucie, that you feel this way. I wish you a pleasant evening. I'll be late for the match, so I'd better ring off."

That night I stayed out on the veranda, rocking myself in the glider until the mountains disappeared into the velvet night sky. For once, I didn't bother to light the candles or the torches. Finally I lay down and fell asleep in my clothes.

Kit was right. Regretting something you didn't do ate at you until it broke your heart.

CHAPTER 21

I spent the weekend pulling weeds and cleaning garden beds around my house. It turned out to be a good way to keep my mind off what was really bothering me, especially after wading blindly into a thicket of ivy-covered pyrocanthus. Not for nothing do they call it the firethorn. From then on I made a point of paying attention to what I was doing and by Saturday night I was so exhausted, bloodied, and dirty that I fell into bed and slept straight through until noon. I was on my knees tackling the last weed-tangled patch by the veranda on Sunday afternoon when Mick showed up.

"We need to talk." He pulled me to my feet.

My T-shirt was drenched and the knees of my blue jeans had stiffened with a thick layer of hardened mud.

"You look very fetching," he said.

"I look like something the cat dragged in."

He threw back his head and laughed. "At least you're talking to me."

We climbed the steps to the veranda. "Don't push your luck."

There was an unopened bottle of water on the glass-topped coffee table. "Care for some water?" I asked.

"You need it more than I do." He cracked open the cap and handed the bottle to me. "Do you really believe I'd pinch your winemaker and never say a word to you?"

"Did you?" I rolled the wet bottle over my face, then drank.

He watched me. "It's like this," he said.

I closed my eyes. If it was like this, then I wasn't sure I wanted to hear it.

"You're right that I did talk to Quinn that morning after I left you," he went on. "I met him by that magnificent tree where your lane branches off. He'd been out jogging. We got talking and he invited me to his place for a coffee, so I went."

"Did he ask where you were coming from at that hour of the morning?"

Mick looked at me sharply. "Yes, as a matter of fact, he did. Why? Is that a problem?"

I said no too quickly.

"Lucie," he said, "is there something going on between you and Quinn? Are you two involved with each other?"

The humidity had loosened the label on the water bottle. I busied myself peeling it off. "Nothing other than a working relationship. And he's involved with Bonita. It's just that I like to keep my private life private, that's all." I set the soggy label on the coffee table.

"That's all but impossible around here. Especially with the old dear who runs the general store and that lot who call themselves the Romeos." He tipped my chin with his hand so this time I had to look directly into those clear green eyes. "And what about you? Before this goes any further. Are you seeing someone?"

I moved my head slowly back and forth. "No."

His kiss was long and lingering and I closed my eyes, surrendering. Did I want this? It seemed like he did. Besides, what was not to like about him? Reason enough . . . wasn't it?

When he pulled away, I rubbed at the dirt I'd transferred to his cheek. "You never finished your story about Quinn."

He sat back in the love seat and slipped his arm around my shoulder. "I didn't, did I? Well, we had a coffee at his place. I said I was meeting the architect I've hired to design my winery. After that, the conversation got 'round to hiring a winemaker. For the next few years all the work will be in the fields, so we talked about that." Mick kissed my hair, then said quietly into my ear, "One thing led to another, love. He said the job sounded right up his alley."

I turned to face him. "So that's when you offered it to him?"

"I told him," he said gently, "that I didn't intend stealing him away from you. But if things ever worked out that he was looking around, he should come talk to me first." He paused, then said, "He said he might be looking around now."

"I see."

"Lucie," he said, "I was under the impression that things weren't going well between the two of you. I can hire another winemaker, you know. There's a chap I'm interested in out in Sonoma and an Aussie I spoke with the other day who was very keen on the position." He kissed me again. "I don't want to ruin this with you. I'll tell Quinn I'm going to hire someone else."

"No." I shook my head. "Don't do that. If he's interested in the job and you want him, it's not right for me to stand in the way. We have completely different opinions on how to do things. Different personalities. Plus I'm a woman. With Quinn, that's another complication."

"Are you sure about what you're saying?" he asked.

"Absolutely."

"What will you do, then, if he leaves and takes the job with me?"

I leaned back against the love seat and rubbed my temples. "I don't know. Maybe talk to your other candidates in Sonoma and Australia. If I could possibly afford them."

"Why don't we cross all those bridges when we come to them?" he said. "I'm not altogether sure Quinn wants to leave you."

"Why not?"

"I don't know," he said. "Just the way he was talking about it. It seemed he hadn't made up his mind what he wanted."

"Well, I guess we'll both know when he does," I said. "And I owe you an apology for the other night. I was upset and rude."

"You were," he agreed, "but I'm going to let you make it up to me. Over dinner. Tonight. My house."

"You haven't even moved in."

"The last time," he said, "we spent the night in that hammock. I happen to have a mattress, which is only slightly less rustic. I figure we'll work our way up to an honest-to-God bed."

I showered and changed while he went to Middleburg for groceries. Then he picked me up and drove me to his new home.

The grounds of the Studebaker place always reminded me of a large English park and the lane leading up to the Georgian-style house with its magnificent two-story columns was lined with saucer magnolias and dogwood trees. In the spring, thousands of tulips and daffodils bloomed along the edge of their private road. Jim Studebaker had employed a professional horticulturist to identify all the trees—copper beech, tulip poplar, Japanese maple, English elm, golden larch, and others—with landscape labels.

Mick gave me a complete tour of the house, which had been built in the late 1700s, around the same time Hamish Montgomery had built Highland House. With the place empty of furniture—except for the mattress on the floor of the master bedroom—the rooms echoed eerily.

"Did you know this was a hospital during the Civil War?" he asked, tracing a finger around an old hole in the dining room door. "See this? It's an old bullet hole. They never repaired it."

Though I knew the house well, I didn't want to spoil his pleasure in showing it to me. "It's fascinating," I said, smiling. "And I did hear about the hospital."

He looked sheepish. "I reckon you know more about what went on here than I do. Your family's been here for . . . what, two hundred years?"

"Longer," I said. "But I do know a thing or two about its history. When is your furniture arriving?"

"In about a fortnight," he said. "I'm flying back next weekend to sort out a few details."

"I thought you were leaving tomorrow or the next day."

"I was," he said, "but I gave Ross use of the place and my boat to get away for a few days. He needed a break. I don't know if he told you that he's seriously considering relocating to Florida."

I nodded. "He really is going to leave, isn't he?"

"Looks that way."

We toured the grounds, finishing in the sunken rose garden, with its fountain surrounded by perennials. "It's like Versailles," I said. "You really bought yourself a palace."

"Wrong country," he said. "It's like Queen Mary's Garden in Regent's Park in London."

"'Oh, to be in England now that spring is here'?"

He laughed and kissed me. "Not England," he said. "Right here."

We had dinner outdoors. The stone fireplace from the original summer kitchen had been converted into an outdoor grill, so we fixed chicken and skewers of vegetables, eating everything with our fingers. I brought the wine—a Pouilly-Fuissé from Leland's wine cellar.

"I thought we'd go for a moonlight swim," he said after we cleaned up.

His house—like mine—was built on a hill so that part of the back-yard fell away to a breathtaking view of the Blue Ridge Mountains, much like ours. Jim Studebaker had taken advantage of the steep slope of the land to put in what was called an infinity pool—a swimming pool with no edge or rim on one side. As a result it seemed as though the water flowed out and disappeared, almost as if it joined the sky. In reality it cascaded like a waterfall into a smaller pool below. The effect, however, was stunning.

The other night Mick hadn't really seen my twisted foot in the dark when we were lying together in the hammock. But if we went swimming it would be so . . . visible.

"I don't think so—" I began.

"Lucie," he interrupted, "it's all right. My oldest sister had cerebral palsy. She was one of the most beautiful women I knew."

"Was?" I could feel the color in my cheeks.

"She died of a brain aneurism when she was thirty," he said.

"Oh, God, Mick, I'm so sorry."

He stood up and scooped me up in his arms. "About that swim . . ."

"I didn't bring a bathing suit," I protested.

"I know," he replied. "Neither did I."

Afterward, he led me to his cavernous bedroom. The mattress was surprisingly comfortable, when we finally fell asleep in each other's arms. The Studebakers had sold him all the curtains, but we didn't close the heavy brocaded drapes so we could see each other as we made love in the scuffed silver wash of a nearly full moon.

I woke at daylight, briefly disoriented as to where I was. Then I saw his tousled head next to mine and reached for my watch on the floor. Five-forty. He must have felt me stir because he opened his eyes and pulled me into his arms.

"You don't need to get up this early," I said as he kissed me.

"I do if you want a lift home."

I was suddenly self-conscious about my foot again, which he seemed to realize. I showered alone in his spa-like granite bathroom while he made coffee.

"When can I see you again?" he asked as he dropped me off at my house.

"How about tomorrow? It's primary day. Come by the Inn after the polls close. Seven o'clock. Noah's going to win and I'm sure there will be a victory celebration," I said. "Though it'll probably be muted, under the circumstances."

"I'll try. I've got more meetings with my architect. If I can't make it I'll ring you." He kissed me until I was dizzy and left.

Quinn was in his office when I got there shortly after seven. I called out good morning without sticking my head through his door and continued down the hall. A moment later, he stood in my doorway, tossing his tennis ball in the air and catching it.

"Something wrong?" he asked.

"No. Why?"

"You didn't stop by."

"Sorry. I know I'm late," I said.

"In a hurry to get to your desk chair?"

"Ha, ha." I covered my mouth, stifling a yawn.

"I thought I'd check the Chardonnay and Riesling," he said. "The boys have been tying up the vines and pulling leaves the past few days. Want to come along?"

"All right."

"I'll get the Gator," he said. "Meet you out front in five."

"They've been working in the south fields," he said when I joined him. "We've got three new guys this season. I want to make sure they did this right."

"Isn't Manolo keeping an eye on them?"

"Sure he is." He sounded surprised. "But I want to see for myself."

If he left, I would miss his thoroughness. Jacques had been attentive, but Quinn was downright obsessive.

The tasks of tying up the vines to the trellis wires so they don't hang down and pulling leaves off by hand, exposing the grapes to sunshine and air, are mind-numbingly tedious. Come harvest time we're always glad we made the extra effort because of the difference it makes in the taste of the grapes. What Quinn wanted to check was to be sure there were no leaves covering each bunch of grapes. Otherwise the ripening process would slow down, robbing the fruit of the sunshine needed to increase flavor and sugar.

He turned down the service road toward the orchard. It was as good a time as any to get this over with.

"I talked to Mick," I said. "I heard you're thinking about leaving here and going to work for him."

He was sitting with his profile to me, but I could still see the visible shock that went through him. "He told you that?"

No point involving Bonita in this, even though she was the one who spilled the beans. "Yes," I said, and yawned.

"How'd the subject come up?"

"We were talking about vineyards."

He grunted. "Opportunity's good. Pay's better."

"So you're going to take it?" I asked.

"I don't know."

My mouth felt dry. "What's stopping you?"

He turned down a row in the Riesling block and stopped the Gator. We both climbed down and he reached out, touching leaves, trellis wires, and bunches of grapes as we slowly walked down the row. Honeybees buzzed and tiny black flies alighted on the Gator. A hot breeze blew and I regretted not grabbing Eli's Mets cap off the credenza in my office.

Quinn, who'd been walking ahead of me, stopped abruptly and turned around to face me. I nearly collided with him in the middle of another yawn.

"Hey, sleepyhead," he said. "I'm asking. Do you want me to stay?"

Here it was. My chance to ask him not to go. "Of course I do."

"I'm bowled over by your enthusiasm."

"Quinn," I said, "I don't want to stand in your way if a better opportunity comes along for you."

"And this is a better opportunity," he said in a hard voice. "Plus it's not like I wouldn't see you anymore, being as you're getting so tight with Mick."

It was on the tip of my tongue to make a retort about Bonita, but instead all I said was, "So you've made up your mind, then?"

"Let's go check the Chardonnay," he said abruptly. "The crew is doing an okay job here."

We went back to the Gator. He started it, shifting quickly through the gears until we were really motoring and I had to hold on to the edges of my seat to keep from falling out.

"I'll miss you," I said softly, but he didn't turn his eyes away from where we were going or acknowledge that I'd spoken. He probably hadn't heard me. It had been hard enough to say it once.

I let it go and we continued in silence, checking the Chardonnay block. After that we headed toward the equipment barn. I was surprised when he drove past it.

"Where are we going?" I asked. "North block? I thought you said the crew hadn't done it yet."

"They haven't."

"Then why are we going there?"

"We're not. We're going to your place," he said. "You know what you need?"

"A winemaker?" I said.

The look on his face was completely inscrutable. "No," he said. "A nap."

Bonita called me Tuesday morning when I was still home. "Hey, Lucie," she said, "you just got a call from someone at Seely's. Apparently we, like, never paid them for some bedding plants they dropped off a few weeks ago. She said you're always so, you know, punctual that she wondered if you didn't get the invoice."

"I bet it was the shipment that arrived the night of the freeze," I said. "And the night Georgia . . ." I didn't finish.

"Oh." She sounded flustered. "Want me to ask her to, like, send another one?"

"She could fax it. Unless your mom has it. I think it was her order."

"I'll ask her."

"Thanks. Just leave it on my desk. And tell Seely's I'll send a check right away. I'll be in as soon as I finish voting."

Bonita had propped the nursery bill, still in the envelope, against my lamp with a note that read, "My mom says sorry she forgot to give this to you."

The bill, for seven hundred and forty-eight dollars and fifteen cents' worth of bedding plants, was signed by Jennifer Seely. "Thanks for your business. Jen." There was another paper in with the bill. A sketch of a rose and "C U 2NITE" written inside a heart.

Randy was supposed to pick up that delivery and take care of it. If he'd done that, he would have seen the bill before anyone else—and removed that note. I fingered the paper. The red roses in the shipment weren't from Noah. They were from Jen and they were meant for Randy. He was supposed to take them before Sera got the rest of the plants.

I was right, after all, that Jen had been lying about being with Randy the night Georgia was murdered.

Say it with flowers, indeed. She'd just said plenty.

CHAPTER 22

Dominique closed one of the Goose Creek Inn's dining rooms to the public on Tuesday evening so Noah and Claire Seely could host a victory party with friends, neighbors, and their campaign workers. As expected, it began as a somewhat subdued celebration, but there was no mistaking the giddy look of elation on the faces of the volunteers who—until a few weeks ago—thought they'd be drowning their sorrows in beer rather than toasting each other with champagne. The staff at the Inn set up a podium with a microphone for Noah's speech and someone changed the large "Seely for State Senate" sign that hung from the mantel of a large fireplace, crossing out the "for" and inserting "is going to the" in its place.

Noah's first remarks—met with grimly polite silence—were about Georgia, but then his ruddy face broke into a big smile and he looked like someone had just handed him the winning ticket to the Mega Millions lottery. After that he spoke more earnestly about November and their chances of unseating his opponent. Frankly, he could have recited the phone book and the cheering would have been just as loud. Tonight everyone wanted only to savor an unexpected win.

Kit came up and nudged my elbow, a reporter's notebook in one hand and a champagne glass in the other. "I thought Ross might show up," she said. "I was hoping to talk to him now that he's back from Florida."

"How do you know where he went? And how do you know he's back?"

"I bought coffee and a Danish at the general store on my way to work. I know everything."

"Good Lord. How did Thelma find out so fast?"

"Because Ross needed milk and bread and some other stuff. Thelma gave me the whole list, but I forgot. He stopped in just before I did."

"He's not coming by," I said. "I talked to him on the phone right before I left the house. It's Noah's night. Ross didn't think his presence would add anything to the evening." That was putting it mildly. No point telling her how angry and resentful he'd sounded. The few days in Florida seemed to have only stoked his belief that folks had turned against him. I clinked my champagne glass against hers. "Are you working?"

"Yep. Left a half-eaten burrito and a Diet Dr Pepper at my desk to swill champagne and find out if this campaign's got what it takes in November to unseat the Big Bad Incumbent. I still think Ross should have come to make nice-nice with Noah. Who cares if they mean it?"

"God, what a cynic you're becoming. Ross is avoiding the press because you'd just glom on to the Randy and Georgia story all over again."

"Not me. I wouldn't."

"Maybe not you, but the guy over there who looks like a tube of mega-hold gel exploded on his head would." I pointed across the room. "I've seen him on one of the network morning shows. He does gossip and fluff and weird stories about people being abducted by aliens. You think he's here to ask Noah's views on repealing the personal property tax in Virginia?"

"Okay, one slime-bag. Big deal." Her head swiveled around. "You know who else is missing? Hugo Lang."

"Speak of the devil," I said. "Look who just showed up."

Kit drank champagne. "This ought to be interesting."

"Seems like he's popping up in a lot of unexpected places lately. The other day I saw him—well, his car, anyway—driving away from Ross's clinic. Wonder what he was doing."

Kit shrugged. "Constituent visit? Except most of the patients don't vote."

Hugo worked the room on his way over to Noah. By the time they met up, I had a feeling Noah wasn't at all surprised to see Hugo. In fact, it seemed more like he had been expecting him.

Noah stepped back to the podium and quieted the crowd, introducing Hugo as the next vice president of the United States. More wild cheering as Hugo joined him and the two men embraced and spoke quietly into each other's ears, before clasping hands in the air, the quintessential symbol of victory on election night.

"They look pretty happy," I murmured.

"Cue the speech of reconciliation, party unity, and mutual respect," Kit said. "And let us not forget victory in November for the people of the great Commonwealth of Virginia."

Hugo's speech was brief and to the point. It was Noah's night and he hoped, he said with a broad smile, that he'd have his own chance to thank supporters—maybe in San Francisco come August. Everyone roared and whooped and hollered until he finally held up his hands for silence.

"We all mourn the loss of a fellow candidate who was a friend and neighbor to many of us," he said. "But tonight is a night of reconciliation, of healing, and of unity. I have the utmost respect and admiration for a fine man—Noah Seely. Tonight I pledge my full support to do whatever it takes so that in November the people of the Commonwealth of Virginia will send this good man, my good friend, and the next senator from the Thirty-first District, to Richmond where he belongs!"

Under cover of the cheering, I leaned over to Kit. "Did you write his speech?"

She grinned. "Honey, I could *give* his speech. What did you expect him to say?"

"He never mentioned Georgia by name."

"Yeah, he didn't waste a lot of time on her, did he?"

Hugo hung around for a while for more back-slapping and politicking. As he got near the doorway on his way out, I happened to catch his eye. We hadn't spoken since Austin Kendall's fund-raiser at the vineyard. And I didn't think he realized I had seen him leave the clinic. His face, for once, was grim as he stared back at me, then turned toward the door.

He may not have killed Georgia Greenwood. But something in the way he'd looked at me made me think that he was anything but sorry she was dead.

"Lucie." Kit elbowed me. "I just said I've got to go. You leaving, too?"

"I'll stick around for a while."

Mick Dunne hadn't shown up yet.

"I'll call you. I've got a hot story and a cold burrito waiting for me."

But as the evening wore on, I began to wonder if Mick was coming after all. I didn't have his mobile number, though something told me he wasn't the kind of man you kept tabs on.

"Hey, cupcake, what's up? Something bothering you?" Joe Dawson stood at my elbow, holding a glass of champagne. "You want this? Yours is empty. I can get another one."

"No, thanks. I'm fine. Probably going to leave soon, anyway."

"Well, cheers, then." He looked around the room, nodding. "Good turnout for Noah. I bet he can pull it off in November."

"Hugo Lang just endorsed him."

"Yeah, I heard. Good career move. Hugo needs to put as much distance between himself and Georgia as he can right now, considering what Ross is up to."

"You mean moving?"

"What?" Joe looked surprised.

I never should have opened my mouth. Joe wasn't a Romeo, but he was one of their conduits. "Oh, God. I thought that's what you meant. I shouldn't have said anything. Please don't repeat it."

"Ross is leaving town?"

"Yes. When this is all over he wants to make a fresh start somewhere else."

"Smart move." Joe sounded grim.

"What do you mean?"

"He contacted one of the big auction houses the other day about selling that Jeff Davis letter. And he's planning to make a stink in the press about it. Says he's donating the money to the clinic, in honor of his wife. I swear to God some of the Romeos are so mad they're ready to lynch him."

"Why'd he do it now? He's right back in the limelight again."

"You talking about Ross, sugar?" Mac Macdonald joined us. "The sooner he leaves town, the better, as far as I'm concerned. His behavior has been anything but honorable."

Mac had overheard, too. Great.

"The only reason he's doing this now is to embarrass the folks who doubted his innocence," Mac continued. "With the Middleburg reenactment coming up he means to make us look like a bunch of crackpots."

In another week—June 17 through 19—it would be the anniversary of the Battle of Middleburg, which had been part of the 1863 Gettysburg Campaign. On those days nearly a century and a half ago, General J. E. B. Stuart valiantly fought a succession of fierce battles along Mosby's Highway, skirmishing with the Union troops of Alfred Pleasanton in an effort to screen Robert E. Lee's move north to Pennsylvania through the Shenandoah Valley. Mac was one of the more zealous Romeos who participated in reenacting this and other Civil War battles. This year they'd planned to re-create the engagements at Aldie, Middleburg, and Upperville. They'd been talking about it for months.

"He had the letter authenticated?" I asked.

"Says he did," Joe said.

"Maybe I can talk to him," I said. "Get him to rethink this."

"Be my guest," Mac said. "But I doubt he'll back down, now he's gotten this far. And by the way, I've been meaning to call you, Lucie. Remember the book of floral prints I was telling you about? Client changed their mind and returned it. So it's all yours."

Nice of him to think of me, though of course Mac always did have his eye on the bottom line. "Thank you. I'll come by to see it."

"The price is right. Don't you tarry, though. I'm holding it for you, but I did have someone in today who was asking about it."

"All right. I'll be in tomorrow."

I left after that conversation. Mick wasn't coming and I had no intention of calling him to ask why.

Jen Seely was climbing out of her car as I walked out to the parking lot. She seemed surprisingly late for her father's victory party.

I walked over to her. "Hi, Jen. Got a minute?"

She smiled a tight-lipped smile. "Hi, Lucie. Not really. I ought to get inside and be there with my dad."

"The party's winding down," I said. "Are you avoiding anybody in particular or a lot of people in general?"

"I don't know what you're talking about." She sounded defensive.

"You don't want anyone to know you were at my barn the night Georgia was murdered, do you?" I said. "What happened, Jen? What did you see?"

"I wasn't there."

"Yes, you were. You sent Randy a bunch of red roses and left him a note in the envelope with the invoice. He was supposed to find it so he'd know you were coming that night. Instead he got waylaid and ended up helping me." I banged my cane on the ground and she jumped. "You were there and you've been lying about it."

"You can't prove that."

"You didn't know about Georgia until you showed up that night, did you?" I persisted. "When you got to the barn, she and Randy were up in the hayloft. You heard them and figured out what was going on. You were furious."

She folded her arms across her chest and said coldly, "That's a pack of lies."

"I don't blame you," I continued. "He lied to you, didn't he? Of course you were mad. While they were still together you had time to think, to decide what you were going to do about it. That's when you came up with the methyl bromide. It would completely disfigure Georgia. So you waited until she left Randy's bed, then you confronted her on the south service road. Then what? Did you go back and have sex with Randy? How did you get him to White's Ferry?"

Until this moment I realized I hadn't actually suspected her of killing either of them. But as I pieced together the scenario, it seemed more than a little plausible.

"I did not kill anybody," she hissed. "You are wrong about everything. How dare you accuse me of something I didn't do!"

Her eyes flashed.

"But you were there that night." I wasn't wrong about everything. Some of this was right.

She wiped her eyes, but the tears came anyway. "I didn't do anything to anybody. I heard them together and I left. That's all. They were both alive and . . . well, alive . . . the last I knew."

"Why didn't you say something?" I asked. "You should have told the sheriff."

"What's to tell? I didn't see anybody. No one knew I was there. Not even the two of them. All I'd do is get mixed up in the investigation. Plus I felt like such a fool for believing Randy. He really was a bastard." Her anger seemed to shift from me to Randy.

"You've been defending him. Helping his sister pack his things. You even told me his relationship with Georgia was all business."

"Sounded better than all monkey business, didn't it?" Her smile was bitter. "I didn't want to get involved. And as for helping his sister . . . I asked for my letters back. I burned them."

"Oh."

She chewed her lip. "I don't see the point in bringing any of this up. It's over, done with . . . nothing would change if the sheriff knew I was there. I didn't see anything. Just . . . well, heard things. Do I need to draw you a picture? I didn't kill anyone. I was mad and hurt and jealous. That makes me human, not a murderer."

I scratched a line over and over in the dirt parking lot with the tip of my cane.

"Look"—she pointed to the Inn—"my dad just won the primary. He's a good man and he's going to do good things in Richmond. If my name gets dragged through the mud now, some of it's going to stick to him. He deserves better than that."

I was silent.

"I need to get inside. Good night, Lucie."

She left and I was alone again in the parking lot with a lot of churning thoughts. Jen had gotten into the barn without anyone knowing about it—except me.

Another guilty secret, and once again, I was an accomplice.

CHAPTER 23

Mac had the book of Virginia wildflower prints on his desk when I stopped by the antique store the next morning. He beamed as I walked through the front door.

"Well, well, well. Glad you came right down here, sugar," he said. "I'm so happy to see you."

Sure he was. Me and my wallet. "Thanks, Mac."

"Sit right down and have a look. Aren't those colored plates just gorgeous? They're all hand done, and this is a limited edition, of course. Only two hundred and fifty copies printed. This one's number sixty-three."

I sat. This book was going to set me back plenty. But as I leafed through the pages and examined the hand-colored plates of wild bergamot, witch hazel, azalea, bloodroot, and spicebush on the thick cream-colored paper, I knew he was right that it was a real gem. I closed the book and cradled it in my lap.

"How much?"

"I'm going to make a big sacrifice here. Practically give it to you."

Of course. He always said that.

He rocked back and forth on his heels. "Six hundred dollars."

"Six hundred? Lord, Mac, that's a fortune!"

He looked hurt. "Now, Lucie, I could remove those fifteen prints and sell each one of them for a hundred dollars, easy. I know you want this book and I want you to have it. That's why I'm making you such a wonderful offer."

He wasn't going to budge on the price. And he had a point about selling the prints individually for more money. Even if Quinn and I decided not to use them as wine labels, I still wanted the book. Assuming Quinn still worked at the vineyard in three years—or even in three months. Maybe someone else would be making the decision about those labels with me.

I set my credit card on his desk. "I'll take it."

Mac gave me a big bad toothy smile and a roguish wink. "I knew you'd come 'round. You're not going to regret it."

As it turned out, neither of us had any idea just how much I would regret it. Owning that book changed everything.

I left the book of prints at the house. Better than leaving it at the villa where Quinn might see it. We'd only argue again. Right now I didn't want to risk any more arguments. We'd had too many already.

On Thursday I met with a cute blonde from the corporate events department of a large Tysons Corner company. We sat on the terrace of the villa and discussed the fact that her boss was looking for a venue for their international sales meeting.

"Gee whiz," she said wistfully as she stood up and reached for her leather-bound folder, "I'd love to work at a place like this."

I nearly opened my mouth to say we could use some help with public relations and marketing when she added, "Just hang out all day and plan parties and drink nice wine. You must have so much fun. I bet it beats having a real job, huh?"

I smiled brightly. "You have no idea."

She grinned. "Yeah. Wow. I'll be in touch. I just love this place."

After she left I called Quinn's mobile. He said he'd be in the barrel room racking over the Cabernet Sauvignon. Bonita had asked for the afternoon off to drive Hector and Sera to a cardiologist appointment in Leesburg. Quinn's phone went to voice mail. He'd probably set it down in the lab and was out of earshot in one of the alcoves. I decided to go over and talk to him.

Both Quinn and Mick Dunne were standing by the stone wall at the far end of the courtyard as I walked through the archway, heading toward the barrel room. Quinn gestured expansively with his hands as he talked. Mick's head was bowed as he listened intently, hands in his pockets. I moved into the shadows of the loggia where they wouldn't see me.

By the looks of things, they were having the will-you-or-won't-you talk. My car keys were in my pocket. I couldn't watch any more.

I drove to the cemetery, the place I always headed to when I needed to get away, ever since I was a kid. Here, at least, I could count on a loyal group of relatives to hear me out, whatever my problem.

The Memorial Day roses Eli, Mia, and I had left at the graves ten days ago had withered in the heat. I touched the petals of the one by Leland's headstone and they dropped off, leaving a naked stem. I tried to arrange them as they'd been, but what was done was done. In the distance, clouds drifted to make dappled patterns of light and shadow on the peaceful Blue Ridge. Off to the right I could see a narrow green tree line, the boundary that separated Mick's farm from ours. I left the fractured flower and went to my mother's grave, leaning on her headstone for support as I sat down.

If, as the old Indian legend went, the stars in the sky were openings in the floor of heaven where loved ones could shine down to let us know they were happy, then was there some tangible reverse way we could let them know about us here down on earth, if we needed them and we weren't happy?

I did not want Quinn to leave, plain and simple. But what I did want was impossible—the kind of relationship my mother and Jacques shared. A partnership where we made decisions together. Jacques was old-school European and his gallantry and politesse in the way he treated not only my mother, but our clients, had made him enormously popular and well-liked. Quinn, with his loud Hawaiian shirts, big cigars, and in-your-face attitude, was the polar opposite; a man Kit once said would benefit from a few sessions in charm school. He wanted to run the show, treated me like I knew little or nothing about the business, acted brashly and abrasively—and so we clashed on almost every issue. But, as they say, the heart wants what the heart wants, however illogical or irrational.

And mine wanted him to stay.

That night a heavy blanket of clouds rolled in and no stars shone down from the sky. No telling if my mother was happy or not. But if she wasn't, that made two of us.

On my way to work Friday morning I found my mobile phone on the demilune table next to the charger. Only one bar on the battery. I unplugged the charger and brought it and the phone with me so I could recharge it in my office.

Quinn was already at the villa when I drove up. He showed up in my office with two cups of coffee.

"Morning." He handed one to me and his eyes strayed to the red light on my desk. "Forgot to charge our phone again, did we?"

"Thank you," I said, indicating the coffee. "I think it's the battery. It doesn't hold a charge very long anymore."

He raised his eyebrows and blew on his coffee. "What would you do if somebody needed to get in touch with you and it was life or death?"

"We didn't always have mobile phones," I said. "My mother and Jacques managed fine without them."

"You and I are not your mother and Jacques," he said.

"No," I said. "We're not."

"You bring them up all the time, you know?"

"I do not!" I opened my desk drawer and pulled out a box that once held a roll of wine labels, now filled with packets of sugar. He took his coffee black, so I didn't bother to offer him any. I ripped open two sugars and dumped them in the coffee, then stirred it with the eraser end of a pencil.

"Yeah, you do. You ought to listen to yourself sometimes." He shoved a pile of *Virginia Wine Gazettes* on my desk out of the way and sat on the edge, so he was staring down at me.

I said, flustered, "Well, I don't mean to."

"Talk to Mick recently?" he asked abruptly.

"No," I said. "Why?"

"Just wondered." He drank his coffee in noisy gulps. "I'm going out with the crew. They're doing more leaf-pulling in the north vineyard and I need to spray the Cab."

I wanted to ask him the same question he'd just asked me, but I couldn't bring myself to do it. Instead I said, "The Mosby dinner is tonight, so I'll take care of setting up. You know after the dinner Joe's giving the talk about Mosby founding the Partisan Rangers, since today's the anniversary."

"How could I forget?" he asked. "Atoka's patron saint."

I ignored that. "You think we ought to risk having it at the Ruins with this weather? If it rains, we're sunk."

"Why not move it here?" he asked. "Then we don't have to worry."

"Because it's better to have it right there. Everyone will be at the exact spot Union soldiers burned while they were looking for Mosby," I said. "Besides, his ghost still shows up on cloudy nights looking for men in blue coats."

"You believe that crap?" He picked up my coffee-stained pencil and examined it.

"When we were kids we used to scare each other with stories that we saw him," I said. "I never did, but I know people who swear his ghost is still around."

He stood up. "I better take off. Bonita's waiting for me in the barrel room."

I dunked the pencil in my coffee so I didn't have to look at him. "I forgot to ask her how Hector's visit with the cardiologist went."

"He might need a pacemaker."

"Oh, God."

"Better than the alternative. I'll call you." He motioned to my mobile. "Turn that thing on, okay?"

After he left I picked up the phone and opened it.

"Hey!" He was back in the doorway with one hand behind his back. "Got something for you."

I closed the phone, grinning like a giddy schoolgirl. Flowers, maybe? "What is it?"

He whipped his hand around and held it up. Just like a bouquet of flowers. "A spoon," he said. "That pencil's really unsanitary."

I started to laugh and so did he. For once it was completely heedless and lighthearted. Then our eyes met and the old cautiousness returned.

"Turn on your phone," he said. "I gotta go."

"Sure."

I punched the button and the display came up. A second later the message icon blinked. Three messages and two missed calls. Both missed calls were from Mick. Last night. The first message, at 9:47 p.m., also from Mick, asked me to call him.

The second message was from Eli. 10:13 p.m. "Luce. Me. I can't get hold of Mia and I need to talk to her about dinner at our place tomorrow night. Have her call me, will you?"

Mick left the final message twenty minutes ago. "Lucie," he said. "I'm just about to board my flight. I rang you last night at home and on this number several times. I wish we'd been able to talk before I left for Florida. Quinn and I spoke yesterday afternoon about the . . ." The commotion in the background drowned out the rest of whatever he'd been trying to say. Finally I heard him shout, "No use! I can't . . . ring you from Miami . . ." The line went dead.

So that's why Quinn asked if I'd spoken to Mick. They did have the job talk, after all. If Quinn was leaving, why didn't he tell me himself? Had he decided to stay? Or did Mick want to prepare the terrain with me first because he'd just hired my winemaker?

The two of them were turning my life upside down. I didn't know what to think anymore.

I phoned the house and left a message for Mia to call Eli. She'd slept at home last night and was probably still in bed. Then I called Quinn.

"Yeah, what?" He sounded harassed and irritated.

I lost my nerve. "My phone works."

Silence. Then, "I'm very happy for you. Now can I get back to business? The damn sprayer's acting up again."

"Sure. Sorry."

He disconnected and I closed my phone, feeling foolish.

We held the Mosby dinner at the Ruins after all, and by some miracle it didn't start raining until we'd finished cleaning up.

"This'll be good for the grapes," Quinn said. "At least it held off long enough for the spray to take on the Cab." We were back in the parking lot. He leaned against his car. "Guess I'll see you at Dominique's shindig on Sunday. Bonita and I are heading down to Virginia Beach, but we'll be back in time for her citizenship party."

I bit my lip, glad for the darkness so he couldn't see my eyes. "I didn't know you liked the beach."

"I'm a California boy, remember? Bonita said they've got a store there that sells tie-dyed Hawaiian shirts. Gotta check that place out."

"Right. Something new for the collection, huh?" I said. "Well, enjoy it. When are you leaving?"

He glanced at his watch. "'Bout half an hour. She wants to watch the sunrise on the beach. If there is one. Maybe they're not getting rain down there."

My legs felt suddenly unsteady and I leaned on my cane. "I hope not, for your sake. Have a wonderful time. See you on Sunday."

I did not sleep well at all that night, though the last time I remember looking at my alarm clock it read just after four a.m. When the phone rang, it was already light outside. Six-thirty. Not Quinn—he was gone. And it was Saturday.

I picked up the phone. Mia. She sounded like she was drunk or crying or both. "Lucie, it's me," she said through hiccupy sobs. "I'm at the hospital. Catoctin General. The police are here. They say I killed someone."

CHAPTER 24

⎯⎯⎯∞⎯⎯⎯

She made no sense except that I gathered she'd been driving and hit another car.

"Oh, God," I said. "When? After you left Eli's?"

"I never went there," she sobbed. "He canceled. Look, can we talk about that when you get here? You gotta get me out of here." She sounded panicked. "I didn't do it, Luce. I don't even remember getting in my car. I don't care what they say."

I closed my eyes. On top of everything she had blacked out, too. How much worse could it be?

I reached for my cane next to the bed. "I'm getting dressed right now, Mimi. I'll be there as soon as I can. I'm going to call Eli and Sam Constantine. I'll see you in less than an hour."

"Please hurry," she begged. "I'm so scared."

I hung up and called Eli. Not surprisingly, I woke him up. "Aw, Jesus H. Christ," he said. "What did she *do*? I don't need this right now."

"Next time I'll get her to plan her hit-and-run or whatever it is around your schedule," I said coldly. "And for the record, she should have been with you last night. Getting the sober-up-or-else talk. What happened, Eli?"

"Don't you blame me for something she did," he yelled back. "I had to postpone dinner because a client wanted to meet last night. So I told her we'd do it another time."

"When did you tell her that?" I said. "She told me she was going to your place last time I talked to her."

"Right before she was supposed to come over," he said wearily. "I had my back to the wall, Luce. I have a family to feed, you know. Client wants to meet, I say, 'How high?' That's the way it is."

"Well, then we both let her down," I said. "Meet me at the hospital. I'm calling Sam." I hung up before he could say anything.

I finally reached Sam on my mobile on my way to Leesburg.

"Where is she?" he asked, sounding sleepy and not too pleased to hear from me at this hour.

"Catoctin General."

"She injured?"

"Lord." I was stunned. "I never asked. She was crying pretty hard and she said the police say she killed someone. Says she doesn't even remember getting behind the wheel of the car."

"Aw, Christ." He was wide awake now. "That's bad already. She needs to keep her mouth shut."

"I'm not even sure she's sober at the moment."

He groaned again. "I'll get there as fast as I can. But if you reach her first, tell her to button it and not to sign anything. I'll fax something over to the hospital so we're on record in case I need to make a Fourth Amendment challenge to anything she says. You can bet they read her her Miranda rights, but if her BAC was above point-oh-eight, then she could have heard the Pledge of Allegiance."

I put my foot down on the accelerator and checked my rearview mirror. I had Route 15, once the trail of Indians, to myself. Good thing, too, at my speed. I tried to keep the anxiety out of my voice. "She won't go to jail for this, will she? If it was an accident?"

"At the moment, let's just work on fixing things so they don't lock her up today."

He hung up and I sped toward Leesburg.

I got to the hospital parking lot fifteen minutes later. The same cop who had looked after me the morning I found Georgia was outside the building, talking into a microphone on his shoulder as I walked up to the entrance.

"Are you here with my sister?" I asked. "Mia Montgomery?"

"Just leaving. There's a female officer with her now." He folded his arms across his chest. "Didn't put two and two together that she was your sister."

"Can you tell me what happened?"

"She struck a Jeep Wrangler broadside at the intersection of the Snickersville Turnpike and Sam Fred Road about four a.m.," he said. "Right now it appears she was operating a vehicle while intoxicated. So far there's one fatality. He died in the ambulance. The other passenger is in serious condition."

My voice was unsteady. "Oh, my God. Do you know who they are? The people in the other car."

"Sorry. We're still trying to reach the next of kin."

"Was it kids?"

He hesitated, then said, "What's left of 'em."

I chewed my lip to keep from crying. I felt numb. "I'm so sorry. She says she didn't do it. I know that sounds impossible. But she says she didn't."

Somebody squawked again on his shoulder, like a parakeet. "With all due respect, miss," he said, "they all say that. 'Scuse me, please."

He turned away and I walked blindly toward the emergency room doors. They closed behind me with the same hiss of finality I remembered from the night Quinn and I were here to see Hector. It seemed like a million years ago. This time the person behind the ER waiting room desk was taking orders from the police. I asked to see Mia and was politely but firmly turned down. Sam had no such problem.

"She has the right to counsel," he barked. "Let me back there immediately."

"I'll give you a full report," he said to me as the doors slid open. "Sit tight and don't you talk to anybody, either."

Eli was the last to arrive. God, had he taken the time to shower, shave, and put on pressed khaki shorts and another embroidered Hilton Head shirt? I'd pulled on the first pair of jeans I found, a T-shirt with dull purple stains on it, no makeup, and scraped my hair into a ponytail.

"Sam's with her," I told him. He exuded a powerfully sweet fruity scent. "Whoa. Did you take a bath in your cologne or maybe pour it on your head?"

He fingered the sleeve of my T-shirt. "Unlike you, I decided not to show up in what I slept in. If you must know, I was pretty shook up after you called. Dropped the damn bottle and it broke all over the marble floor in the bathroom. We might have to regrout where the cologne left a stain. At least the house smells good."

"I don't think there's a dress code for when your sister might go to jail," I said. "Eli, she was driving drunk and she killed a kid. The police told me she broadsided a Jeep Wrangler. The other passenger is in tough shape."

He walked me over to the familiar rows of molded plastic chairs. Fortunately the television was off. "Oh, God," he said as we sat down. "That's manslaughter. If she was drunk it might be voluntary manslaughter. I'm not sure, though. Jesus, Lucie. She will do jail time for this."

I swallowed hard. "Maybe she'll get a suspended sentence."

"Not if she killed somebody. Especially if she plowed into the other car. No way to get around that."

"I wonder who the other family is. Or families." My eyes watered and I swiped at them with the back of my hand. "How did it come to this?"

"Yesterday was graduation at all the high schools," Eli said. "One of my coworkers had a daughter who finished at Blue Ridge High. Took the day off. They were having a big party. Probably not the only ones. And hell, graduation night. I'm sure some of those kids weren't drinking lemonade before they started tooling around in Daddy's BMW . . . or the Jeep Wrangler." He pulled a handkerchief out of his pocket. "Here. Use this. It's gross when you use your hand."

I took it and wiped my eyes again. "She doesn't remember getting behind the wheel."

"Great. She must have been really wasted."

"I don't know. I talked to her. She was adamant that she didn't do it."

"Well, who was driving the damn car, then? Elvis? Come on. Her car. She was found at the scene." He held out both hands, palms up, and shrugged. "What's not to understand here?"

The door to the inner sanctum of the emergency room opened and we both spun around in our seats. Sam Constantine strode out, looking like he would dismember anyone who got in his way, then dine on their entrails.

"This isn't good," Eli muttered. He stood up and put out his hand. "Sam. Thanks so much for coming. Sorry I missed you before you went in to see her. What's the story?"

Sam shook Eli's hand. "The story," he said, "is bad." His eyes were the color of tombstones. He glanced at Eli. His nose twitched, but he said nothing.

"How bad?" I asked.

"Her car hit the Jeep. Graduation present for the eighteen-year-old driver, who had his high school diploma in his back pocket. The girlfriend's seventeen. Looks like she'll pull through. Sheriff's on his way to visit the parents and tell 'em. Christ. I don't envy him, knocking on those doors." He ran a hand through his shaggy gray hair and looked up with anguished eyes. "Last thing Mia remembers is being at Abby Lang's house. They were drinking something that goes by the name of 'Southern Smasher.' Cognac, Red Bull, and peach schnapps. God help us all. The Lang kid's boyfriend dumped her and she was feeling sorry for herself. Mia wanted to be a good friend so she kept Abby company. Doesn't remember how many she put away. Said she passed out in the bedroom."

"How'd she get in her car?" Eli asked.

"She hasn't got a clue."

"Oh, God. Where was Hugo?" I asked.

"The senator wasn't home. Just the two girls. Housekeeper had the weekend off." Sam shrugged. "Next thing she knows, she's face-down on the ground next to her car. Lights and sirens everywhere. The other driver and the girlfriend were drinking, too, but she hit them, so it's clearly her fault. It must have stopped raining by then, because they had the top down, the whole nine yards, so it was like she hit a dune buggy or a golf cart. The driver didn't have a prayer."

I covered my mouth with my hands and clamped my lips shut, afraid I would scream.

"What does Abby Lang say?" Eli asked.

"That's where I'm headed right now." Sam sounded grim. "Assuming she's in any shape to talk."

"What about Mia?" I asked. "Is she going to jail?"

Sam looked at me with eyes that said he'd spent a lifetime talking

to people like me after someone they loved had accidentally committed a felony and he was their salvation to make it go away.

"Honey," he said, "right now I'd say the odds are pretty good that
she will. They're gonna draw blood here at the hospital to see what
her BAC is. They've agreed to defer her arrest until they get the tox-
icology report because she's known in the community and I said she
wasn't a flight risk."

My throat was dry. "How long?"

"Three to four weeks."

"Then what?" Eli asked.

He sighed again. "If it's above point-oh-eight, she'll be charged
with vehicular manslaughter because she was DUI. In that case
she'll do time. Below that level . . ." He shrugged. "We might get it
knocked down to involuntary manslaughter. Suspended sentence
and community service. Teach an alcohol awareness class in schools
for a year, eighteen months. And go to AA."

"What do we do now?" I asked.

"Besides wait?" he said. "Well, they're going to release her shortly.
So get her home and chain her to something, because if she so much
as puts a whisker out of line before that tox report comes back,
they'll lock her up before you can say jackrabbit."

"Yes, sir," Eli said.

"Do you think she did it, Sam?" I asked. "What if she's telling the
truth?"

"She is an unreliable witness," he said, eyeing me. "But I'm going
to talk to the Lang girl."

"How can we thank you?" I said.

He smiled without showing any teeth. "Oh, don't you worry," he
said. "There's a little something I like to call 'the bill.' All the thanks
I need."

He left and I looked at Eli.

"God," I said, "what has she gotten us into?"

Dominique became a U.S. citizen later that afternoon. Joe took her
down to the community center in Alexandria where, along with two
hundred or so others, she signed her naturalization document in

front of the judge, then pledged allegiance to the United States of America. After that, she was an American.

The only people allowed in the crowded room were the newly minted citizens-to-be, so Joe never got to witness the big moment. When they got back to the vineyard, we carried on with plans for a family dinner at the house, though the atmosphere was more like a funeral than a party. No one spoke about what had happened, but it was like trying to ignore a hundred elephants in the room. Fortunately, the presence of a baby—Eli and Brandi had brought Hope—provided a welcome distraction. Mia excused herself when we brought out the cake and Dominique didn't want us to serve the champagne, but I insisted.

The party we'd scheduled for all of her friends on Sunday afternoon at the villa was now up in the air, especially after the news of the accident made the front page of the newspapers, including photographs of Mia and the two other kids. The last thing anyone felt like doing was celebrating.

"Why don't we postpone?" Dominique said. "It's terrible timing."

"I'm so sorry about this. Maybe in a few weeks we can reschedule," I said. "But we ordered all the food, so what if we just invite your staff over for a buffet? We can call everyone else. I don't think we'll have to explain much. If we miss anyone or someone does show up, they can join us."

"All right," she said. "I'll get a couple of my waitresses to make the calls."

"I've ruined her citizenship party along with everything else I've done," Mia said the next morning as she sat cross-legged on my bed, watching me change into a sundress. "She's waited years for this. I'm not going, you know, even if it is just the staff from the Inn. Everyone will look at me like I'm a monster." She pulled a pack of tissues out of the pocket of her jeans, tears streaming down her face. "I can't believe I killed that boy," she said. "I just can't."

"You don't remember anything," I said. "So what makes you so sure you didn't? You already have a history of drinking and driving. You pushed your luck that you didn't get caught before. This time you did and you killed someone." I was so angry with her, but so scared for her, too.

"No," she insisted. "That's not true! Okay, I drank. But I *never* drove, not even after one drink. I'm not stupid. I always went with a DD."

"You actually thought about a designated driver? What about that ticket?"

"Of course I did. And the ticket was for public drunkenness. Just a fine. Not DUI."

"Did any of the kids you were hanging out with drink and drive?"

She made a face like she'd just eaten something nasty. "A few."

"Who?"

"Brad. Abby's boyfriend. Ex-boyfriend. And a couple of the others. I don't know them too well."

"I don't know why Abby didn't take your keys away from you," I said. "'Friends don't let friends drive drunk.'"

Mia swallowed. "She's no friend anymore. Not after what she told Mr. Constantine. She was already loaded when I got there, crying about Brad. She found out he slept with someone else. I thought she was gonna kill him. It's not true that I'm the one who insisted on making those drinks. Anyway, I had a horrible headache when I got there. She gave me something for it and I lay down for a while. When I woke up she handed me a drink."

"What'd she give you for your headache?" I asked.

She shrugged. "I dunno. I thought it was aspirin. Whatever it was, it worked."

"Well, the way this is going down it's your word against hers. Sam said she claimed you took off before she could stop you. Her father said Abby was home when he got in around midnight. In bed. He knew she had been drinking, but she's not underage. Sam wasn't sure Hugo wasn't going to get fined or worse for allowing a minor to consume alcohol on the premises, considering what you did after you left there. The fact that he wasn't home doesn't get him off the hook, but it's probably a mitigating factor."

She buried her head in her hands. Her voice was muffled. "God, I just don't know. It didn't happen like that, I swear."

"Then how did you end up at the scene of an accident?" I demanded. So far I'd been trying to keep my voice even, but what she said was physically impossible. I ticked things off on my fingers. "You were banged up. You were driving that car. No one else was there except you and the other two kids. What other explanation is there?"

She looked up, her pretty young face ravaged and grief-stricken. "I swear on Mom's grave, Lucie. I think I got set up. But I don't know how."

"Stay here," I said, "while I'm at the villa. And stay out of trouble. The strongest thing you can drink is coffee. Got that?"

"What should I do?" she wailed. "I can't stop thinking about it."

"I don't know," I said, exasperated. "Watch a movie. Watch TV. Read a book. Do your laundry. But do not leave this house under any circumstances."

She nodded, looking completely broken. I swallowed the lump in my throat and left for the villa. I should have hugged her and told her it would be okay. But it wasn't okay and she'd been playing with fire. She had taken a life. The newspaper photographs were the high school photos for all three of them. The boy had been a good-looking kid, though the bow tie of his tuxedo was slightly askew and his smile had a bit of the devil in it. But his eyes were intelligent and hopeful and now there would be one lucky wait-listed person who would take his place at Princeton. At least his girlfriend was reported to be in stable condition, thank God.

Almost everyone who wasn't actually working the Sunday lunch shift at the Inn showed up for the buffet. As expected, it was a sub-dued afternoon. I was in the kitchen removing the plastic wrap from another tray of hors d'oeuvres when Quinn showed up, sunburned from the beach and sporting a new Hawaiian shirt. He looked good.

He leaned against the doorway. "You've had the weekend from hell, haven't you?"

"Not as bad as the weekend the family of the boy Mia killed is having."

He walked over to me. "Why didn't you call me?"

I said unsteadily, "It's a family matter. And you were . . . away."

"I would have come back immediately if I'd known."

I hadn't cried the whole weekend, for the dead boy, for the grief my sister had caused their family, for the absolute tragedy of the situation. "It has nothing to do with the vineyard. You don't need to be involved." The tears streamed down my face and I looked around for a napkin, anything, to wipe them away.

He pulled me to him and stroked my hair. "I'm sorry what I said about Mia before. I had no right to do that. It was out of line."

"It's okay," I said into his shirt. "Don't worry about it."

He kicked the kitchen door shut with the heel of his boot and let me cry it out in choked hushed sobs while he held me. "What if they can hear me out there?" I said, finally. "Everyone will wonder. And I should take this tray out to the terrace."

"Shhh," he whispered. "No one wonders anything. I'll take it out in a few minutes. Calm down and take a deep breath. That's a good girl." He handed me a cocktail napkin that said "Congratulations" on it in flowery script. "You going to be all right?"

I wiped my eyes. "I don't want you to go."

"I'll be right back." He picked up the tray.

"That's not what I meant."

He'd been about to open the door, but he stopped and set the tray back down. "What did you mean?"

I twisted the small napkin into a knot. "I don't want you to leave the vineyard. I want you to stay."

He looked at me for what seemed like an eternity and I could see the futility in his eyes that meant my plea was too little too late and the die was already cast. But all he said was, "I'll be back."

When he finally returned with two more empty trays, I was leaning against the counter with wet napkins pressed against my eyes like compresses. "How do I look?" I took away the napkins and blinked. "Can you tell anything?"

"You look fine," he said. "Come on. Let's get back out there."

The party broke up not long after that. Dominique left for the Inn with Joe. Her staff stayed behind to clean up.

"We've got things under control here," Quinn said to me. "Why don't you take off?"

"You sure?"

He nodded. "What are you doing tonight?"

"Babysitting my sister."

"Call me if you need anything," he said.

"Thank you," I said. "How did it go in Virginia Beach?"

He smiled ruefully. "Okay, I guess. Bonita ran into some friends she knew from around here. She wanted to stay and party with them, so she's still there. I came back alone. She's catching a ride back later tonight with some guy she used to date."

"Oh." I studied him. "Everything all right with you two?"

"Why wouldn't it be?"

"No reason. Thanks for the reprieve on cleaning up. I owe you."

"No, you don't. See you tomorrow." He pulled a piece of paper out of his pocket. "With everything that happened, I've been holding off telling you. But you need to know. We heard from Belcher."

The EPA verdict. "How bad?"

"A fine. We got off easy, considering. They're going to throw the book at Lambert Chemical, though." He handed me the paper. "I'm glad it's over with. This thing with your sister. Georgia. Randy. Maybe now we can start moving on."

"Yes," I said, "now all I can think about is whether Mia is going to jail or not."

He looked at me sadly. "Aw, honey. You poor kid. Go home and get some rest."

I drove back to the house, completely confused. Was he leaving or wasn't he? He never said, one way or the other.

I found Mia stretched out on the glider, drinking something straw-colored and thumbing through the book of prints I'd bought from Mac.

"What is that?" I hadn't meant to sound sharp, but it looked like Chardonnay.

"Apple juice. I swear. Want to try?" She held up the glass.

"No, it's okay. Sorry I snapped at you. But be careful you don't slosh anything on that book while you're lying there. It cost six hundred dollars. I think some of those prints will make nice labels for the new wines. If they get wet they'll be ruined."

She sat up and swung her long tanned legs around so her feet were on the floor. "Six hundred?" She looked stunned. "You paid six hundred dollars for a damaged book?"

My turn to be surprised. "Damaged how?"

"It's got missing pages."

I sat down next to her and the glider rocked back and forth. "Show me."

She opened the book to the flyleaf. "Here. Looks like maybe one page was cut out." Then she flipped to the back. "And here. Two pages. See those tiny edges? If you're going to cannibalize it, I guess it doesn't matter. Where'd you get it?"

"From Mac Macdonald. Someone bought it, then returned it. Mac knew I was looking for wildflower prints."

Mia sipped her apple juice. "Probably whoever returned it found the cut pages after they bought it."

Or maybe that person was responsible for the damage. "Wonder what was on those pages," I said.

"Nothing. They were probably the blank pages at the beginning and end of a book. I bet there was an inscription or some notes on them and somebody decided to remove them."

I glanced at my watch. "I'm going to call Mac and ask him about that."

I got through to the antique store a minute after five p.m. and the phone immediately went to the answering machine. I hung up without leaving a message.

Mia was hungry for the first time all day and I'd been too distracted to remember to bring anything back from Dominique's reception. I fixed her bacon and eggs in the kitchen while she sat at the old pine table and read the comics, like she used to do as a kid.

"Boy," she said gloomily, "my horoscope's dead right. 'Sitting on hold is frustrating.' Too bad I couldn't have Mom's. Taurus always has good ones. 'Out of your efforts springs something magical.'"

"What's mine?"

"Cancer. The crab." She looked up and grinned. "'Push yourself to do the very thing you don't want to do.' Ring any bells?"

"Too many," I said. "Put that away."

She went to bed after dinner. I cleaned up and threw the newspaper in the recycling bin. But not before I read the rest of my horoscope. "A great deal is accomplished alone and in silence."

I got the book of prints and went to the library, which had been Leland's office until the fire destroyed most of it. His extensive collection of books on Thomas Jefferson had literally gone up in smoke and none of the furniture had been salvageable. My mother had once gone tartan-mad in decorating the room—heavy doses of red and green plaid on a heathery purple background, the colors of our modern tartan. It had always seemed a bit eye-popping and agitated to me and I didn't spend much time there.

After the fire I knew I wanted the original floor-to-ceiling bookshelves rebuilt and then, in honor of my clan—my family, my history—I again used the Montgomery colors, though this time opting for our ancient tartan in the calmer shades of sage green and Wedgwood blue. I sat in a tartan-covered wing chair by the fireplace and turned on the three-way reading lamp to its full wattage. Not that I needed it.

The uneasiness that had been haunting me all evening had bloomed to real fear. And anger. Mac wouldn't have lied to me about the condition of the book. He was an eccentric businessman, but he was an honest one. I flipped through the pages one more time. I'd seen that distinctive thick cream paper somewhere else.

The letter Jefferson Davis wrote to Judah Benjamin.

If Ross had cut out the pages before returning the book to Mac, then to whom had he given them so that person had been able to forge the letter? Had he done it himself? The forgery had obviously been good enough to fool some expert analyst who believed it was genuine. Meaning the forger had to be a real master at what he did.

I left the book in the library and got a bottle of one of our best Chardonnays from the wine cellar. This time I went to the summerhouse.

Ross told me once that in medical school he'd been taught to diagnose disease and illness by their own version of Occam's razor—that usually there is a common, logical, and easily understandable diagnosis for a patient's symptoms. When you hear hoof beats, first think horses, not zebras. Assume the easiest and most obvious explanation.

But as I sat there watching the stars for the second time in two nights, wishing Quinn were here with his telescope to distract me, I couldn't help myself. There were exceptions to every theory. And God help me, this time I did not think horses.

I thought zebras.

CHAPTER 25

I finally fell asleep in one of the Adirondack chairs. When I woke at daylight it felt as though I had a crushing weight on my chest and then I remembered all of it. Mia's accident and everything that lay ahead for her. And Ross.

By now I was positive that the Jefferson Davis letter had been written on a page excised from my book. The paper would be the right age, for one thing. But did Ross forge the letter himself, or did he obtain the paper for someone else?

Either way, why had he done it? He didn't need the money. Was it for the thrill of trying to get away with something this audacious?

I finished most of a pot of coffee after a shower and breakfast as I watched the layered Blue Ridge change from gray to heathery blue as the sun rose in the sky. Quinn would wonder where I was. Finally I called him.

"Sorry, I overslept," I lied. "And something's come up. I'll be in after lunch."

"Are you sick?" he said.

"No."

"What is it?"

"Nothing."

"Aw, jeez. You're a horrible liar, you know that? Is it something about Mia?"

"No, I need to talk to someone, that's all."

"Lucie," he warned. "Don't con me."

"I'll call you later. Word of honor." Then I hung up.

First I had to see Mac. Right before I left, I woke my sister.

"I've got some errands to do. Middleburg and Leesburg. I'll be back later," I said. "You know the drill."

She sat up sleepily and scratched her head. "Yeah, no booze for breakfast."

"Very funny."

"You still trying to figure out who cut the pages out of that book?"

I had tucked it under my arm. "Not anymore. See you later."

I got to Macdonald's Antiques just after ten. I found Mac straightening a painting of someone's ancestor that hung next to an antique barometer. His eyes fell on the book.

"What have we got here? Don't tell me you're not happy with that gorgeous book?" His smile was strained. "I don't understand why something as beautiful as that keeps coming back here like a boomerang."

"I'm not returning it, Mac," I said, and watched him relax. "I'm just wondering if the reason Ross returned it was because of the pages that had been cut out of it."

"Oh, so he told you he had it on trial?" Mac said. "And, sugar, no pages were cut out of it. I checked it over myself. That book is in absolutely pristine condition." He held out his hand. "May I?"

I clutched it to my heart. "No, that's okay. I'm going to take it apart anyway, for the wine labels. Thanks so much. Sorry to bother you. I've got to go." I was babbling, but I didn't want to hand the book over, now that he'd confirmed my suspicions.

"Something wrong, Lucie?" He straightened a lace doily on a small oak table. "I know you've had a lot on your mind lately."

"Yes," I said, "it's been rough. Thanks, Mac. See you later."

Then I drove to Leesburg.

If Ross was the forger, then this wasn't the only document he'd faked. What about his collection of Civil War papers? Were they all phony, or just some of them? Lord, he'd sold dozens of items he'd turned up over the past few years, earning himself a respected repu-tation among historians. Had he duped everyone?

And if he could fake Jefferson Davis's signature well enough to fool the experts, then how hard would it have been to fake someone else's handwriting, who was less well known?

Randy.

What about that note that supposedly came back with Georgia's dry cleaning? And the suicide note? Dear God.

I went to the clinic. They didn't have visiting hours until the afternoon. Hopefully no one would be there except Ross, and maybe Siri. What was I going to do or say when I saw him? Accuse him of forgery . . . and murder? Two deaths? I'd helped him get off, hadn't I? He had relied on my loyalty, my faith in him, my devotion—and I'd delivered.

I parked by the side entrance next to the black Explorer. The only other car in the lot. He was alone.

I tried the door, though I knew it would be locked. Then I banged on it until finally he opened it. He seemed surprised to see me.

Bobby told me once that the hardest thing about being a cop was seeing the look of betrayal flash in the eyes of a criminal when you slap handcuffs on them because they really believed you meant it when you said, "If you put down that gun nothing's going to happen."

"They give you this big, dumb look," he'd said. "Like cows. And they say, 'You promised.'"

I held up the book of prints. Ross's eyes met mine—which I know were filled with fury—and that look of betrayal came into his.

"You want to tell me about this?" I asked.

"I'm not sure what you're talking about."

"I'm sure you are," I said. "Where's the letter Jefferson Davis wrote to Judah Benjamin, Ross? Can I see it again?"

"I don't have it anymore," he said. "I dropped it off at the auction house yesterday."

"Well, I guess there's hope that one of their experts will figure out it's a forgery before they sell it," I said. "If I can do it, it can't be too hard. Though I wonder how you fooled whoever vetted it for you."

His eyes grew dark and hard then, and I knew. "Oh," I said. "Your expert gets a share of what you sell it for, is that it?"

Ross took my arm. "Let's go to my office, shall we?"

I shook my arm free. "Don't touch me. I can walk fine by myself."

"No," he said, still my doctor. "You can't. You need a brace for that leg and you're in denial about it." He shoved me into his office and closed the door. I heard the sound of a deadbolt. "I need you to be reasonable, Lucie. The money is going for the clinic."

He walked around to his desk and indicated that I should sit down in one of the two chairs facing him, just like we were going to have a little chat about my blood pressure. He sat. I did not.

He straightened up some papers and, though I'm not good at reading upside down, I know a prescription pad when I see one. It looked like he'd been busy writing prescriptions, too. I felt sick. Where did it stop?

My voice shook. "You forged those notes from Randy, didn't you?"

"He wrote that note that came back with her dry cleaning," he said calmly. "But I knew he was screwing Georgia before I saw it."

"So you killed her."

"You can't prove that."

God, I was right. "You killed her because she was having an affair?" I was incredulous. "Wouldn't a divorce have been less messy? You won't go to jail for that."

"I won't go to jail for anything," he said in that same even voice. "I had no choice. She knew too much."

Now I was confused. "About what? The historical forgeries?"

If his eyes hadn't strayed to the prescription pad before meeting mine, it would have taken me longer to work it out.

"All those pills," I said. "They're not all from dead people, are they?"

"Lucie." He stood up and put his hands on his desk, leaning toward me. "Don't screw up something you don't understand. I am trying to *help* these people. And I will do whatever it takes to circumvent the system. The people who come to this clinic are the poorest of the poor. They have nothing! Do you understand that?"

"So you forge prescriptions for drugs? Someone still has to pay for them," I said. "Don't they?"

He cleared his throat. "They are paid for by the generosity of other patients, who can afford them."

"In return for what?"

He folded his arms across his chest. "Certain controlled medications are just that—controlled. I can help someone who's suffering unnecessarily get around those limitations. It's about helping, Lucie. It's always been about helping."

"Hugo Lang is one of your suppliers?"

That caught him off guard. "No."

"You're lying, Ross. He's on some kind of medication, isn't he? And he doesn't want anyone to know about it. He never did get over his wife's death. What is it? Antidepressants?"

"None of your damn business."

"So Georgia found out about the fake prescriptions? What was she going to do, turn you in? Though that doesn't sound like Georgia. No offense, but she didn't have much of a conscience."

"She was a lying, scheming little bitch," he said, and this time the calm façade cracked, and I saw contempt and hatred. "She was going to blackmail everyone. I couldn't let it happen."

"That's why Hugo endorsed her, isn't it? Because she knew about the drugs."

"The man is grieving, Lucie. After all these years. Georgia had no right to do what she did."

"So you killed her and then you killed Randy. And you got Emilio and Marta to lie for you. Those babies weren't born that night, were they? Emilio called his son a little bull. Angelina, too. At first I thought he was talking about how strong they were, but he was referring to their zodiac sign. Taurus. I just read my horoscope last night and that's when I saw the dates. They couldn't have been born May twenty-first because they'd be Geminis. The twins."

"Aren't you clever?" he said sarcastically, but I could tell he was unnerved by how I was piecing things together.

"Did you kill them both the same night?" I persisted. "Why did Randy have to die, too?"

"I didn't kill anybody. You helped prove my innocence, remember? You're in it with me." His eyes glittered like a madman's. I'd once trusted him with my life.

"Not anymore," I shouted. "Don't you dare say that! Now I know why you got so quickly to the place where Georgia was killed, but the sheriff and fire trucks got lost. Because you knew where to go."

He said nothing, just kept staring at me.

I held the book up. "One of the missing pages in this book is the paper you wrote that letter on," I said. "If I show this to the sheriff and he starts investigating, how short a straight line does he need to draw to connect two dots?"

"You won't do that, Lucie," he said coolly, "because I have something you want more than anything else in the world."

I wanted to scream at him that there was nothing he could possibly have that I wanted, after what he had just taken from me. Trust. Loyalty. Devotion.

He waited.

"What is it?"

"Your sister's life."

I shook my head. "I don't believe you."

He smiled and laid down a winning hand of cards. "She didn't kill that boy."

My voice shook. "How do you know?"

"That is what it will cost you to not turn me in to the police. And believe me," he added, "I *know* what I'm talking about."

I felt sick. "I can't."

"Then she'll go to jail," he said. "Guaranteed. Her BAC will be well over the legal limit when that tox test comes back. She's going to hang for this. Unless you save her."

"How do you know I won't agree to your terms, then turn you in anyway?"

"Because I know you, Lucie. And because I'm going to set this up so that if you ever do renege on your promise, you'll feel the pain."

"If you know something," I said desperately, "then the police will find it out, too."

He raised an eyebrow. "Want to bet on that? You want to gamble on that beautiful, fragile angel surviving and going on to live a normal life after she's done time behind bars?"

"No." I gripped the book so hard my knuckles turned white. I felt like I was going to pass out. "Ross, you're a doctor, for God's sake. Do no harm. How can you do this?"

"You know," he said, "it's really true what they say. The first time's hard, but it gets easier. Now, do we have a deal or don't we?"

"You can go to hell! It's where you belong." I picked up my cane and started for the door.

"Where do you think you're going?"

My hands shook so badly it took me a few seconds to unlock the deadbolt. "The sheriff's office. Thank God it's only a few blocks away." I reached for the doorknob.

"You're not going anywhere. Turn around, Lucie, and move away from the door. Or I'll pull the trigger and kill you now. I swear to God I will." The gun was pointed at my heart.

"Since when do you own a gun?"

His expression changed into a sneer. "It's easy enough to get one in Virginia. Now shut up. You think you're so clever. I'm going to get away with it, Lucie. Marty told me the ME's about ready to rule Randy's death a suicide. Don't forget it's an election year and the sheriff's running again. They could close the case once and for all, if they decide Randy killed Georgia, then took his own life. Tie it up with a bow and no one will remember, come November."

"What about me? What are you going to do with me?" My voice sounded far away. Would he really kill me in cold blood? If he did, it wouldn't be here. He couldn't afford to. There'd be blood everywhere.

"Let's go," he said, reading my mind. "This can't be messy. And I need to get back here before the clinic opens at two."

"Of course. God forbid shooting me should keep the good doctor from opening ten minutes late."

"Don't goad me. It's not a good idea."

Outside his office, I heard the outside door open and bang shut. Then someone—it sounded like a woman wearing high heels—came toward us.

Ross drew a finger across his lips. No talking.

What the hell? What did I have to lose? At least if he shot me he'd be caught.

The doorknob rattled and Siri's clear musical voice said happily, "Ross? You in there? Can I come in? I've got coffee and muffins."

It was over before it started. As she opened the door, I turned and threw the book in his face. He moved instinctively to deflect it and I raised my cane, bringing it down like a sword on the arm that held the gun. As it flew out of his hand, I yelled to Siri, "Get his gun! Now, or he'll kill us both!"

"What?" She stood there, dazed and stunned, holding a paper bag from the bakery and a cardboard holder with two large coffees in it.

"The gun!" I screamed. "Get it! Siri, now! He killed Georgia and Randy! He'll shoot us, too!"

Her hesitation gave Ross enough time to dive for the gun, which was under his desk. When he stood up this time, I knew he wouldn't hesitate to pull the trigger. He didn't. I had no idea what kind of shot he was, but at this close range, he couldn't miss. He pointed the gun at me.

From the corner of my eye, I saw Siri hurl one of the coffees as the gun went off. Someone screamed. Later I realized it had been Ross, scalded by the blistering liquid.

I swung my cane and he gave up the gun more easily this time. No one noticed the blood seeping through my shirt until the police showed up.

CHAPTER 26

I had to stay overnight at Catoctin General. The bullet had grazed my ribs, a minor miracle. I think Ross had been aiming for my heart.

Bobby Noland came to the hospital while they were fixing me up. I told him everything, including what Ross had said about knowing what really happened the night of Mia's accident. Turned out she'd been right. She hadn't even been driving. Abby had been behind the wheel, on her way to see the promiscuous Brad, who had decided he wanted to kiss and make up. With her car in the shop for a previous fender-bender, Abby took Mia's keys and managed to pour Mia into the backseat, where she passed out. When Abby hit the Jeep, she panicked and called Brad. Their lucky night, to have no witnesses—especially among the passengers in the other car—so they moved Mia to make it look like she'd been driving, wiped Abby's fingerprints off the steering wheel, then took off.

When they got back to Abby's place, Brad called Ross, who made another late-night house call, putting two and two together the next day when he read the morning papers.

Bobby told me later the CSI team lifted a nice set of Abby's prints off the back of the rearview mirror of Mia's car.

"Happens almost every time," he said. "As many cop shows as there are on TV, you'd think enough people would remember to wipe the mirrors for prints. Every day I get on my knees and thank God for stupid criminals."

I did not see Ross again. There would be no reason for me to testify at his trial. Like he'd told me, he knew about the affair and knew Randy and Georgia were meeting that night. He faked the call from Emilio and Marta and got Georgia to agree to switch cars—he'd already delivered the children the night before. Then he waited until he saw the Explorer head over to the barn. He slipped inside and heard them and that's when he found the flashlight. Furious, he hid Georgia's Roadster in the bushes off Atoka Road and jogged back to the vineyard, collecting a canister of methyl bromide. And waited. After he knocked her out, he made sure that his beautiful wife would be so disfigured no man would ever want to look at her again.

After that he needed to set up Randy, making it look like he killed Georgia, then himself. He returned to the barn, pretending to be an intruder. When Randy investigated, Ross's judo skills trumped Randy's size. The rest was improvised, but easier than he'd expected. Randy's car keys were on the lanyard on his belt. Ross put him in his own car and drove to White's Ferry, where he shot Randy and dumped him in the Potomac.

The trek back to Middleburg was a terrific trial run for someone training for a marathon, though Ross barely managed to get home, shower, and change when my call came in. It wasn't in the plans for Georgia to be found so quickly. Randy, on the other hand, took far too long floating down the Potomac until he washed up on T. R. Island. And Emilio and Marta screwed things up by disappearing, too.

Now they were going to disappear for good. In return for Emilio testifying against Ross, he would not do jail time, but he and his family were being deported back to El Salvador.

"You know, if Jen had shown up at the wrong time, or even waited around for Randy, she would have seen Ross," I said to Quinn. "He might not have killed Georgia that night, or Randy, either."

We were sitting on the terrace at the villa at the end of the day. I'd just returned from the hospital, where my bullet wound had been cleaned and dressed again. Quinn had brought out a bottle of Chilean Chardonnay. "Thought we'd try this. Jen would have been in the way. No telling what Ross might have done."

"More Chardonnay?" I asked. "Ross managed to get away with two murders. He never could have talked his way out of three."

"Nearly managed, you mean," Quinn said. "Bobby never bought that murder-suicide story. Then you figured out about the forgery. And yes, more Chardonnay. Tasting for next year's vintage. Never too early to start."

"So you're staying here, then?"

He uncorked the wine. "I've come to the conclusion that you need me more than Mick does."

"What is *that* supposed to mean?"

"Take it any way you like." He smiled. "There's something else."

"Yes?"

"Bonita's moving in with me. I hope you're going to let Hector and Sera stay at their place for a while, even if he's retired. Bonita loves her folks, but they drive her nuts, and vice versa. So this seems like a good solution." He handed me a glass of wine. "Okay?"

I stared into my wine. "Okay," I said. "How did Mick take it when you turned down his job offer?"

Quinn seemed surprised. "Haven't you spoken to him?"

"Once, after Ross was arrested," I said. "He was pretty devastated by the whole thing. Said he had no clue what was coming."

"I thought you two were . . ." Quinn didn't finish.

"Were what?"

"Together."

"Not really." I shrugged. "I don't know."

He clinked his glass against mine. "There's a Spanish proverb that goes, 'With wine and hope, anything is possible.'"

"One out of two isn't bad."

"No hope?"

I wrinkled my nose. "No wine. This stuff's corked. How about another bottle?"

"All right," he said. "Let's start over."

WHAT'S THE DIFFERENCE?
Virginia Wines vs. California Wines

As they say in real estate, the difference between a Virginia wine and a California wine can be summed up in three words: location, location, location. In wine-making the term is *goût de terroir,* which literally means "the taste of the land."

"In California, because they have endless sun, you can get wines that have a higher alcohol content than Virginia wines," says Juanita Swedenburg, owner of Swedenburg Estate Vineyard in Middleburg, Virginia. "California wines tend to be more robust and often more heavily oaked, while Virginia wines are more delicate."

John Delmare of Rappahannock Cellars in Huntly, Virginia, agrees. The favorable growing environment in California is conducive to intense fruit flavors, which he says are the result of ripe, and even overripe, fruit. "When that happens you get a wine that has what's called a 'chewy' taste," he says.

Delmare owned a vineyard in California before moving to Virginia in the 1990s—and still has strong ties in California wine country—so he's in a good position to explain the difference in terms of taste and technology. "It's a lot harder to grow grapes in Virginia where you need to be an expert farmer," he says. "There's also a finite selection of grapes that can be grown. But what you get in Virginia are more complex and balanced wines, reminiscent of French or European wines."

Gordon Murchie, president of the Vinifera Wine Growers Association, points out that California and Virginia don't grow the same grapes, either. The top five California varietals produced are (in order): Chardonnay, Cabernet Sauvignon, Zinfandel, Merlot, and French Colombard.* In Virginia, that list consists of Chardonnay, Cabernet Franc, Merlot, Vidal Blanc, and Cabernet Sauvignon.†

"We grow a host of French hybrids in Virginia that aren't grown in California. Three prime examples are Vidal Blanc, Sevyal, and Chambourcin," Murchie says.

So how can you tell the difference between a California and Virginia Chardonnay, the number-one grape grown on both coasts? Part of the answer is in the barrels used in fermenting.

"Because of the 'fruit-forward' taste of a California Chardonnay," John Delmare explains, "forty to fifty percent of the barrels can be new, meaning they impart a strong oak flavor. In Virginia, we use mostly older barrels because we don't want to overpower the more delicate fruit with other tastes—especially oak. A Virginia vineyard wouldn't use more than twenty to thirty percent new barrels."

It was a Virginian—Thomas Jefferson—who first promoted the idea that the newly formed United States ought to have its own wine industry. Though he'd hoped Virginia would lead the way, he'd undoubtedly be pleased at the way things turned out—according to Gordon Murchie, there are now wineries in all fifty states.

"Jefferson understood that the soil and the climate make the wine," Juanita Swedenburg says. "When he was ambassador to France, he drank wines from all over Europe, so he appreciated this difference. Today, we can taste wines from anywhere in the world. That's the fun part—to be adventurous enough to try something new and see if you like it."

---

    * Source: Final Grape Crush Report, 2004 Crop, California Department of Food and Agriculture
    † Source: Virginia Commercial Grape Report 2004

ACKNOWLEDGMENTS

It takes a village to make a book, although this one seems to have taken a state (or commonwealth, to be precise)—and that would be Virginia. I am indebted to many people throughout the Old Dominion who have generously helped me with research and fact-checking. As always, if it's right, they said it; if it's wrong, it's on me.

First and foremost, heartfelt thanks and gratitude to Juanita Swedenburg of Swedenburg Estate Vineyard in Middleburg, Virginia, for all the technical assistance and hands-on experience to make Lucie's vineyard run so well. Thanks also to Jon Wehner of Chatham Vineyards in Machipongo, Virginia; John Delmare of Rappahannock Cellars in Huntly, Virginia; and Gordon Murchie of the Vinifera Wine Growers Association.

Lieutenant Rich Perez and PFC Tommy Thompson of the Fairfax County Police Department and John French, crime lab supervisor, Baltimore Police Department, helped with police matters and forensics. Steve Bussmann of Bussmann Aviation in Vienna, Virginia, answered questions about the use of helicopters to treat frost in a vineyard.

I made extensive use of local historian Eugene M. Scheel's series *Loudoun Discovered: Communities, Corners & Crossroads* published by the Friends of the Thomas Balch Library, Leesburg, Virginia, and also owe him thanks for taking the time to talk to me and set me straight on historical details.

More thanks for research help go to Tony and Belinda Collins,

Skipp Hayes, Stan Kerns, Sarah Knight, Jim Malone, André de Nesnera, Andrew Thompson, and Lyle Werner.

Donna Andrews, Cathy Brannon, Louise Branson, Mary Featherly, and Catherine Reid read and commented on drafts of this book. Thanks, also, to Carla Coupe, Laura Durham, Peggy Hanson, Val Patterson, Noreen Wald, and Sandi Wilson.

In New York, I'm grateful for the support and talent of many people at Scribner, but especially Brant Rumble, Katie Monaghan, Susan Moldow, Anna DeVries, Andrea Bussell, and Whitney Frick, as well as Maggie Crawford at Pocket Books. Finally, deepest thanks to Dominick Abel, who made it all happen.

ABOUT THE AUTHOR

Ellen Crosby is a former freelance reporter for *The Washington Post* and was the Moscow correspondent for ABC News Radio. She has spent many years overseas in Europe and the former Soviet Union, but now lives in Virginia with her husband and sons. Crosby is the author of *Moscow Nights* and *The Merlot Murders*. She is currently writing the third book in the Wine Country Mystery series.

Visit her website at www.ellencrosby.com.